# Delta ON MY Mind

Thanks for
your support

DeAnna

ISBN: 978-1-936824-29-8
Library of Congress Control Number: 2013943866

Manufactured in the United States of America
10  9  8  7  6  5  4  3  2  1

# Delta ON MY Mind

- A novel -

## DeeAnna Galbraith

ETCETERA PRESS
Richland, WA
2013

*For Ross. My First Edition.*

# Acknowledgements

To Courtney Hall-Mullen and Melinda R. Haynes.
BETA readers extraordinaire. Thank you.

To Darcy Carson, Marcella Burnard, Lisa Wanttaja and
Connie Wescott. Best of the best critique partners.

To Ellen Tomaszewski. Thanks for helping me channel
my indie dream.

# Contents

# Contents

# Chapter One

"Well if she's going to die anyway," Charlotte grumbled, leaning against the porch railing. "I wish she'd hurry. I'm bored."

Delta Jameson couldn't recover from her shock fast enough to respond. Molly Brisco, the object of Charlotte's complaint, did it for her.

"I'll turn up my toes when I'm good and ready, girl. Not before."

Admonishing Charlotte for her appalling lack of feelings would be a waste, so Delta shook her head, gazing toward the open bedroom window above the porch where she and Charlotte stood. Apparently, her grandmother's hearing was just fine.

"Sorry Gran," Charlotte quipped as she brought a cigarette to her lips. "It's too hot to be polite."

Molly Brisco gave no ground, although her voice grew fainter. "That's a poor excuse for your lack of manners,

Missy. And don't go lightin' one of those nasty-smellin' cigarettes."

Charlotte snapped the lid of her gold lighter closed and rolled her eyes. "No, Gran." She fanned herself and leaned in to whisper to Delta. "At the risk of repeating myself, this is boring. Like everything in this miserable little town."

She tipped her head toward the empty, tree-lined street, then back at the house. "I'm going in for a Co'cola. Want anything?"

Delta held up her glass of ice water. "No, thanks."

For the second time that afternoon she wondered why, given her attitude, Charlotte had bothered to come and stand vigil with the rest of the family. It seemed a very un-Charlotte-like thing to do. Gran wasn't even her blood relation, a circumstance which Southerners viewed as highly accountable. Delta shook her head, swishing her ponytail and shedding her mean-spirited thought.

She leaned back and closed her eyes, sadness washing over her. When Molly Brisco, known to all as Gran, passed, she would be the last of her generation in the close-knit group Delta thought of as family.

Molly Draper Brisco, Lydia Nash Pierson and Victoria Trask Parker had grown up close as sisters and forged life-long friendships. Delta saw the three in her mind's eye.

Each of the women raised one daughter, and the daughters in turn, produced four children. Molly's daughter, Suzanne, gave birth to Delta and her brother, Van. Lydia Pierson was mother to Caroline Richmond, who had Blue, and Victoria's daughter, Winnie, was Charlotte's mother. Charlotte, Delta, Van, and Blue were more like cousins by association than unrelated friends.

Charlotte reappeared with not only a Coke, but freshly applied lip-gloss. She never left the house without every blonde hair in place and every eyelash coated.

Delta looked at her sandal-shod feet, and shorts topped by a faded Atlanta Falcons t-shirt. Once, she would have needed to appear perfectly turned out too, but for a different reason. These days, she chose comfort over sleek trappings. Besides, Gran loved her no matter what she wore.

Charlotte rolled the cold can across her forehead and above the low-scooped top of her short dress. "By the way," she said, sliding her gaze down the street again, "Blue's coming."

Pleasure slid through Delta at the thought, then the missing puzzle piece fell into place. Blue's arrival was the reason for Charlotte's presence, and no doubt also for the way she was dressed. Charlotte was not a woman to let pass the opportunity to impress an eligible man.

The blonde continued. "He's going to stay with Dewey at Aunt Caroline's. Dewey and I have kind of a thing going and he's living there while Aunt Caroline's staying with Gran. The old man Dewey was renting from died and his daughter couldn't get Dewey out fast enough so she could sell the house. Anyway, it's probably better to have Aunt Caroline's place occupied and all."

Delta only half listened. She wasn't surprised Blue was on his way. He would be so good for Gran. She'd been fading fast, seemingly before their eyes. Blue always found time for her, though, and Gran adored him.

"... and Dewey can't move back in with his folks. His deputy job has weird hours and his younger sister still lives there and we'd have absolutely no privacy."

Charlotte patted her hair. "I was living in Marietta, married to that no-good John Pilcher, the last couple of times Blue came to visit."

*Leave it to Charlotte to juggle Dewey while making a play for Blue.* "I always liked John," Delta said. "And he was crazy about you."

Charlotte dropped her gaze, then snapped it back to Delta's. "He still is, but you can have him. Crazy's not good enough. John promised he'd set the business world on fire. Make me lots of money. He didn't keep that promise." The glint in her eyes hardened. "You drove in from Atlanta last night. Come and go as you please, but I'm stuck here, living with my parents and working part time at the same bank my father worked at. I purely hate ever' minute of it."

She wiped the back of her hand across her forehead and straightened. "I bet Blue's still good looking. And I hear he made a bushel of money in Chicago." She frowned. "Too bad about his brains."

Delta felt her eyebrows draw together. "Blue is extremely intelligent."

"I know," Charlotte sighed, tapping her temple. "I like men on the light side up here. Easier to keep 'em occupied."

True, Delta thought. Charlotte had always preferred the easy-going, non-verbal type. And she almost never failed to get who or what she wanted. Artfully highlighted blonde hair, green cat-eyes in a heart-shaped face, and a perfect petite figure were hard for most males to resist. Poor Blue.

The object of her misplaced pity strolled into view and Delta smiled upon seeing one of her favorite people. He still moved with a languid male grace that a dozen years' absence from the South hadn't defeated. Unfortunately, he was in for a close encounter. Luckily, Blue Richmond could handle himself.

Blue slowed his approach to Gran's. The walk from his mother's house had been too short for him to arrange his thoughts. He was bone-tired from a flight with an extended layover and depressed about Gran's health. Even though she was not his flesh and blood, Blue loved Molly Brisco as his Gran.

There were only a few people he really cared about, or allowed himself to care about, and he was here to wait for one of them to die. On top of that, the unusually dry September weather had released some sort of pollen and his eyes and nose itched.

The weight of his thoughts didn't keep Blue from reveling at being back. He'd grown increasingly tired of the incessant traffic, crowds, and noise of Chicago. Could be it was time to make a change.

Two figures occupied the front porch of Gran's house. He set his teeth. *Great.* He'd hoped to slip in, find his mother, and take her for a walk. Partly to give her a break, and partly to discuss Gran's condition. As he neared, the fading light revealed the two as Charlotte Canfield and Delta Jameson. He'd not seen Delta in almost half a year and Charlotte even longer.

Blue felt a lightness work its way up his chest. He could always count on Delta's presence to settle his mood. Even though she was two years younger, they'd always gotten along, in sync with each other when it seemed adults or peers couldn't quite fathom one or the other's state of mind.

Delta looked more approachable than she had in a while. The first year after her divorce she'd been on edge, her gaze not making contact when she was in a conversation. It had made Blue want to go to Atlanta and have an up-close physical discussion with her ex.

Blue had not been part of the 'A' crowd in high school, but his stature as a winning long distance runner afforded him a certain rank in the boys' locker room. There, he overheard any number of times that Delta's smoky grey eyes, slender figure, and dark, curly hair would be more than welcome in the back seat of any car she chose to grace. Much to the frustration of the boys she occasionally dated, however, Blue was pretty sure she'd never made that choice.

A football jock once intimated that Delta had put out for him. Blue had stood and stared at the Neanderthal.

After a minute, the other boy shrugged and mumbled something about Delta being too skinny for him to make the effort.

Blue walked up the porch steps and stopped in front of Charlotte. She'd be expecting a compliment, so he obliged. "Hey, Charlotte, you look nice. Broken any hearts, lately?"

The blonde wet her lips. "Why, thank you, darlin'. You're looking particularly fine, yourself. Now that I've got rid of John, I'm free as a bird and twice as happy. How 'bout you?"

"Not happy about the circumstances," he said. "But Gran asked for me and here I am."

Charlotte moved closer, her gaze telegraphing something entirely different than sorrow. "I know. We all feel just awful." She stood on tiptoes, her hands softly patting his shirtfront. "Let Charlotte make it better."

The realization that she was going to kiss him hit Blue at the same time as the overpowering urge to sneeze. The sneeze won. When he straightened, Charlotte had backed off. Blue glanced at Delta and swore she smothered a smile.

"Bless you," she said.

He nodded at her. "Thanks."

"Is that my Blue?" Gran's thready voice called.

"Yes, ma'am," he answered. He'd hoped her health wasn't as bad as his mother thought, but Gran sounded weak.

She had anchored his small world as he grew up. Among other things, telling him stories about his father. A soldier who had died in a military training accident before Blue was born.

"Come on up here and let me rest these old eyes on you," she urged.

"Coming, Gran."

He took a shallow breath and stepped over to Delta. "Jameson. How are you?"

Sad eyes studied him as she lifted a shoulder. "Okay. Considering the reason we're here."

Blue liked Delta this way, without the big city veneer. Another side effect of her divorce. Not entirely true, he reflected. *That cool edge layered over her Southern belle softness was an intriguing combination.* He mentally refocused and nodded, then took in her attire. For some reason that bit of casual display in the midst of the family heartache, cheered him. He grinned. "You can't take the country out of the girl. Talk to you later?"

# Chapter Two

Delta smiled. She felt an odd mixture of emotions at having Blue around – he always lifted her spirits – but Gran's passing would make him so unhappy.

Charlotte watched the door close behind Blue and tipped her chin up. "Well. He certainly acted standoffish."

Delta strove to keep the sarcasm out of her voice. "He might have been thinking of Gran."

"Maybe," Charlotte considered, her brow furrowing. "Or he could have a cold."

Delta was willing to bet her small bank balance Charlotte hadn't even flirted with the notion that it might be lack of interest. "He could," said Delta, mentally gratified at the outcome of Charlotte's blatant maneuvering. She sighed, sipped her ice water and started to stretch when Blue opened the door.

"Gran wants to see us."

Charlotte glanced at her watch. "I hope this won't take long. I have a date tonight." She looked at Blue from beneath her lashes. "A casual date. You understand."

"She only wants to see Delta and me this time, Charlotte," Blue said.

"Suits me to the ground," she responded. "Y'all can join us at Tinker's later if you've a mind. If not, I'll stop by here with my folks tomorrow morning."

Delta watched Charlotte leave and envied her uncomplicated decision-making process. It never seemed to go beyond the bounds of the last event to present itself in her favor.

"I hadn't even realized Gran turned eighty-eight last May," she said. "Do you think this is it? The last time we'll get to talk to her?"

Blue shook his head, holding the door for her. "I don't know. Mother's with her now and Aunt Suzanne said Gran wants to see us when they're done."

Delta brushed damp palms on her shorts. "I hate this. Gran's always, you know, been there."

He flashed a sympathetic grin. "True. And she's always gotten her way, so come on."

She followed Blue into the cool house where they saw her parents and Van talking in the kitchen down the hall. Blue's mother, who Delta had always called Aunt Caroline, descended the stairs as they closed the door. Something was wrong. She looked almost on the point of collapse.

Blue saw it, too. He stepped forward. "Mother, what is it?"

Aunt Caroline smiled on seeing Blue and hugged him, closing her eyes tight. She straightened her already perfect posture and shook the soft pageboy she'd worn since high school. "I'm a bit tired, is all. You look wonderful, honey." She headed for a chair next to the staircase. "I'll wait here until Gran finishes talking to you, then I'll get her settled for the night. We can take a walk after that."

He looked uncertain. "Could I get you some iced tea?"

Aunt Caroline fluttered her hand. "Go on, now. She's anxious to see you."

Blue headed up the stairs reluctantly, glancing back at his mother. Delta followed.

They entered the large front bedroom, a room that hadn't changed in anyone's recent memory. Its familiarity welcomed them. Linen dresser scarves with intricate tatting matched the coverlet folded neatly at the foot of the bed. The heavy mahogany furniture shone with hand-rubbed wax, and braided rugs graced the spotless floor.

Gran lay on the near side of the bed, her pale eyes lighting at the sight of them. "My Blue. Gives me a treat just looking at you."

Delta stayed back, hesitant to intrude as Gran took Blue's hand and pulled it down to her soft cheek. The old woman's gaze focused on him for a minute, then found her. "Don't stand so far away, girl. Come up here by Blue."

Delta approached the bed and smelled the faint scent of lilacs and camphor. She stood slightly behind Blue.

"Been saving my time to tell you something before I go," Gran said to Blue. "I'll hurt telling it because you'll hurt hearing it, but I made a promise."

Delta saw Blue's shoulders stiffen, but he spoke lightly. "Can't be that bad."

Gran shook her head. "I don't regret one bit what happened back then. I want you to know that, first."

She released Blue's hand and blinked wearily. "I married my Henry during World War II. Right before he was inducted into the Army. They sent him off to North Africa two weeks later."

Her glance strayed to the waning light at the window. "I was a mess, but Toria, Trask she was then, and Lydie Pierson, my two best friends on this earth helped me through his leaving. Lydie's husband, Bill, had just shipped out to somewhere in the Pacific, so she knew what I was going through."

Gran hurried on, a faint smile on her lips. "Toria was a spitfire. Wild and red-haired and always leading us to the very edge of trouble, Lydie and I only daring things because of her.

"She got this idea that we should all go to the Bell Bomber Plant in Marietta to see if we could get jobs. She convinced Lydie and me we could earn extra money, so when our husbands returned we could buy our own houses that much sooner.

"Toria's parents refused to let her go at first, but since Lydie and I were decent and had a speck of sense, they finally agreed.

"We thought it was a grand adventure and got hired on the first day. Toria wanted to go to a jazz club to celebrate." She sighed. "We should have stood firm, Lydie and I, but gave in to her wheedling, partly because we'd never get a chance to see a place like that once we returned to proper married life."

*Grand adventure indeed.* Delta had never heard this story, and could only imagine the freedom the three small town women must have felt.

Gran's eyelids fluttered, her mind focused on another time. "We can't take back our mistakes, and I don't hold with laying blame, but Toria acted crazy that night, drinking beer and sashaying around that 4-F trumpet player. That man reeled her in like he was fishing for redheads and knew the exact bait to use. Three weeks later she knew she was pregnant and the daddy long gone."

Delta tried to get her mind around a vision of a wild, careless Victoria Trask Parker, but the image wouldn't gel. Grandmother Parker, as Delta had called her, had always presented herself as the picture of calm, firm propriety. It must have come as quite a shock when she came home unmarried and pregnant. The secret must have also been tightly held because Delta had never heard the slightest whisper of a 'family failure'."

Gran had gone quiet and Delta thought she'd drifted off to sleep, but Gran directed her gaze to Blue. "Water, please?"

Blue slipped his arm behind her shoulders and lifted her gently while he held the water glass to her lips.

Gran nodded when she'd had enough and lay back. She bunched the bedspread with thin fingers and moisture gathered in her eyes. "Toria got hysterical, threatening to kill herself. Then Lydie came up with a plan. The three of us made a pact, agreeing to stay in Marietta until that baby was born. Then Lydie would bring it home as her own."

Delta couldn't control the gasp that escaped any more than she could avoid curling her hand around Blue's wrist. Aunt Caroline was Victoria Parker's natural daughter, not Lydia Pierson's. That meant Blue ...

# Chapter Three

Blue stood unmoving and said nothing. Gran pulled his hand to her heart and searched his face. "You aren't blood, boy, never have been in the true sense, but you're still mine, no matter who your grandma was. Nothing's changed."

Delta felt his pulse pound as she held onto him. He could retreat as clean and pure as if he'd left the room, a skill she marveled at and was instantly jealous of the first time she'd perceived it. They had been teenagers and Charlotte's father had arrived home early to find her drunk. Blue was working in Gran's yard nearby and Delta had gone inside to get them a sandwich. Charlotte's father came out of his house and seeing Blue, had a meltdown, blaming Blue for his daughter's state. That detached look was in place now, fathomless and unblinking.

She sought a way to give Blue time to absorb the shock. "Gran, are you sure you're not mixed up? It was a long time ago. What about Grandpa Pierson and Gramps? Did they know, too?"

Gran gave a trembling smile. "Yes, girl, I'm sure. Toria begged us – it would kill her parents – and she was as good as engaged to Hollis Parker. I wrote your grandpa right away and he was wonderful. Took the secret to his grave, like he promised.

"We were lucky women, Lydie and I. After she wrote to her Bill, he wrote back sayin' he was going into some heavy fighting and how he wanted her to take that baby to have someone to love in case he didn't make it. Turned out to be a blessing, too. They couldn't have any children and adored Caroline."

Delta leaned down and patted the older woman's shoulder. The whole story was surreal. In less than two minutes, her grandmother had rocked the foundation of Blue's world. "I still don't understand, Gran. The three of you were only an hour or so away."

Gran nodded, her focus now entirely on Blue. "We made a couple of trips home, Lydie wearing bunched up clothes and Toria loose. Later we used long shifts for the war effort, weather, and gas rationing as an excuse that we wouldn't be back for a while." She smoothed Blue's fingers. "When we did come, everyone accepted your mama as Lydie's baby."

She blinked back tears. "Say something, boy. Tell me you forgive us."

Blue heard the blood rushing in his ears. Delta was his link, her slender fingers wrapped around his wrist. He shook his head. "Of course. You did what you thought best." He forced words from a brain used to shelving personal problems and solving them later.

Now he knew what had upset his mother. He pulled his hand from beneath Gran's and patted it. "I need some time with Mother and you're tired. I'll come see you again tomorrow morning."

Molly Brisco nodded, anxiety clear in her eyes. "Yes, boy. You go spend time with your mama."

Delta ran her hand lightly up his arm, a balm to his hurt. "Take as long as you need," she said. "I'll stay with Gran until Aunt Caroline comes back."

Blue turned, his steps to the bedroom door by rote. His mother stood as he came down, worry etching her features. She tried to smile. "I always wondered where on earth those dark red highlights in your hair came from."

Blue ran his hand over his hair as if to remove the offending color. He had always considered his hair dark brown, but she was right. Time in the sun brought out auburn streaks that he'd never liked. "Guess there are answers to questions we haven't even thought of yet." He wrapped her in his arms and put his chin on top of her head. "Delta's going to sit with Gran. Let's go for that walk."

She stepped away to retrieve a sweater. "Yes, let's."

The evening air had a crisp tinge to it, confirming the onset of autumn. Blue took a deep breath, wondering how to begin, but his mother started speaking quietly.

"I always knew something wasn't quite right. The way Grandmother Parker favored me. Even over her Winnie at times. Come to think of it, Gran favored us, too. I thought it was because your daddy died so young and she and Gramps were trying to make it up to us."

She stopped and reached to stroke his cheek. "Some people haven't got anything better to tend to than what they believe are shortcomings in others." Acceptance flickered in her eyes. "Word will get around, and they'll have Gran's secret to turn over and talk about. Remember, though. They can only hurt us if we let them."

Blue marveled at his mother's capacity for letting life's unfairness wash through her, then coming out strong. "I don't care about other people," he said. "How are *you* doing?"

She seemed surprised by the question. "I keep thinking of the fear that secret caused. The love and trust they shared must've been unlimited. Gran passed that on to us."

They walked for a while in silence, then reached the point where the streetlights ended and the rural area began. His mother's house lay a little beyond, nestled in a shelter of trees. He saw Dewey's patrol cruiser in the drive and a couple of lights on.

His mother stood on tiptoe and kissed his cheek. "We'll be fine."

Blue peered into the darkness. Sleep would escape him tonight. In the morning he'd get up and run a half dozen miles. Now, as in high school, running helped him think.

The walk back was quiet. When they reached Gran's, he paused. His mother read his mood. "I'll go in and you wait to take Delta home, would you?"

He nodded, looking at the pale square of light from Gran's window.

When he'd applied for and won a mathematics scholarship to the University of Illinois, his extended family was surprised that he'd want to go so far away. He'd been eighteen, though, and had convinced himself his outlook would improve with a fresh start in a place far away from the small closed-in town where he'd grown up believing he was a misfit.

After college graduation, Chicago seemed a logical place to stay. He'd liked it because he'd never felt roots there. Just a place to live and work – no attachments required.

# Chapter Four

Delta came out in a large sweatshirt that barely skimmed the bottom of her shorts. It looked oddly sexy with her long bare legs and sandals.

She walked toward him and stopped, her gaze direct. "You okay?"

Before he could think of a lie, she stepped close and slipped her arms around his waist, hanging on tight.

Blue breathed in her fragrance and closed his eyes, relaxing. "Not the best news I ever got."

Delta tipped her head back. "Yeah? Worse than being told you had to take me to the Junior Prom?"

He groaned, remembering one of his rare visits home from college. Delta's date had had a death in his family and she was left without an escort. Blue had been shanghaied into the role. She spent the evening at their table, declining offers to dance, choosing instead, to talk to him.

It struck Blue as he stood in her arms letting her feminine comfort surround him, that Delta was just being nice, the way she was to everyone.

He grew warm. "It sounds worse than it turned out."

"Maybe Gran's news will, too," she said, giving him a final squeeze before moving away. She cocked her head. "People are way more liberal about this kind of thing these days. Most of the time it barely causes a ripple."

"Most of the time," he said. "But people can be hurtful in small towns." *Towns where families go back generations and people are still judged by the character of those families.*

Blue headed them in the direction of her parents' house. The Jameson, Brisco, Richmond, and Canfield homes fronted the Patchet River and all lay within the same half mile.

Family memories swirled in Blue's mind. "Gramps left us money when he died." He, Charlotte, Delta, and her brother Van had received $25,000 each.

"And you think what?" Delta asked, stopping to fist hands on her hips. "That you didn't *deserve* it? Get over it. You heard Gran. He knew exactly what he was doing." Her voice rose. "So don't you dare spoil the gesture of that sweet old man."

Blue lifted a shoulder, still absorbing the fact that he was descended from an entirely different set of grandparents, one of whom they knew nothing about. "Cut me a break, Jameson. I'm trying to sort things out. Not everyone is going to feel the way you do, either."

Delta flipped a hand in dismissal. "Like who? This won't change anything for Van or my parents. As for the town gossips, well, they'll be jealous because it's all so risqué and because they have only sad little lives and no ambition."

Blue smiled at her odd speech, which actually made him feel better. "This, coming from a woman whose own ambition single-handedly set the world of architecture in Atlanta on its ear."

She stepped back, the shadow behind a streetlight blocking her expression. "What makes you say that?"

He grinned. "I keep up. Besides, Mother sent me a copy of that article in *Atlanta Architecture*. I believe the term the author used was 'one of the most brilliant green architects on the East coast.'"

Delta stepped out of the murkiness, pure pleasure in her expression. "Yeah. It was pretty great. Got me a couple of new clients."

"I also read you're moving into a building you helped design. High rent district."

Her eyes rolled up and worry tinged her voice. "Maybe. The whole financing thing has gotten a little wobbly. I had to cut out my primary investor. He decided he wanted a say in how my business would be run."

"Not good," Blue said. "On the other hand, I'm always looking for a solid investment."

Delta laughed. "Okay. Be prepared to drop a couple hundred thousand."

He raised an eyebrow. "Offer's open."

She cleared her throat to cover the very real belief that he could back up his offer, and started walking again. "Still trading options on the Chicago Board Options Exchange?"

"Part time," he said. "I've developed other interests."

Nice segue to a distraction, she thought. "Other interests? Still in the financial arena?"

He hesitated, then cut his gaze away. "Not exactly. One of my clients is Maxwell Carter."

Her mouth dropped open. "The most successful green contractor in the Midwest?"

Blue nodded. "Nice guy. And he got me interested in his projects and after a few visits to his worksites, I ..."

"What?" she prompted. "Invested in his business?"

"Spent this year getting my LEED Accredited Professional Building Design and Construction certification," he said quickly.

Delta couldn't believe what she heard. When it fully sank in, she was beyond delighted. Before she could stop to think, she threw her arms around his neck and kissed him soundly. "Congratulations!"

Blue stiffened a little, but as she stepped back, satisfaction showed on his face. "Thanks."

Delta grinned. "So, have you done any work with Carter?"

"I consulted on a small housing project. He offered me a permanent position and I'm thinking it over. Not sure how much it'll affect the work I do on the Exchange for the handful of clients I have left."

The rosy mist surrounding her dissipated as Delta contemplated losing this man to design and construction of green housing, a passion which she knew from experience could keep him endlessly occupied. "Great," she said. "Great. I'm sure you'll be successful at whatever you decide."

Blue looked at her with a steady gaze. "I'm lucky to have found two careers I'm good at."

He seemed about to say something else, but stopped.

"Well, watch out for Charlotte," she teased, changing the subject. "You more than fit her criteria for eligibility. Male, prosperous, and breathing."

Delta had expected him to laugh, but he'd stopped, his smile rueful. "I don't think even Charlotte would pursue a relationship with a first cousin."

She grimaced. The conversation had wandered, but Blue's mind was still on Gran's revelation. "Sorry, I didn't think," she said.

"Whole new ballgame," Blue responded, extending his hand. "I'm Blue Richmond, by the way. Descended from that fine old family, the Parkers of Peck's Bluff, Georgia."

# Chapter Five

Her hand slipped into his. *Okay, he had a right to be derisive.* "Pleased to meet you. You must be very proud."

Blue's expression was wary. "Jury's still out."

She turned, not taking the bait, then saw they'd reached their destination. "Hey, looks like there's life at my folks' house. Come in and say hello."

When he didn't respond, she glanced over and saw the closed-off look in place again. He still wasn't convinced his new status wouldn't affect his welcome. Victoria Parker suddenly seemed like a very selfish person.

Blue pinched the bridge of his nose, avoiding her gaze. "I'm beat, and this has been a weird day. Tell your family I'll see them tomorrow."

She'd expected some withdrawal, but didn't think Blue would avoid family. Sadness pushed at her chest. "No."

"What?"

Delta sighed. "You say that like they're casual acquaintances, but my parents have known and loved you since you were born. Their personalities and feelings aren't going to change because your natural grandparents are Parkers and not Piersons. So, take two minutes and say hello."

This time his gaze caught and held hers. "At least one of them was a Parker. And suppose you're right? Suppose everyone in your family treats me exactly the same. How does that alter the way *I* feel?"

Frustration was a feeling Delta knew intimately. She'd felt sorry for herself a long time after her marriage to Slayton ended and didn't want to see Blue sink deeper into his shell.

She leaned forward and poked him in the chest. "Because feelings are a reflection of people's reactions to how you feel about yourself. This is all about you, however. Never mind how it affects your mother or the rest of us."

Muscles clenched and unclenched in Blue's jaw, his voice rising. "Thanks for the insight. Since I've already talked to Mother and nobody else matters, you can butt out!"

Delta would not let him get away with his pity party. "If nobody else matters, why aren't you going inside with me?"

The front door to the Jameson house opened and Delta's father looked out. "I've got a bullhorn if y'all want your conversation heard everywhere."

Delta's heart rate clipped right along and she could feel warmth in her face and neck. From the pulsing of Blue's jugular vein, adrenaline was jumping through him, too. "Sorry Daddy," she huffed. "Blue's being contrary."

Her father turned his attention to Blue. "The Jameson women tend to worry a body 'til he sees things their way, so the only things you're raising besides your voices are your tempers and the neighbors' interest. Why don't y'all come inside?"

Blue shot Delta an accusing look, then nodded to her father. "Yes, sir. Sorry."

Delta felt secure on her high moral ground as they entered the house. Then her mother and brother turned unsettled glances toward them and she wavered in her victory.

*Nothing to do but make the best of it.* "Look who's here," she said brightly.

Blue stood inside the front door, fists jammed into his jacket pockets.

Suzanne Jameson's chin wobbled and Delta's regret grew. She was so used to making herself face unpleasant situations since her divorce, she'd forgotten confrontation didn't work for everyone. Especially Blue. He needed time to work through things and she'd just bulldozed him into a corner.

Delta turned to her father. "Daddy, guess what? Blue's earned a LEED AP BD+C."

Fuller Jameson raised his eyebrows. "Care to put that in terms a small town lawyer can understand?"

"L E E D is Leadership in Energy and Environmental Design. It's the national organization that sort of oversees the green building industry. Blue's received an Accredited Professional status in Building Design and Construction. He's consulted for the best green contractor in the Midwest."

Delta's father held out his hand, genuine admiration on his face. "Well done, Blue."

Suzanne Jameson came over, kissed his cheek and hugged him. "We're very proud of you, honey. And just so you know, your mama and you still hold the same places in our hearts."

Blue hugged her back, his mind calmed at her words. Delta had been right about her family on that point. "Thank you. That means a lot."

Van stood and stepped forward, his gaze direct. Blue hadn't seen Delta's brother in a while and he looked good. He was wearing his dark hair a little longer and he'd put on a few pounds, but he seemed to be the same laid-back guy he'd always been.

"Great seeing you, man. Let's plan on getting together before I go back to school. Right now, I gotta go. Merrilee's waiting."

Aunt Suzanne frowned. "Really, Van. You can stay and visit for a while since Blue's here."

Van's pained expression almost made Blue laugh. "I only met Merrilee once and she seemed nice. How're things going?"

Van rolled his eyes. "Driving me crazy with details about the wedding. You'd think it was next week instead of next June. And before I forget, you plan on being one of my groomsmen, okay?"

Aunt Suzanne's mouth dropped open in horror. "Van Jameson. You mean to tell me you haven't asked Blue, yet?"

Blue bit his lip. Van looked like a kid with his hand caught in the cookie jar.

"No, ma'am. I haven't had the chance, 'til now. How 'bout it, Blue?"

Blue felt a stab of envy. Delta's brother was in his last year of law school, had a fiancée, and a plan for his life. "Sure. I'll plan on it."

Van grinned as he turned toward the door. "Thanks, man. One more thing to cross off my endless list. The thing is growing faster than kudzu."

Van left and Delta turned to her father. "Daddy what do you think of the Falcons' chances this year?"

Her father brightened. "I hear there's a lot of hope for that second string quarterback they signed. With their defense, it'll be the fresh start they need." He turned to Blue. "What about the Chicago Bears? How've they turned out this year?"

Blue rubbed his forehead. "Sorry, I don't follow football that closely."

Delta slipped her hand around Blue's arm and came to his rescue as quickly as she'd browbeat him into the visit. "Blue's had a difficult day. Why don't we let him get on home?"

Her parents nodded as Delta turned a wry expression on him. "Can I buy you breakfast at Mackie's tomorrow before we see Gran? I doubt Dewey has anything in the fridge except buttermilk and Ho Ho's."

Blue laughed. He'd checked out the food situation before walking over and those items, plus something unidentifiable wrapped in aluminum foil were exactly what was in the refrigerator. "Sure. Seven o'clock?"

Delta nodded and walked him outside into the chilly night air. She hugged herself. "About pressuring you ..."

Blue shook his head. "No. You were mostly right." He turned to leave and she shoved him from behind.

"I won't let this get to you," she said.

"Too late," he said softly.

# Chapter Six

Blue walked toward his mother's house, hoping Dewey was either in bed or hadn't heard the news. Discussing Gran's revelation didn't appeal to him right now.

As he approached, the glow of the television screen showed through his mother's sheer curtains. When he stepped into the living room, Blue got his second good laugh of the day. Dewey sat watching *ESPN*, eating Ho Ho's and drinking buttermilk from the bottle.

His friend smiled and held up the drink. "Want some?"

Blue realized he hadn't eaten since the airline lunch, around midday. He'd seen lots of food on the kitchen counters at Gran's, but hadn't been hungry. "No, thanks. You backwash."

Dewey looked at the bottle. "Oh. Right." He reluctantly held up the carton of snack cakes. "Some Ho Ho's left."

Blue waved away the offer and sat down. He and Dewey had a friendship that didn't require constant communication, so they kept in touch through infrequent phone calls and emails.

"How's it going?" Blue asked.

A smile, replete with buttermilk mustache, stretched Dewey's face. "Great. Dad's got a dynamite lineup this year."

Dewey's father, Coach Harcourt, was the pride of the Peck's Bluff High School Athletics Department. Especially during football season. Every year he coaxed, cajoled, and somehow molded pure eagerness into gridiron glory.

Dewey had made his father proud. He still held the record for most quarterback sacks made by a Peck's Bluff Buccaneer lineman.

Dewey's father was the track coach, too. For three seasons, Blue had run the mile and Dewey had thrown the shot. They'd fallen into a friendship that had endured. When Blue left for college in Illinois, Dewey had stayed in Peck's Bluff and gotten an AA in police science from the junior college. Now, he was a senior deputy out of the county sheriff's office.

"Wasn't one of his star players recruited by the Packers?" Blue asked.

Dewey grinned. "True. And hey, I'm dating Charlotte Canfield." He tried and failed to look threatening. "So, she's off limits."

That answered Blue's question about Dewey knowing he and Charlotte were cousins. "No problem," Blue said, then briefly wondered at Charlotte's admission barely an hour ago that she was going on a date tonight. Dewey was in sweats. Obviously, any exclusivity in the relationship applied only to him.

Blue changed the subject. Dewey would find out about Charlotte soon enough and maybe he wouldn't care. "So, what else is going on?"

Dewey frowned in concentration. "Bad news and good. The flooring factory had to lay off almost half its production crew. Most of the lines are too expensive to run and still make a profit. The county passed a special tax rate to keep them here, but I don't think they could afford to relocate anyway. Might not matter, though. Bobby Dean Tyler's got a pile of money and he's thinking of building some kind of theme park around here. You know, like Dollywood?"

That bit of news took Blue by surprise. The local boy turned country-western superstar had not seemed the theme-park type. Blue remembered Bobby as the quiet kid who had borne the jibes of his peers all through junior and senior high school as he dragged his old guitar around and talked about nothing but music. Immediately after graduation, he took off for Nashville.

Bobby was talented and lucky. His releases now hit the top of the charts regularly. But Peck's Bluff and a theme park? Blue shook his head. "Sounds far-fetched."

Dewey nodded and talked around a mouthful of cake. "Yeah, folks are either all for it, or totally against it. I'm mostly for it, since it would bring in jobs and money."

Blue nodded as he glanced around his mother's living room. Pale cream walls met a thick, dark gold carpet. Dark teal overstuffed chairs with sprigs of cream-colored flowers flanked the fireplace, and a tobacco-colored sofa with the same flowers fronted the big-screen television. He had insisted on bumping out the back wall of the house year before last and adding a bath to his old bedroom and updating his mother's. She had thought it too expensive, but he convinced her it would count as Mother's Day, birthday, and Christmas for the whole year. She finally gave in.

Dewey finished off the buttermilk. "So, how long can you stay this time?" He ducked his head. "I mean with your family business and Gran?"

"Been thinking about staying permanently," Blue said, wheeling over an ottoman from in front of one of the chairs and sitting down. "Mother's getting older, and I'm really tired of the winters in Chicago." He lifted a shoulder. "Settle down, start a family, the whole, 'livin' the dream' thing."

A genuine smile lit Dewey's face. "That's great, man." He rubbed the side of his chin. "Can you work from here?"

Blue waved his hand to indicate their surroundings. "Virtual office. I can keep my hand in for my Chicago clients in an hour or two a day. Plus, I earned this certification for green contracting. Thinking about buying older houses that have been on the market for a while, then updating with recycled products for about a third of the cost." Blue let out a puff of air, glad he'd shared his thoughts with his old friend, but at the same time, wondering why he hadn't with Delta.

His friend's smile widened, an interested glint in his eyes. "Well, if that doesn't beat the band. If anybody could make that recycle thing work in this economy, you could. I can swing a hammer with the best of 'em, too. So if you need help in that area, let me know. Been saving for a couple of years now, to buy my own place, and I could use the extra money."

"I have a better idea," Blue said. "Going to schedule a meeting with the managing director of the flooring factory to discuss the viability of converting one of their closed production lines. There's a huge market for green products and there's no reason Peck's Bluff can't profit from it. Got a few investors in mind. You interested?"

"Heck yeah," Dewey said. "You're a regular Walter Buffet."

The laugh that rolled out of Blue felt good. "I think you mean Warren, but I'll take it as a compliment."

Dewey's laid-back, 'take it as it comes' view of the world prompted Blue's next decision. He stared at the rug. "I got some news tonight."

Perception sparked in Dewey's eyes. He muted the television. "Yeah? Not bad, I hope." His voice softened. "I mean, your Gran ..."

"It's kind of in a category by itself," Blue said. I found out my mother isn't a blood relation to the Pierson family, which means I'm not either. Victoria Parker is, or was, my natural grandmother."

Almost a minute of silence stretched before Dewey spoke. "So, are you okay with that?"

Blue raised his gaze to his friend's one of concern and had to smile. Dewey had a way of boiling things down to their most elemental level. "Don't know, yet. It's somewhat of a curve ball. I can't change what happened over sixty years ago, but it's a hell of a shock to find out you've been sawn off the original family tree."

Dewey laughed, then furrowed his brow. "Dad always said there's a positive side to everything, but this one's tough." He put down the buttermilk and held up his index finger. "There aren't any Parkers left, but the Canfields are real nice."

Blue didn't share that assessment about all the Canfields, so he said nothing.

After some more consideration, Dewey beamed and punched the air. "Charlotte's your cousin. Perfect."

"I can see the advantage for you," Blue said wryly. "Any imagined threat I might have posed as dating material for Charlotte is gone. However, the part about the wagging tongues in town having a field day at my mother's expense sucks."

Dewey started nodding before Blue finished. "Maybe, maybe not. Your mother is so nice most folks won't say anything. Beside, like you said, it was over sixty years ago."

He swallowed another bite of snack cake and smiled. "I just thought of something really cool. Delta's been divorced for a while. I always thought you two would be great together."

Blue was totally unprepared for the warm rush Dewey's pronouncement gave him.

He'd dated in Chicago, of course. Mostly friends of co-workers, until he'd started working at home. He'd been invited to a few social functions by his clients, but they were mostly interested in the money he could make them, not his personal life. His one serious relationship had been with Sara, a woman he'd met while running in the park near his townhouse.

They had lasted a whole year until Sara voiced her disappointment about the lack of time he spent with her family and the fact that she'd never met his mother. They'd split amicably.

Blue missed the companionship, and Sara's warmth in his bed, but considered himself lucky. Two months after she moved out, he had a hard time remembering her face. That would never happen with Delta. But dating her sounded too weird.

His gaze snapped to Dewey's. He was embarrassed at having been caught considering Delta as a serious date. "I don't think I'll go there. We know too much about each other. Like dating your cousin. Know what I mean?"

Dewey continued to grin. "It can't be all bad, man. You've always liked each other. That's a big deal. If I hadn't been busy trying to date every blonde in school, I'd have paid more attention myself. She was a pretty girl, but she's turned into one fine-looking woman. Too much brains and class for me, but perfect for you."

Blue couldn't argue with the fine-looking woman part. Nobody could. It was also a fact that he and Delta liked each other. He slowly nodded. "True, but the next step is huge."

"You never know 'til you take it."

He was definitely out of his comfort level, so he didn't quite meet Dewey's gaze. "You're full of backwoods crap, Harcourt."

His friend laughed and seemed so pleased with himself, he'd apparently forgotten about Blue's new lineage. Blue stood. "Think I'll finish unpacking and hit the sack. Keep that bulletin about me possibly moving back, under your hat. Oh, and I might get up early to run, so if you hear someone moving around at dawn, don't shoot."

# Chapter Seven

Blue punched his pillow for the tenth time. Tonight's news had opened old wounds. His newly acquired uncle, the esteemed Joseph Tremont Canfield, had taken every opportunity when Blue was young to remind him he was fatherless and would never quite measure up. As he got older, Blue consciously avoided the man.

Then there was Blue's mother.

If he chose to, he could go back to Chicago after Gran died and the rest be damned, but his mother had to live here. Victoria Parker had had two natural daughters, Caroline Richmond and Winnie Canfield. If Joseph Canfield, or anyone else, balked at accepting that, they would have Blue Richmond to deal with. Having made that decision, Blue's brain and body finally succumbed to sleep.

Delta had the dream again. She stood in front of Slayton, ready to go to a social function. He ignored her until his parents came into the room. At their appearance, he

made a big fuss over her, speaking endearments and com-
plimenting her dress while he smiled at their cold stares.
He smiled wider and nodded at them until they smiled,
too. Then the three of them started laughing and pointing at her. Her face grew warm, but she never spoke, just
stood there, letting it hurt.

It had taken two years of marriage for Delta to realize
her in-laws were never going to like her, much less accept
her into their family. She kept trying, though, kept wanting to be the perfect wife and daughter-in-law.

Slayton finally admitted after drinking too much one
night that he'd married her to irritate the hell out of his
parents, not because he loved her. He despised them and
they had hated the thought of him marrying out of the
prestigious section of Atlanta that included their own
childhood area of Buckhead. He had told Delta she could
deal with it or leave, he didn't care.

The next day she'd taken stock of her situation. She
was emotionally stripped but decided to leave while she
still had a shred of pride left. Her architect's degree and
the support of one or two socially important matrons
had helped her decide. As it turned out, Slayton had lied
about not caring. He'd been furious when she'd walked
out.

The pre-nuptial agreement left her with nothing so
Delta had used her small inheritance from Gramps to
rent an apartment and some office space with shared resources. It was hard work and it made her hard, too. She

vowed to never be used as an emotional crutch again. By anyone.

Delta opened her eyes, surprised at where she was. She'd never had the dream in her parents' house. It must have been brought on by her anxiety about Gran's impending death.

Turning the clock to the wall didn't help, so she got up. If she hurried, she could make it to Mackie's fifteen minutes before they opened and talk to her close friend and confidante, Patience Mackie.

She showered, pulled her hair into a ponytail, and slipped into jeans and a thermal T. As an afterthought, she stopped at her mirror to make a pass with her lip gloss before she left. Aunt Caroline, Gran, and Blue had occupied her thoughts late into the night, then the dream happened. The resulting puffy eyes were not becoming. She stuck out her tongue at the mirror and left.

Delta brought her face close to the glass door of Mackie's. She could see the light blinking on the coffee maker. Patience made the best coffee in town. It was dark and rich, a big draw for the farmers and truckers who came in as regulars.

She shifted to one side of the faded letter that proclaimed it the Rainbow Freedom Café. Everyone called it Mackie's, and Patience was owner, cook, and took up the slack waiting tables when things got busy, which was often. She showed up every day at four to start the baking for breakfast and most days didn't leave until two. Mackie's closed after lunch.

Most of Delta's crying and punishing introspection had taken place with Patience, who had repeatedly told her how lucky she was that her marriage failed. After all, she'd said, grinning, Slayton and his parents still had each other to deal with.

The swinging kitchen doors parted and Patience appeared carrying two pies. Delta's mouth started to water. *Oh, please, let one of them be apple.* She tapped on the glass with a quarter to get her friend's attention, and was ignored for her trouble. She grinned and tapped the Georgia Tech fight song. The rhythmic sound worked.

Patience looked up and her wide mouth stretched in greeting. She walked to the door and opened it. "Lord, look what the cat dragged in. Come here, girl."

Delta stepped into a hug as Patience spoke close to her ear. "Sorry about Gran."

"She says it's time," Delta said.

Patience nodded. "Leave it to Molly Brisco to know."

Delta took a cleansing breath and headed for her favorite booth in the back. Patience poured them coffee and brought two warm pieces of apple pie to the table.

The pie was heavenly and after a sip of coffee, Delta sighed. "So, give! When I was here last, you hinted at getting married but were very coy about his name. It's been driving me crazy."

A freckled snub nose tilted upward in defense. "That's because he doesn't know yet. He's only got a few days left, then I'm going after him. We're perfect for each other."

Delta studied her friend over the rim of her mug. Patience Mackie was a tall, slender redhead with a generous mouth and serious brown eyes. "Whoever you've decided on is extremely lucky. I mean that. You have a lot to give. But don't count on things being perfect. It seldom works that way."

Patience knitted her brow. "Guess you'd know, but Dewey's pretty uncomplicated. At least what I've seen of him coming in here the past ten years."

Delta squealed and leaned forward, completely delighted. "You want to marry Dewey Harcourt? That's so great. When did you decide?"

Patience flushed under her freckles and glanced at the front door. "It was in the cards," she said solemnly. "They confirmed what I've been thinking for a while."

This is just what I need, Delta thought happily. A total distraction with a best friend. She shook her head. "You went to New Orleans again and had a Tarot card reading."

"Several times," the redhead confirmed. "Once by a Voodoo priestess." She flapped her hand in the air. "I know what you're thinking. Dewey's partial to blonde, fluffy-headed little things. Well, I'm going to change his mind."

Delta didn't doubt it. Patience was a very focused woman. "What happens in a few days to give you the go-ahead?"

"Autumnal Equinox," Patience replied. "Then he'll be open to new relationships and I'll be ready."

"Couldn't happen to nicer people," Delta said.

Patience nodded. "Thanks. You want some biscuits with ham and redeye gravy to wash down that pie?"

Delta looked wistfully at the plate where the pie had been. "I'm waiting for Blue. Maybe in a few minutes."

A small crowd pressed through the door and Patience stood to gather the empty dishes. "My early birds await. I'll bring y'all some more coffee 'til he gets here."

The place filled up fast and Delta was about to relinquish her booth when Blue walked in. He smiled at her and Delta warmed to her toes. Suddenly, her slapdash, low maintenance appearance mattered. A little foundation and blusher wouldn't have hurt, she thought.

Blue slid into the booth. He looked tired, too. Then he brightened. "Was the apple pie good?"

Delta followed his gaze to her shirt. Sure enough, a glob of apple with crust crumbs rested atop her right breast. She grabbed a napkin and plucked it off. "Yes, as a matter of fact, it tasted fabulous."

"I intended to run this morning, but couldn't talk myself into the effort. Maybe I'll try the pie and burn it off later."

"Knock yourself out," she said. "I'm paying."

Blue picked up the menu and glanced down the page. "Anything new here?"

"Didn't look," Delta answered, then found herself scrutinizing Blue. Dark hair and lashes, fine-toned skin and a slightly crooked nose. When had that happened? Or had his nose always been that way? She didn't think so.

All in all, he wasn't outlandishly handsome, but definitely good looking.

He dropped the menu and caught her perusal. "Hopefully there aren't any telltale Ho Ho crumbs on my shirt."

Delta shook her head.

"Then what?"

She held his gaze and lied. "Adding up the pluses."

He looked surprised. "For who?"

Delta pushed it. "Both of us."

Blue focused on his paper napkin, folding it into precise creases. "You, maybe. I'm not feeling very fortunate."

Her lack of sleep and Blue's continued self-pity made her cranky. "Yeah, my life's a real pip," she said. "It took me over a year after the divorce to get my first decent design contract. And I'm going to be broke for the next five years when I open the new office. But this isn't a contest." Delta's voice rose. Maybe if she pressed the issue again, he'd get it out of his system. "I don't get it, if you're going back to Chicago anyway, why you even care what people think?"

"You're talking about things," he shot back. "Those are just things, not ... not being here when people are hateful." He tapped the table hard. "My mother has to live here."

"Aunt Caroline is loved by everyone who knows her and is a lot stronger than you give her credit for. She'll be fine."

Patience walked over with the coffee pot. "If I'd known y'all were going to put on a show, I would've hired extra waitresses and printed tickets. As it is, there's only me and I got to get back into the kitchen, so what'll you have?"

Delta felt instant chagrin. Why had she continued to push his buttons? The thought that if she didn't stop, Blue would simply not see her any more made her panic. Her heart thumped. "You're right, Patience. I started it and I'm sorry. We have enough to deal with, now that Gran's made up her mind."

The bands of red across Blue's cheekbones receded, but a shadow remained in his eyes. He forced a smile, glancing up at Patience. "Nice to see you again. I'll have the number four and a large chunk of apple pie. And please pack an extra piece for Dewey. I have to replace some Ho Ho's I ate on the way over."

Patience grinned. "Nice to see you, too. I'll pack the chocolate. He likes that better."

"Thanks," Blue said, leaning back. "I'm impressed how well you know your customers."

Patience winked and Delta laughed out loud. "I'll have the same," she said. "Without the pie."

When Patience left, Delta covered Blue's hand with hers. "Give the rumormongers a couple of days and they'll be whispering about someone else. They aren't worth wasting your time on."

Blue didn't comment.

She shook her head. "I did it again, didn't I? Started pushing you to let go of things you feel strongly about when I haven't managed to do that myself."

Interest sparked in his eyes. "Like what?"

Delta took advantage of his shift in attention. "Like how I let myself be treated by that arrogant horse's ass I was married to."

His mouth quirked. "Told you so."

She winced. A month before her marriage to Slayton, she'd come home for the weekend to introduce her fiancé to friends and family. Blue had flown down and she'd asked him in private what he thought of Slayton. She'd discovered he had big reservations. He told her flatly that she was making a mistake, that Slayton wasn't the man he wanted her to think he was. It hurt her feelings at the time, but she had fancied herself in a great love match, so she'd ignored Blue's warning.

"Thanks so much for the reminder," Delta said. "I'd almost forgotten."

He turned his hand over and squeezed hers. "You wouldn't even let me come to Atlanta and break his nose."

Delta sighed. "Speaking of not being worth it ..." She squinted at Blue. "And speaking of noses. Has yours always been crooked or am I seeing things?"

Blue ran his finger self-consciously from bridge to tip. "I broke it last year in a kickboxing match. Didn't duck fast enough. The bandage itched, so I took it off and this is the way it mended."

She tilted her head to one side. The comfort level she'd always felt around Blue stretched into a new dimension. It confused her and left her uncomfortable, so she buried it. "The look adds character, but I don't think I could watch you fight. Isn't there a chance of loose teeth and blood and stuff, if not worse?"

Blue laughed. "There's always that. Although you try not to think of those things right before a match."

A vision of Blue with light gloves, shorts and a glistening body popped unbidden into Delta's mind. She blinked and pulled her shoulders against the tufted seat, banishing the image.

Patience brought their food and they ate ravenously. The trucker-sized breakfast left Delta warm and somnolent after her lack of sleep. Blue looked in the same state.

Three women came in as they stood to leave. One of them was a girl who worked at the bank with Charlotte, and who Van had dated once. Delta thought the girl was selfish, nosy, and crass. Of course the three headed straight for her booth.

They looked like Stepford Wives in pastel suits, perfectly coiffed and made up. Charlotte's friend spoke up. "Hey, Delta. Y'all about to leave? We just have to get our morning coffee and it's terrible in the break room at the bank."

Delta scraped up her change. "Go for it."

They were close to escaping, but the girl stayed in front of them. She smirked at Blue. "Supposing what Mrs. Brisco said is true. Are you hoping to ride on the Canfield coattails?"

Customers at nearby tables stared, and a tirade on what a miserable excuse for a human the girl was, hovered on Delta's lips.

Blue looked at her until the girl began blinking uncomfortably, then he turned toward Patience, held up the Styrofoam container with chocolate pie in it, and smiled. "Thanks again." Ignoring the girl, he walked out.

# Chapter Eight

Blue stood on the sidewalk, cooling off. *Typical.* Less than twelve hours since Gran's revelation and the whole town knew his mother was illegitimate and were taking sides.

When Delta didn't follow immediately, he glanced through the window at the scene inside. It had all the drama of a silent movie. Without the subtitles. Delta's cool posture and narrowed eyes radiated anger. A bad sign for the girl and her friends who wisely leaned back from the force of it even as the rest of the patrons leaned forward so as not to miss anything. When she finished, Delta dismissed their presence and strode out.

"I *cannot* believe she said that. What is wrong with her?"

His own anger hadn't subsided and Delta's actions frustrated him. "I handled it fine. There was no need to defend me."

Total surprise crossed her features. "Defend you? What are you talking about?"

He took her arm and moved them away from the window. "Then what was going on in there?"

Her eyes widened in comprehension, her mouth forming an O. This time she focused on him. "For your information, Ms. Know-it-all is a friend of Charlotte's. She heard about Gran's story from Uncle Joe when she called their house last night. Thought she'd get personal points by siding with the Canfields in public. After you left, I told her Gran does not lie and to stay out of my family business, period."

Blue's anger faded. "Oh. I assumed you ... Sorry."

Delta grinned. "Told you it's not always about you. Apology accepted."

The churn in his stomach abated and he returned her grin. "Point taken."

"Okay then," she said with a quick nod over her shoulder. "Can you tell me what men see in that, that, fake she-cat?" She huffed and pursed her lips. "Forget I asked. When she's not in her latest-fad suits, her clothes are tighter than a tattoo."

An idea crept in behind Blue's smile. "Really? Now that I think about it, she is kind of pretty."

Delta took the bait. "Well, maybe. But that doesn't overcome conniving and gossipy. Oh, and I've seen her mother. She will not age gracefully."

He burst out laughing. Delta's observations, though not, he was sure, delivered especially to cheer him up had done so while making a point. She was right about people like that. They weren't worth his time. He looked toward the café. "Almost makes me feel sorry for her."

"She doesn't deserve your sympathy," Delta sighed. "She's an irritating, narrow-minded simpleton and I let her annoy me."

Blue gave her a light hug in agreement and they walked the rest of the way to Gran's in silence.

As they approached the porch under Gran's window, he couldn't imagine being so close to anyone that you would keep quiet about a lie as big as the one Molly Brisco had held for Victoria Trask Parker.

The front door jerked open and Charlotte nearly barreled into them, a red mask of fury on her face. She looked from Blue to Delta, then back to Blue. "Momma told me about Aunt Caroline last night, but I came to see for myself. This ruins everything."

He sighed, in no mood for Charlotte's tantrums. "Why does Gran's secret about my mother ruin anything for you?" he asked.

Her jaw tightened. "Never you mind."

He shook his head. "Okay."

Long, manicured nails drummed on her hip as Charlotte looked over her shoulder into the house, then back at Blue. She reached for his jacket, pulling him down to her level. "Welcome to the family, darlin'. You're gonna hate it."

Charlotte covered his mouth with hers and held on, kissing him deeply. Finally letting go, she licked her lips.

"What a waste. Good thing I've got a back-up plan." She flipped her hair and stalked off the porch.

Blue wiped lip gloss off with the back of his hand as he turned to Delta. "What the hell was that about?"

Delta arched an eyebrow. "It would seem you've been crossed of Charlotte's list of eligible bachelors," she said. "See? Some good did come from Gran's news."

Although he shuddered at the thought of being the object of a real pursuit by Charlotte, Blue puzzled over Delta's remarks. She looked all worked up and he'd never known her to be unkind. Yet, in the last fifteen minutes she'd put down the girl in Mackie's, and now, Charlotte.

His mother opened the screen, smiling through her fatigue. "Winnie, Joe and Charlotte came by early, too. Are y'all hungry? I can fix something while you're with Gran."

"We ate at Mackie's," Delta said. "Is there anything I can do to help?"

Blue's mother took her hand. "No, thank you, honey. Gran wanted to see you and Blue as soon as you got here."

"How is she?" Blue asked, wanting the answer to be a miracle turn in Gran's health.

"About the same. Anxious to spend some of the time she has left with the two of you."

Gran wasn't through with them when it came to surprises, Blue thought, but there was no avoiding it. He hoped whatever she had in mind wasn't as consequential as last night's. He squeezed his mother's hand, then took Delta's and headed up.

Daylight washing through the lace curtains emphasized the shadow of the woman who'd always been his Gran. Her weight loss seemed dramatic, although she'd never been heavy and the pronounced hollowness around her eyes was new. *She's made up her mind,* he realized.

"Come talk to me," Gran said. "I have things to say and not much time." She reached for his hand. "How are you, boy?"

"I've been better," he said, not lying to spare her because she would know anyway.

"Couldn't be helped," she whispered. "I promised."

Delta stroked the small of his back, soothing him.

"I know, Gran. It'll work out," Blue said.

"That bein' said, I have a request," Gran whispered.

Blue smiled in spite of the stomach churn that had returned. No one ever turned down one of Gran's requests and he wouldn't start now.

"I've always had plenty in this world," she stated, eyes closed. "I know that's not what the two of you are about, but I wanted you to hear this from me."

Blue seriously hoped she was not going to bequeath him something important out of a misplaced sense of responsibility. "Gran ..."

"Let me get on with it, boy." Her eyes opened and her whisper turned raspy. A terrible loss filled Blue. She was using her last breaths and he could do nothing to change it. He nodded.

"The house'll go to Van. He and Merrilee will need a proper home after they're married. My Henry did some pretty smart investing, bless his heart, and Charlotte will inherit that."

Blue needn't have worried. Gran was leaving her main bequests to others. But why hadn't she mentioned Delta?

Gran's next words were made with effort. "Toria left a few pieces of jewelry in keeping for your mother, boy. There's more, but it'll wait."

He drew a sharp breath. He would have to get used to thinking of Victoria Parker as his flesh and blood grandmother.

A tug on his fingers brought him back, and he saw moisture glisten in Gran's eyes.

"None of the other grandchildren know about their inheritances, but you and Delta are so special to me," she said, "I wanted to tell you myself. Since I married the last of the direct line of Brisco males, I'm leaving Brisco's Folly to the two of you."

# Chapter Nine

Relief battled with amazement as Gran's words sank in. Brisco's Folly was a worthless one-hundred-sixty acre chunk of marshy bottom land, most of which was too wet to be farmed or used for anything commercial, even if it was cleared.

Blue had heard the story a hundred times. The President of the Confederacy, Jeff Davis himself, had awarded the land to Captain Sinclair Brisco for heroism and loyalty. The captain and his ragtag band of rebels had engaged a much better equipped troop of Yankees for almost two days, allowing a shot-up contingent of Robert E. Lee's army to get back to the safety of their own lines. Brisco and his men were captured and spent the remainder of the war in a filthy Yankee prison, where more than half had died.

The parcel had been called Brisco's Folly since anyone could remember.

Blue had almost forgotten it existed, and now it was being given to him and Delta. "Thank you, Gran," he said, knowing what it meant to her. "That's very generous."

Delta leaned forward. "We're honored, Gran."

The old woman smiled, a serene and peaceful look. "Sell it. You'll find a use for the money and it'll help the town."

That made no sense to Blue, so he just patted her hand.

"I've named you co-executors," Gran said. "Delta's daddy'll help y'all."

Cool, dry fingers clasped Blue's hand. "I've told you some hard things, boy. But you have your mama's compassion and your daddy's strength in you, so I have faith."

Apprehension rose to fill him. Facing her death was hard enough.

"Promise me," she said, her words paper thin. "You have someone to make peace with. Promise you'll try."

Blue didn't have time to consider how or what she knew, but wondered what Delta would make of Gran's request. In any case, refusing was not an option.

Her fingers curled tighter in urgency. "I know it's not fair to ask," she said. "And that stubborn look's set on your face, but please, boy?"

"Whatever makes you happy," Blue managed, his throat tight.

Her hand slipped to the coverlet and pale blue eyes held his gaze. "It's not me needs bein' happy," she exhaled on a shallow breath. "I'm tired, but I want to see my girls one more time."

Blue heard a soft sob from Delta as he bent over to kiss Gran. "You behave yourself up there," he said, and was rewarded with a weak smile.

Delta kissed her too, and whispered "'bye, I love you," before straightening and turning sharply for the door, her face wet.

Blue found her, shoulders curved inward and shaking, standing out in the hall. He held her in his arms until the shaking stopped, then they headed down.

His mother, Aunt Suzanne, and Winnie Canfield stood at the bottom of the stairs, faces pale.

"She wants you," he said, then followed Delta out to the front porch. She stood, arms wrapped around her middle, taking in gulps of air.

Blue led her to sit on the porch swing. "It's going to be sad not having her around."

Delta nodded, her lips pressed together.

He had the strongest urge to pull her to him and kiss her temple, but the impulse shook him to the core. She'd already been in his arms twice in as many days. Both times for comfort, true, but deep down, he wanted more. If he followed through on those wants, Delta would be so distressed that he would lose her friendship. Besides, he felt he had less to offer any woman now than he had even a day ago. Let alone a woman like Delta.

She curled her legs under her and leaned in to him. "We've been so lucky."

"True," he said. "She's one of a kind."

As she spoke, her warm breath penetrated his cotton shirt, creating havoc on his skin. She made an odd sort of chuckle that turned into a sob. "Brisco's Folly. What are we going to do with it?"

Blue barely registered the question. He risked a glance at the angled profile of the beautiful woman next to him. The morning sun threaded the dark wisps of hair framing her face and tears glistened on her eyelashes. Damn, she was almost flawless, even up close. And she smelled like the sheets he used to wrap himself in when Gran took them off the line out back, all warm and fresh. Guilt and heat spread through him at unbidden thoughts of a warm, soft Delta in his arms.

"Hard to say." He swallowed. "We'll have to do some investigating. Gran sounded as if it could actually be usable, but I can't imagine for what."

Delta sighed, her breath warming his chest again. "It's probably not worth a Confederate dollar, but Daddy can tell us. He's handled Gran's legal affairs for years."

The possibility that Gran was slipping away as she rocked here in the morning sun depressed Delta beyond belief. On a logical level, she knew people couldn't live forever, and Gran had led a long, happy life. But on a selfish, emotional level, she wanted Gran to always be there for everyone who loved her.

She realized as they sat there what a good friend Blue was. With his interest in green construction, maybe she could talk him into moving to Atlanta. He could stay in touch with his financial clients digitally and maybe even partner with her on projects. Besides, she could really use someone to confide in after a tough day. They'd always been close, right? Maybe that confiding and closeness could lead to something else entirely. Something that had occupied the back of her mind on and off for years. She felt her face warm and stopped her selfish musings.

Exhaustion and grief took their toll and she fell asleep. The next thing she knew, Aunt Caroline gently shook her shoulder. "Delta honey, your mother needs you. Gran's passed."

As Aunt Caroline turned to go into the house, Delta blinked and focused on Blue's face. The pain and sorrow she saw matched her own and she laid her hand on his cheek. He turned his head and brushed her palm with his mouth.

She slipped her hand down to his neck and hugged him briefly before straightening. "Thank you for being here," she said.

The immediate family gathered in the private chapel of Gran's church. Her casket sat at the front of the small room. Delta had already shredded a half dozen paper tissues before her mother gave her a lace-trimmed handkerchief.

Suzanne Jameson's dimple appeared at the same time her chin bobbled. "From Mother."

Delta smiled. Leave it to Gran to remember proper cloth hankies for her own funeral.

Charlotte wandered in with her parents. She appraised Delta's navy blue silk suit and cream-colored blouse. "Very Atlanta Junior League."

Delta was in no mood for Charlotte's ill-mannered jibes. She took in Charlotte's black bolero jacket over a tiny black dress. "Very ... obvious."

The blonde shrugged. "The fashion in this town is depressing." She mock-shivered. "Women dress like they're middle-aged by the time they're thirty." Her attention brightened as she saw someone arrive. "Speaking of clothes. There's a man I wouldn't mind seeing without any."

Delta knew before she turned that she would see Blue. He wore a charcoal gray suit and white shirt that molded well to his athletic build. He nodded when their gazes met, and that discreet contact made her feel better. He walked Aunt Caroline to a chair in the front row.

Charlotte leaned in to whisper, the slight hint of alcohol on her breath, "God, he looks so brooding and damaged. I would love to recharge those batteries."

"Pull in your tongue and shut up, Charlotte. This is Gran's funeral, not Tinker's Roadhouse. Besides, you seem to have overlooked a teensy little fact. He's your first cousin."

# Chapter Ten

The private service was brief, followed by a public ceremony given to a standing-room-only assemblage. All too soon, they walked to the old cemetery behind the church. Molly Draper Brisco would occupy the last family plot.

Delta looked around at the gathering. Very different from when she was a member of her ex-husband's family.

She had attended only one funeral as Slayton's wife. Several generations of Atlanta's social elite and their indulged children were in attendance, a coup for Slayton's mother whose uncle had passed away. Even the press stayed outside the vaunted gates of that section of the cemetery. The household staff had been allowed one representative who stood quietly at the fringe of the mourners. It was a cold, see-and-be-seen affair more than a tribute to the man's life. She'd hated it.

The people at Gran's graveside formed a structure, too. But it bled at the edges. Old Peck's Bluff families had been infiltrated by assorted escapees from the big

Southern cities and Yankees come down to establish businesses where the taxes and labor were cheaper. Molly Brisco had known everyone worth knowing and many who others thought were not. She had been liked by everyone.

Delta held tight to her mother's hand when they lowered the casket. She felt numb from grief, and wanted to go back inside. Suzanne Jameson was no Steel Magnolia and Delta feared the quiet façade would crumble when the medication her mother had taken to help her relax wore off. She also dreaded the long line of people waiting to pay their respects. As it started to form, Caroline Richmond and Winnie Canfield stepped back. Her mother would have none of it though, and took their hands, pulling them to stand with family. As Blue leaned to kiss her mother on the cheek, tears welled anew in Delta's eyes.

Blue watched the three women accept more offers of condolence from the people crowded into the Brisco house. His mother blinked heavily from time to time and he glanced at his watch. Fifteen more minutes and he would insist she go upstairs and rest. He looked around the room at heads bent in quiet conversation, some of which he knew discussed him and his mother and their new relations. He took a deep breath. Delta was probably right. After a few days, it would be old news.

His gaze found Delta and her paleness concerned him. She hadn't left her mother's side for more than a few minutes all day. He quashed the desire to go and just be with her. He'd come to the conclusion that he'd best stay away from the beautiful Delta Jameson for his own peace of mind.

The energy from his morning run had been sucked away by the forced sitting and interactions with the mourners. Blue stood beside the short hallway to the kitchen biding his time. He was about to move away when he heard loud female laughter from the kitchen. Blue rolled his shoulders and went to investigate. He found Charlotte, Dewey, Van and Merilee standing by the table laden with food and punch. Charlotte held up a small silver flask, apparently offering to spike the punch. She had no takers and shrugged, giggling. Spotting Blue, her eyes lit. "Cuz!"

"Hey, Charlotte. Celebrating something?"

She licked her lips. "Sure am. The reading of the Will."

"Hasn't been read yet," Blue said, mildly.

Charlotte took a sip from her flask and winked. "Found a copy in Daddy's desk when I moved back home a year ago. Interesting reading."

Silence fell on the group and everyone looked uneasy.

"What?" Charlotte asked. "Gran wanted us to be happy. And my own, personal happiness lies far away from here." She raised the flask. "So, here's to Gran."

The others held up their glasses. "To Gran."

Everyone's quiet thoughts were interrupted when a voice carried from the hallway. Blue recognized the speaker. Joe Canfield.

"... of course the old girl could have made the whole thing up to get attention. I'm going to have the story investigated. There are more than a few people who would like to claim a blood relationship to the Canfields and Parkers. For the Parker money alone. I'd feel no compunction requesting a blood test to keep my wife's family reputation clean."

Blue's hand curled into a fist as it all came flooding back. The put downs and constant intimation that he was not worth anything. This time, though, Blue wasn't a little boy. He stepped around the doorway to stand in front of his new uncle.

Joseph Canfield's pupils widened, but he showed no remorse. The man he'd been speaking to hurried off.

If Blue expected an apology, he wasn't going to get one. He leaned into the older man's space. "Listen carefully, Joe. You will not denigrate this town's opinion of Molly Brisco or my mother. That includes subjecting my mother to any kind of test to prove she is Victoria Parker's daughter. *Any kind.*"

Joseph Canfield flicked an assessing glance around them and licked his lips. "Having proof would eliminate any speculation. It would help your mother's case."

Blue didn't care who looked on. Anger heated his blood and tensed his jaw. "My mother doesn't have a *case.*"

"Ah don't mean case in the formal sense," Canfield said, lengthening his spine to his full five foot, seven.

Blue changed his expression to one of concern. "Oh, you mean so everyone would know for sure?"

"Exactly," his uncle replied.

"Then you wouldn't mind if I returned the favor?" he asked. "Have the Canfield name and financial standing investigated back several generations? And the Parker money or whatever's left of it? I wouldn't want my mother exposed to any unpleasantness. Any more than I'm sure you would."

Blue knew he'd hit a nerve as his uncle drew a quick breath through a pinched nose.

"That would be costly and unnecessary," he stammered. "I'm sure we can agree your mother is a lovely, discreet woman, and more than welcome as an extended member of the Canfield family." As a clear afterthought he added, "You are too, of course."

"My mother deserves nothing less," Blue replied. "My opinion of your offer is somewhere south of that."

Charlotte's high-pitched giggle inserted itself and her father turned his attention toward the kitchen. He stepped away from Blue, not bothering to hide a smirk, and leaned in. "We're leaving. Be ready in five minutes."

Blue saw the blonde's demeanor change instantly. "No."

He had no interest in bitter words between father and daughter. His own frustration stilled burned. After seeing his mother engaged in a quiet conversation with a friend, he forced himself to walk calmly through the screen door and down the back steps. He headed for the river path.

Before he reached the treed avenue, he heard someone approaching.

"Blue, please stop. What's wrong?"

Hearing Delta, he slowed, but didn't stop. Her steps quickened and she caught up with him as he reached the first trees.

"Uncle Joe?"

Blue paced across the path and back. He jerked a hand into the air in front of him. "That son of a bitch wanted to subject my mother to a blood test. Otherwise he would deny the family connection as a figment of Gran's imagination."

Delta gasped. "He couldn't have been serious."

Blue hit the closest tree with the side of his fist. "Of course he was serious. He even intimated she was after the Parker money. Which is pure bullshit."

She ran her hand from his elbow to shoulder and back. "He was just blowing off steam because he was taken by surprise at the news."

Her words didn't diffuse his anger. "That was two days ago. Does that give him the right to trash my mother?"

Delta glanced toward the house. "Of course not. He was wrong and narrow-minded. He'll realize that and apologize."

Blue took a breath, trying to push out the build-up of heat in his chest. "No, he won't. He's always been a rude bully. I threatened to have his family name investigated."

Small crinkles winged at the corners of her eyes. "You didn't."

Blue shrugged and nodded. "Gran's been buried less than half a day. I get the opportunity to forgive someone and what do I do? Retaliate for some stupid remarks."

"I don't know why she asked you that," Delta said. "But you know she'd forgive you. Everyone's emotions are strung out."

"My mother's worth ten of Joe Canfield."

"I agree," she said. "And you deserve the same respect."

"I don't care what anybody thinks about me."

She pulled her hand from his arm, shaking the index finger in his face. "Really? Well, stop feeling sorry for yourself. You come from respectable people and have always acted accordingly. No amount of sleazy gossip or speculation is going to change that. Start accepting the respect you deserve. Take it if you have to."

The adrenaline had nowhere to go. He stepped toward her, the dappled sunlight softening her beautiful features, her pale face colored pink by her indignation.

She saw his intent and swallowed; her eyes wide. "This is not what I meant." Her gray gaze searched his. "I meant for you to ..."

Blue leaned closer, watching and wanting her mouth. He slipped his hand inside her jacket and splayed it across her lower back. Her eyes drifted shut and she tilted her head. He brought his mouth to hers, puffing words against her lips. "Just taking what I want."

# Chapter Eleven

Delta stilled. Did she want this, too? She waited. Nothing. The moment passed and she opened her eyes.

Blue studied her face. "Sorry."

"No apology necessary," she said, every corpuscle screaming for a completed kiss. "I was pushing you, again."

He eased his hand from her back. "You didn't deserve being pounced on."

Delta laid her hand lightly on his chest. Now that she was this close, she knew she wanted more. "I could have moved away."

Blue's shoulders dropped and he relaxed. "Thanks."

*Did he seem a little too happy to have dodged the bullet?*

"Next time, follow through," she said, smiling. "We might learn something."

Blue smiled back, a hint of promise replacing the self-condemnation in his eyes. He leaned, kissed the tip of her nose, and Delta thought she might get her wish.

"How cozy."

Delta jumped at Charlotte's voice and looked for its source, her heart still pounding. The blonde stood a ways down the path, a cigarette dangling from her fingers. She walked toward them, a sly expression on her face. "Dewey's looking for you," she told Blue. "Something about a silly game."

"I need to get back too," Delta said, ignoring Charlotte's insinuation. "Daddy's going to read the Will in a couple of hours and Mama's exhausted. I'll talk her into lying down for a while." She turned her attention full on Blue. "Don't forget we have a meeting with Daddy tomorrow morning at eleven to go over our executor duties."

"I know someone who'd take Brisco's Folly off your hands for a good price," Charlotte blurted.

Surprise, then suspicion crossed Blue's face. "To what end?" he asked. Then cocking his head slightly, "Since when did that become public knowledge? Delta and I haven't even discussed if selling's an option."

Charlotte lifted a shoulder and took a puff of her cigarette, but her gaze didn't meet Blue's. "Told you I saw a copy of the Will. Besides, what else are you going to do with it and why do you care what anybody wants it for? It's just a nasty hunk of marshland." She turned toward the house. "Anyway, keep it in mind."

"What do you make of that?" Blue asked, once Charlotte was out of earshot.

Delta raised an eyebrow. "If Charlotte's involved, there's probably a man and money to be had somewhere. Not necessarily in that order."

Blue laughed and squeezed the hand against his chest. Had he followed through on the kiss he wanted so badly, and Charlotte not interrupted, he would still be kissing Delta. When he'd told Dewey it would be like dating his cousin, he'd been dead wrong. Until a couple of days ago, he didn't have any cousins, but he was sure being with Delta wouldn't compare. He was also sure that keeping his distance from her would not be easy. Yep. Moving back to Peck's Bluff was going to be hard on his self-control.

Delta glanced down before stepping back onto the path and it overwhelmed him what a beautiful, fine woman she was. His sense of euphoria waned and he sucked in a breath to try and loosen the palpable yearning.

Dewey trotted down the back steps when they approached the house. He put his arm loosely around Charlotte. "I got a great idea."

Charlotte rolled her eyes.

"The next couple of days are supposed to be real nice," he said. "How about we go out to Tinker's tomorrow night? The new cook makes a mean hamburger and they have a live band on Wednesdays. Can't dance worth a darn, but it'd give me a chance to hug on my woman. Thursday we could play flag football at the park around ten then have a picnic afterward. It's been a long time since we've all been together and Miss Molly wouldn't have wanted everyone moping around."

His friend's infectious grin lightened Blue's heart. Dewey was right. They'd been buried in their grief and Gran wouldn't want that. Besides, some of his fondest memories included fall days and flag football. "I'm in. How about you, Delta?" At her nod, he continued. "We'll need at least one more couple. Maybe Van and Merrilee?"

"No luck there," Delta volunteered. "Merrilee wants Van to herself before he goes back to school next week. They're talking to florists and bakers Wednesday and Thursday." She nodded eagerly, her mouth curling up on one side. "But I know just the woman for the flag football game. She'll even bring the picnic."

"Great!" Dewey exclaimed. "Who is it?"

"I have to confirm with her first," Delta said, grinning. "But you're going to like my choice."

"Okay," Dewey said, "One more guy and we've got six."

"Leave that to me, darlin'" Charlotte piped up.

Dewey shrugged. "Then we'll see y'all around six tomorrow night."

Delta's father tapped his pen on the table. "I know we're tired and saddened by the events of this day, but Molly asked that her Will be read, and I quote, 'The same day I'm planted.' Luckily, it's short and straightforward." He looked around the table. "Before I begin, however, and so there are no misunderstandings, I want y'all to know this Will is airtight. Any attempt to circumvent its intentions would be useless."

As the reading of the Will began, Blue wondered why Delta's father chose to stress that point. Had someone in the room already questioned Gran's final wishes?

His gaze sought Delta. She sat beside her mother and held her hand. Both women were pale and tired.

It had only been a couple of hours since their unsettling talk. Heat and desire curled in his stomach as he remembered her beautiful face tipped to his in expectation. And his own chagrin at letting his anger turn into unchecked want.

He knew physical need was only part of a relationship. There were a hundred areas where sex could not overcome differences. Even if he got past his issues with Uncle Joe, there was family. Her father was a respected attorney and her mother was the daughter of the venerated Molly Brisco. Eventually Gran's revelation might matter. It would be better to put that near-kiss and the feelings that blossomed from it, behind him.

His mother gently tugged his arm and Blue snapped his attention back as Delta's father read his name.

"... the boy I loved as my own grandson, and Delta Jameson, my beloved granddaughter, I give Brisco's Folly, free and clear, to do with as they wish."

Blue felt an intense stare coming from his left. His glance engaged Charlotte's for only a second before she turned away.

Fuller Jameson continued. "To my grandson Van, and per his parents' wishes, I leave my house, so he and his betrothed can start their married lives in a home of their own."

Van and Merrilee gasped. She hugged him with tears in her eyes.

"... and to Charlotte Canfield, and per her parents' wishes, I leave a matured stock portfolio, in her parents' guardianship until she reaches thirty years of age."

"No!" shouted Charlotte, standing abruptly, her expression furious. "That was mine." She pinned her father with a look of hatred. "You did this. Went behind my back, you interfering old bastard. I'll never forgive this and you better not touch a penny of it." She looked around the table. "He *helped* Grandmother Parker invest and his incompetence cost her nearly everything." Charlotte turned and jerked the door to the meeting room open and slammed it behind her.

Joseph Canfield stuck out his chin, his expression sour. "Ungrateful girl. Doesn't know what she's talking about."

Winnie Canfield blushed to the roots of her hair. "She's upset, but she'll get over it once she sees it's for the best. Please excuse her."

Blue felt sorry for Charlotte. Her 'sure thing' had been yanked from her grasp. Even if the bequest had been immediately available, she'd probably have blown through it. The part about Grandmother Parker's money was interesting, though. And in direct conflict with what Joe Canfield had claimed after the funeral.

From what he was hearing, Blue concluded that the three women closest to Gran had been consulted and agreed that certain bequests would skip a generation.

Caroline Richmond reached over and patted Winnie's hand.

"If there are no further interruptions," Delta's father said, "I'll finish. To my daughter Suzanne and the daughters of my heart, Winnie Canfield and Caroline Richmond, I leave designated pieces of furniture, jewelry, and mementos. I also leave equal shares of the cabin on Spoon Lake."

The three women smiled and dabbed their eyes.

A short while later, everyone talked quietly for a few minutes, then people started leaving. Blue led his mother to his car. She would stay in Gran's house while she, Suzanne, and Winnie sorted and cleaned everything out for Van and Merrilee.

For the first time in the dozen years since he'd left for college, and despite his new family status, Blue was looking forward to moving back home.

# Chapter Twelve

Delta took her mother home, got her settled, then dressed
in casual clothes before calling Patience. Her friend lived
alone in a big old farmhouse outside of town. Delta needed to talk to someone about Gran and her growing feelings for Blue.

When she got there, the Mackie house showed little
change from a visit of almost a year ago. Had she really
been that busy?

The façade of the house always made her smile. It had
started small and been added onto with alarming capri-
ciousness. As an architect, Delta couldn't help her fascination. Gingerbread trimmed windows on the ground floor
hid behind Doric columns holding up the large second
story porch. Eyelid windows and a solar panel peeked over
the edge of the roof. The Mackies had been nothing if not
eclectic.

Delta took in the barren farmland behind the house.
She'd once heard Patience's grandfather lament the only

successful crop he ever grew was a malcontented son. That son now lived with Patience's mother in Taos, New Mexico. They were two aging, and somewhat selfish, to Delta's way of thinking, parents who left for the West before the ink was dry on their daughter's high school diploma. Patience's older brother didn't want anything to do with the little farm, either. He lived in Albuquerque.

A large white candle burned in the window as it always did when Patience was home. She answered the door wearing a gauzy dress, bare feet, and a sprig of tiny red leaves in her hair.

Delta leaned forward to examine the leaves. "Are those real?"

Patience laughed. "Yep. My Bonsai Maple is losing leaves." She stepped back. "Hey, come on in. I'm sorry. I made it to the viewing but missed the service. Wanda, my fill-in waitress, promised to take her grandmother to pay her respects and I couldn't get away. Should have closed down for all the business I had."

Delta stepped inside, accepting her friend's warm hug. "I think half the town was there. Not many left of Gran's generation to say good-bye to." She glanced around the room before heading for her favorite overstuffed chair and sitting down cross-legged.

Patience made herself comfortable on a big floor pillow nearby. "When do you have to go back to Atlanta?"

"Can't for a while, yet." Delta said. "Blue and I are executors of Gran's estate." She shook her head. "And I have no idea what we're going to do with Brisco's Folly.

Could be there's an endangered marsh bug of some kind living out there and the EPA will make us leave it untouched in perpetuity."

Understanding dawned on Patience's face. "You mean she left it to you?"

"Actually, Blue and I are co-inheritors, if there is such a word. Gran left it to us fifty-fifty."

Patience smiled. "People love that area. The Briscos never fenced or posted it, so over the years folks have kind of made trails. You know, for Sunday walks and bird watching, that sort of thing. You should go out there, it's beautiful. Take Blue."

She hesitated. "I heard 'bout his new, um circumstances. Unfortunately, he got Joe Canfield as an uncle in the bargain. That man walks around like he's better than everyone else. From what I've seen at the café, though, he's stingy and sad with a permanent black aura." Patience cocked her head. "Yours is a little greener than usual. It always is when you're around Blue. He brings out the healer in you." She leaned toward Delta. "Speaking of Blue, now there's a lovely man. You going to do something about him?"

Delta was still stuck on Patience's observation of her healing aura. "What?"

Her friend's eyebrows bobbled. "You know, Blue. Tallish, dark hair, all that heart built up and no one to share it with. Just like you."

Delta laughed to cover her embarrassing thoughts. "We kind of tested the waters earlier this afternoon."

"Do tell," Patience said with a nod.

Delta sighed. "It was a very intense almost-kiss. That's the only way to describe it."

Patience cocked an eyebrow. "I believe the intense part. I don't know Blue that well, but he used to come into the café after school, order a burger, and study. He was quiet, polite, and always kept to himself."

"At the end of football season, my Dewey started sitting with him. From what I could see, Blue helped Dewey get through his math requirement. He helped a lot of other guys, too. Right into the start of track season. Since Blue's gotten back, looks like he's all wound up again." A corner of her mouth lifted. "There's one sure way to relax him. Guaranteed."

Warmth crept into Delta's cheeks. "That's occurred to me, too, but this whole change in his family history and the way he's always felt, sort of push his emotions around, you know?"

"Never been in that situation myself," Patience answered. "I can imagine it's frustrating."

"If it wasn't for the fact that it's Blue, this whole issue would be downright annoying."

"Meaning?"

"Meaning, Slayton's family didn't think anyone was good enough for him. Blue, who's as fine a man there is, doesn't think he's good enough for any woman."

Patience pulled her head back. "Why the heck not?"

"Because of things that happened while he was growing up. Things he won't talk about. Now that he's found out his maternal grandfather was some kind of jazz Gypsy, he's backsliding."

Patience frowned. "He had any repressed urge to play a musical instrument?"

Delta laughed out loud. Patience always brought light into the most serious discussions. "Not that he's mentioned." She closed her eyes and hung her head. "Damn his stubborn hide. I don't know if this relationship is going anywhere, but I'd love for Blue to at least understand he has so much to offer. He's funny, smart, and damned sexy. Any woman would be lucky to have him."

"True, and exactly my point," said Patience. "You and he live two time zones and two busy lives apart. If y'all are going to act on that mutual attraction, you better not dawdle. I think once you realize how good you are for each other, convincing Blue he's truly wanted won't be that difficult."

"You really think we'd be good for each other?"

Patience grinned. "Don't need to go to the cards on this one. You and Blue together was the first thing I thought of after I decided on me and Dewey."

For some reason, that made perfect sense to Delta. "I've still got a few issues of my own," she said, then snapped her fingers. "Speaking of you and Dewey, can you arrange to take the rest of the day off after the breakfast rush on Thursday?"

"Sure. I'll ask Wanda to make up her time. Why?"

Delta grinned. "I promised Blue and Dewey I'd bring a woman friend to play in a flag football game at the park starting around ten. I said she would provide the picnic lunch."

Patience laid a hand on her chest and fluttered her eyelashes. "Little ol' me? Who can outrun a rabbit and cook like an angel?" She crooked an eyebrow. "I s'pose Charlotte'll be there?"

Delta nodded.

Patience stuck both thumbs in the air. "Why it hardly seems fair, then. But I'll get over it."

"I'm counting on it," Delta said. "I thought maybe buttermilk fried chicken, some of that wicked cold bean salad, and chocolate pie for dessert."

"Don't forget honey cornbread, fresh from the oven," Patience crowed. She held her hand up for a high five, fairly bouncing on her big pillow. "Okay, now it's your turn."

Delta blinked. "For what?"

"You said you had some issues." Patience leaned forward. "Let's hear 'em."

Pent-up breath pushed from Delta's lips. This was the downside to having Patience as a friend. She listened with her heart.

"Intellectually, I know my treatment as the hands of my ex and his parents was undeserved. Emotionally, I'm still recovering. Guess my healing aura only works outwardly.

"I've known Blue as a friend my whole life and I'm extremely fond of him. I'm just not sure if I'm capable of transferring that into a romantic relationship. If it fails, I could lose his friendship."

"Nothing ventured, nothing gained," Patience said. "In this case, you have a whole, lovely future to gain. Anything else?"

Delta bit the inside of her cheek and swallowed a welling of angry tears. "Blue's got his own problems. He doesn't need mine, too. He deserves better."

Patience patted Delta's knee. "What he deserves is you," she said softly.

Delta didn't say anything. Not trusting her voice. She felt hollow, her earlier hopes that she and Blue could be a couple, tenuous, at best.

"As for that worthless ex of yours," Patience scowled, "If I ever get my hands on him, I'll pin his ears back and feed his privates to the hounds."

Delta smiled at the image. "Oh yes. Then, let's have his custom-made titanium golf clubs melted down and recast into a lawn jockey in his likeness. We could install it by the front drive of his country club."

Patience howled in glee, laughing and wiping her eyes.

When they calmed down, her friend caught and held Delta's hand. "So, what do you think?"

Delta felt a lightening in her chest, as if Blue had entered the room. "I think we've paid our dues and it's our turn."

# Chapter Thirteen

Delta smoothed the front of a butter-yellow sleeveless dress with matching jacket. It was feminine and flattering. She hadn't worn it since leaving Slayton and the round of society parties she'd had to attend with his mother.

When she arrived, Nancy, the secretary for her father's small firm greeted her.

"Hey, Delta. You look great. They're expecting you."

"Thanks, Nancy." Delta smiled at the woman who'd been her father's right hand help for twenty years.

The light of appreciation in Blue's eyes as she entered was worth her careful preparation. She walked around the desk as her father looked at his watch. "Right on time," he said.

She kissed his temple. "I'm always on time, Daddy. You know
that."

Fuller Jameson nodded. "Your mama could learn from you on that count."

Delta rolled her eyes and sat by Blue. "Ready."

"Molly's estate is pretty simple," her father said. "The smaller bequests have already been completed. The larger ones, such as title transfers for the house, the lake property, and Brisco's Folly will be taken care of through this office and Southern Branch Title."

He shook his head. "Charlotte called earlier. She asked if the terms of her bequest could be reversed if she brought her mother in to sign a release. I had to tell her no."

Delta swallowed. "She was counting on that portfolio."

"Charlotte's very focused when it comes to getting what she wants," Blue said. "Especially if it's money. I don't think she'll give up easily."

Delta's father spanned his forehead with his thumb and fingers. "I'm telling you this because in the capacity of Molly's executors, Charlotte may try an end run with one or both of you. Maybe threaten legal action that includes you."

"Can she do that?" Delta asked, uneasy at the thought of being a legal target of Charlotte's anger.

Her father shrugged. "Her only recourse is taking us to court for fiduciary irresponsibility in the handling of her bequest. That would take money and neither she nor Winnie and Joe have any to spare. Besides, they would certainly lose, and Joe knows it." He smiled wryly. "Not that Charlotte would listen to him."

The smile turned genuine. "On the other hand, I have good news for you two. A substantial offer for Brisco's Folly."

Delta and Blue said "From who?" at the same time.

"He'd rather make his offer in person," Delta's father said. "And I think you'll like what he proposes to do with it."

Blue leaned forward. "Sir, I really don't need the money. I could sign a release for my half."

Delta bristled. "I need the money but not the charity." She faced her father. "When can we expect a visit from this mysterious buyer? And what do you mean by substantial?"

Her father's eyebrow inched upward. Delta looked at Blue, but he studied his hands. She felt her face warm. "Sorry. That sounded abrupt and greedy. If the land is actually worth something, I could certainly use the money as soon as possible."

"Something you want to discuss?" her father asked.

Delta bit her upper lip. "Things are tighter than I counted on. I have deadlines for the fees on my new office and furnishings. It would be nice if I had a little breathing room."

"I'd be happy to give you a loan until this comes through," Blue said.

She glanced at him, his gaze steady. He meant the offer sincerely, but he also had no idea how hard won her independence was.

"Wasting your breath, son."

Delta swung her gaze back to her father.

"Her mama and I've offered to help several times." Fuller Jameson gave her a look tinged with understanding. "Unfortunately, she has her Granddaddy's stubborn streak and thinks she has to do everything on her own."

Delta squared her shoulders. "I'll take that as a compliment."

She'd never told her parents how tightly Slayton and his parents held onto their money. Their stinginess even extended to things like personal toiletries and dry cleaning. Of course that cheapness didn't apply to them. Now, she trusted no one but herself when it came to money. She thought back to her conversation with Patience. Maybe she could start by trusting someone with her feelings.

"... be here in the next day or two."

"Sorry Daddy. I missed that."

Her father gave her his best patient lawyer smile. "I said, the people interested in Brisco's Folly should be here in the next day or two. They have an unusual schedule, so make yourselves available on short notice. You'll both want to hear the details."

"I haven't purchased a return ticket, yet." Blue said. "And I can access the Exchange from my laptop."

Delta did a mental inventory. "Most of my design work is with clients for approval. I'll forward my business calls to my cell phone. May I use your home office if I need to?"

Delta's father nodded then sat back, grinning. "I'm very proud of the success the two of you have made in your careers."

Blue nodded. "Thank you, sir."

Delta added her thanks and wondered if her father realized how successful Blue was. He'd been quick to say he didn't need the money from the sale of Brisco's Folly without even knowing the amount.

"That about winds it up," her father said. "I have copies of paperwork for y'all to take and I can answer any questions you might have."

They were both quiet until they stood out front of the small office building.

"Take you to an early lunch?" Blue asked.

Delta smiled, her head full of the possibilities to be realized from the sale of Brisco's Folly. Her father had also said they would like what the potential buyer intended to do with it.

This must be what Gran had in mind for them. Delta shook her head. "Thanks, anyway. I promised Mama I'd help out today. The ladies have decided to clean and paint the house from top to bottom for Van and Merrilee. They won't be married for nine months but Van told me she's talking about moving in and saving the rent money to put toward furniture. I'll see you tonight, about six?"

Blue nodded, his expression showing neither disappointment nor relief. "Right. Gives me time to work up an appetite. I run in the mornings, but haven't done any bag work for a while."

"Bag work?"

"Yeah. My kickboxing exercises."

Her mind again conjured Blue, wearing athletic shorts and dripping with sweat, his dark hair plastered to his forehead. Her throat dried at the vision. "Guess we'll both be hungry," she managed.

Delta changed into jeans and a t-shirt before heading to Gran's. She found her mother, Aunt Caroline, Winnie Canfield, *who she would have to start thinking of as Aunt Winnie*, and Merrilee in the kitchen drinking coffee. She looked for a resemblance between the newly discovered half-sisters, but found none. Aunt Caroline's straight salt and pepper hair was far different than the naturally wavy faded red of Winnie Canfield's and Blue's mother was tall and slender to Winnie's short, more hippy figure.

The women had been hard at work for hours and Merrilee's face glowed as she talked about the house and how she wanted the rooms used on the upper floors. Paint chips and wallpaper samples were spread out on the big kitchen table.

Winnie fingered a pale grey-green chip. "I tried to get Charlotte interested in redoing her room, but she insists she's leaving and not to bother. She was so angry about the bequest she left last night and didn't come back until this morning.

"She threatened to leave and never see us again unless I agreed to sign a document reversing our decision on the portfolio. I finally agreed, but when she called Fuller, he said no, it would break the intent of the Will."

Delta's mother sucked in a breath. "She does seem terribly unhappy since her marriage didn't work out."

Aunt Winnie sighed. "It started long before that and I blame myself." She took Caroline's hand. "Joe wanted a son so badly and when we couldn't have more children, he left Charlotte to me. Mother's response to child rearing had been to eliminate temptation of any sort. Now I know why. I hated it so much I raised Charlotte to do as she pleased."

"Maybe if you sat down and talked to her," Aunt Caroline said. "Helped her make plans. She's what, twenty-eight? Less than two years isn't so long."

Winnie's shoulders sagged. "Waiting isn't Charlotte's strong suit." She looked from Caroline to Suzanne. "When Gran called Joe and me a year ago to talk about her Will, Charlotte and John were married, but struggling. Since the decision on who would inherit was ultimately mine, I chose Charlotte. Joe was very disappointed the portfolio wasn't coming directly to us. When Charlotte left John, Joe talked Gran and me into modifying the bequest. He said it would take time for her to overcome her poor spending habits and I foolishly agreed. Actually, he wanted it modified to read thirty-two years of age or married at least five years."

Winnie shrugged. "We reached the compromise you heard yesterday."

She looked around at the faces in Gran's kitchen. Her gaze stopped at Caroline's. "We three used to do everything together. I don't know how we got too busy, but now that I know we're half-sisters, let's not be strangers."

Aunt Caroline smiled, nodding. "I'd like that."

"Include me, too," said Delta's mother.

Delta hoped this was a new phase of closeness in their lives. If only Gran knew. *Or maybe she had.*

Four hours later Delta dragged herself through the front door at her folks'. Unwilling to dirty her mother's pale chintz, she plopped into her father's leather chair.

She'd just about decided to go upstairs for a hot shower when the doorbell rang.

A private delivery service driver stood on the steps. "Registered envelope for Delta Jameson." He held out an electronic clipboard. "Sign on the last empty space, please."

Delta signed and noticed the return address was her business attorney in Atlanta. *What in the world is so important that it can't wait a few days until I return?*

Halfway through the second page she got her answer. Anger and despair overwhelmed her with palpable energy. She ran to the phone in the kitchen and called her father's office. When he came on the line, she sobbed, "Daddy, Slayton is suing me."

# Chapter Fourteen

Blue knocked on the Jameson's door at precisely 6:00. Delta answered and he knew something wasn't right. "Jameson?"

She smiled lopsidedly. "Yep, Jameson. And gonna stay that way."

He noticed the wine glass dangling from her fingertips. He also noticed her outfit, a short denim skirt with red suspenders and a white t-shirt. She also wore red cowboy boots. Not an everyday Delta outfit, but extremely sexy. He took a deep breath. "Uh, what's going to stay that way?"

She squinted in thought. "Didn't I say? Jameson, silly. Not going to change it again. *Ever.*"

Blue persevered. Whatever had happened to upset her apparently had to do with her divorce. His stomach tightened as he added another tic mark against Slayton. "You want to tell me what's wrong?"

All traces of humor disappeared. "What could possibly be wrong?" she said. "First, Gran dies, then there's the almost kiss, and I have these feelings to deal with. And today. Oh, today was a *stunner*. My loving ex dredges up a teeny tiny clause in our prenuptial agreement that I, never believing it could hurt me, blindly signed."

He shook his head, purposely avoiding her remarks about him and zeroed in on the last part. "Whoa, what does this clause say?"

She waved her empty hand and picked up her jacket by the door. "S'legal. Daddy said so. Now, you and me gotta celebrate my almost successful business 'cause it's almost gone." The jacket in one hand and glass in the other puzzled her for a moment, then she tossed the jacket to Blue, leaving her arm extended for him to help her put it on.

Blue didn't oblige. "Okay, one step at a time. Are your folks home?"

Delta looked behind her into the living room. She turned back slowly and tipped her head toward the glass in her hand. "They're at a bridge tournament. It's just me and Mr. Chablis," she whispered.

He sighed. He'd been looking forward to this evening. It had been too long since he went anywhere with friends to do nothing but have fun. "Why don't I get some takeout? You can eat, then sleep it off."

Delta dropped her arm. "You can be a real stick sometimes, Richmond. You know that?" She started patting her torso. "Keys were here a minute ago."

Blue watched frustration set in until she rediscovered her jacket in his hand and brightened. "Oh, good, you changed your mind." She carefully set her glass on an entry table, grabbed her purse, closed the door, and stepped around him..

Blue rolled his eyes. She'd given him no choice except to follow. Delta didn't drink too often because she got hell's worst hangovers. If she needed this catharsis, he'd watch out for her. Besides, he wanted to help, and to do that he had to know the reason.

By the time he reached the car, Delta was strapped inside, leaning forward. He got in and handed her the jacket but paused before starting the car. "Sure you want to do this?"

She swiveled her gaze to him and said simply, "You're with me."

This was the second time she'd referred to him in what Blue considered a 'more than friends' way. He knew she was tipsy, but her behavior made a serious dent in his earlier intention to quash his feelings.

Dewey and Charlotte were already at Tinker's, holding a table, when Blue and Delta arrived. Dewey rose and cast a questioning glance toward Delta. "We just got here, and I was about to order some drinks. What'll y'all have?"

"White wine."

"Two cokes," Blue overruled her.

Delta faced him, her gray eyes flashing an approaching storm. "I'll have white wine if I have to pay for it myself."

Blue got in her face. "And something substantial to eat."

The tip of Delta's tongue worked her upper lip. *Lord have mercy but he wanted that mouth.*

"Okay," she conceded, looking at him through her lashes.

"Hunh?"

"Ah said, okay," she drawled, her accent and acquiescence a sure sign that she was 'going Southern' as Blue liked to call it when her barriers came down. All bets were off.

Charlotte gave a two-finger salute, sullenness stamped on her features. The look, especially around her mouth, reminded Blue of Uncle Joe's when he was unhappy, an observation Blue intended to keep to himself.

"Y'all know why I'm gonna get sideways," Charlotte said to Delta. "Let's hear yours."

Delta fixed the blonde with a challenging look. "Well, take your ex and multiply your complaints by ten and you might come close to the miserable excuse for a donkey I married. What was I thinking?" She slapped her forehead "Ow!"

Charlotte laughed without enthusiasm and looked around. "I should be clubbing in Atlanta. Celebrating in style with the kind of people who really know how to party." Her perusal stopped on Delta, again. "Present company excepted." She sipped her drink. "I know! Let's blame men. My ex, my daddy of course, and let's not forget the horny trumpet player that made Blue into my first cousin." She giggled loudly. "Get it? Horny trumpet player?"

Both women laughed uproariously as Dewey shrugged at Blue over Charlotte's head. It was going to be a long, but entertaining evening.

The music started toward the end of dinner and Charlotte immediately wanted to join the rowdy dancing. When she and Dewey stood, Blue absently rubbed Delta's shoulder. She'd gone quiet after her second wine, then pulled an eyeliner pencil out of her jacket. Black hearts of differing sizes now adorned the butcher paper covering the table.

Blue spoke above the music. "You ready to go?"

Delta looked at him and blinked. "I wanna dance."

That particular skill still eluded him, but Blue figured the floor was crowded and maybe Delta wouldn't notice. He smiled. "Sure. Next slow one?"

She flashed a Cheshire smile and went back to drawing.

They had their dance and afterward both couples walked back to the table in time to see a stranger approaching. The man dressed a couple of notches higher than the crowd in Tinker's. He wore a custom-cut western suit, white Resistol cowboy hat, and probably, Blue guessed, expensive boots.

Dewey looked dismayed as Charlotte chirped, "I do believe this handsome man and I are going to be friends."

A niggling memory of Charlotte mentioning a casual date just a few days ago had Blue wondering if this was her first encounter with the guy. His sympathy toward his cousin changed to dislike. Charlotte operated at skin level. Every word meant to convey a means to something she wanted, or thought she wanted, and Dewey would bust his butt seeing if he could get it for her. Judging from her interested gaze at the newcomer, his friend was in for a hard time.

"Uh, this is Harlan Braxton," Dewey said. "I met him at the courthouse today. He's looking to locate a business here."

Braxton grinned as he shook Dewey's hand. "Deputy."

Charlotte smiled and got right down to business. "Harlan and I already met at the bank. Y'all like to dance, darlin'?"

He nodded and cast a polite glance at Dewey. "If the Deputy doesn't mind."

She took his hand and headed back to the dance floor, speaking over her shoulder. "Dewey's a sweetie. He doesn't care."

Delta tugged at Blue's sleeve. When he leaned over, she tipped her head toward Charlotte. "I'd snatch her bald-headed for that, but Dewey'll be on the mend by tomorrow. Trust me."

Blue had no time to puzzle what she meant. Delta lowered her voice so he had to lean in even closer. "Besides, we have Brisco's Folly. They'd never find her body."

Blue laughed at the mischievous sparkle in her eyes.

A second later, and before he could react, Delta kissed him softly.

Unadulterated desire shot through him and he knew he'd want her for the rest of his days. Whether he ever acted on it was another matter.

"Nice," she said. "I thought it would be."

He smiled, going for casual. "Nice is for wimps."

She cut him a purely female look from the corner of her eye. "Then we'll call it a good beginning."

There was no response that he could say out loud so Blue shifted his attention to Charlotte and Braxton as they headed back to the table. There was an intimacy between them that wasn't shared by people who were relative strangers. Then again, Charlotte made men friends so easily it was hard to tell.

"So what kind of business are you looking to start?" Dewey asked as they waited for the band to begin again.

"I'm scouting a location for a client," Braxton answered. "Call me Brax. All my friends do."

Blue didn't think much of the answer or the man. And while his feeling was only based on the way Charlotte treated Dewey as a result of Braxton's attention, Blue had no interest in becoming Harlan Braxton's friend.

Delta stood and excused herself. As she walked toward the ladies' room a table full of raucous men tipped their beer bottles and whistled. She didn't even look their way.

Shortly after she returned, Brax and Charlotte got up to dance again. He must be a good dancer, or at least Charlotte thought so. She'd stopped asking Dewey's permission. In fact, she didn't seem to remember she and Dewey were there as a couple.

Dewey mentioned twice that Charlotte needed cheering up because of her disappointment at the terms of her inheritance.

Blue didn't comment and neither did Delta. She stayed quiet and thoughtful as they kept Dewey company. Blue was about to suggest they leave when Dewey stood and pulled out his cell phone. He glanced at the read out. "Sorry, gotta take this." He left the table and went outside. He returned at the same time as Charlotte and Braxton.

"Bad news. There's a nine-car smashup on I-75, inside the county line. They need everyone out. Blue, can you take Charlotte home?"

"Uh, sure."

A stubborn pout transformed Charlotte's face. "I want to dance some more. You promised me the whole evening."

Braxton smiled and touched his hat brim. "I've intruded on y'all's hospitality long enough. Nice meeting you and thanks for the company." He turned to leave.

Charlotte would not be denied. She stamped her foot and put out a hand to stop Braxton. "Just another half hour. Brax can take me home."

Blue noticed how comfortable Charlotte had become with the use of the man's nickname.

The newcomer lifted a shoulder. "I don't mind."

Charlotte stood on tiptoes and kissed Dewey's cheek without waiting for an answer. "Thanks, darlin'. See you tomorrow morning?"

The deputy nodded in capitulation and hurried out.

Delta snorted unladylike and stood. "I'm ready to go. Now."

She reached for her jacket on the back of her chair as one of the men from the table of loudmouths grabbed her hand.

"Let's dance, cutie."

Even tipsy, she gave him a look guaranteed to freeze alcohol and pulled back her hand. "No, thank you."

He was too drunk to get the message.

Delta slipped her jacket on and turned for the door. He reached for her again and this time Blue cut him off.

"She said no."

The guy squinted at Blue, sizing him up, then shoved his shoulder.

Blue tried to kid him out of his intention. "Hey, she's my date and you're making me look bad. We're leaving anyway, so why don't you ask someone else?"

The drunk stared at Delta's retreating back. "'Cause I want to dance with *her*," he bit out.

One of his buddies appeared next to the guy. "He got laid-off at the flooring factory today and has had a little too much. Sorry."

Blue nodded. "No problem," and followed Delta out.

They made it halfway across the parking lot when the Romeo charged out of the door with three friends in pursuit. "Hey!"

Delta turned and raised an eyebrow. "Persistent, isn't he?"

"And about as fried as a catfish," Blue said.

She giggled and pointed to the drunk's droopy mustache. "He even looks like one."

The man advanced and smirked at them. His blinking gaze went to Blue's feet. "City boy's shoes. Too bad. I got some shitkickers gonna kick your shit all 'a way outta town. Then we'll see who's the man."

Delta slipped her hand in Blue's, bouncing on the balls of her feet. "You can take him, sugar. Don't make me lose respect for you, now."

Blue had been looking at his comfortable soft leather shoes, but turned his attention to Delta in amazement. It might be the wine talking, but she had never in all their born days together called him sugar. He sighed. He had to make one more attempt to get through to the drunk.

"Listen, I'm a trained fighter and you're not at your best here. Why don't we call it a draw?"

The guy took two more steps toward them, waving his friends back. Blue slipped his hand from Delta's, gently nudging her away.

"Don't go anywhere honey," the drunk said. "We still got that dance comin.'"

Blue rolled his shoulders and widened his stance. The guy's friends stood back, but that could change.

"Not really a city boy," he said, trying to sound reasonable. "I'm in town for family business. Know the Briscos?"

"Not interested in your f-ing family tree," the man growled.

Delta hissed behind him.

The drunk moved quickly, leading with his head, fists curled tight. He grunted and dived, one shoulder coming up high, aimed at Blue's chest. It was a brute attempt to knock down an opponent twenty pounds lighter than him. Blue sidestepped the charge easily and the drunk did a face plant in the gravel.

Blue reached down to help him up but the man rolled over and kicked him a glancing blow to the thigh. Blue stepped back. The guy couldn't see past his last beer long enough to tell he was outmatched. And now he had a bloody nose.

"Sorry," Blue said. "You need to get some ice on that."

The three friends recognized the futility and came forward. One of them squatted down. "Hey, man, you get any more busted up and your wife's gonna have your balls for breakfast."

"Wife?"

Blue heard Delta's indignant outburst, but kept his guard up. The drunk wasn't finished.

He stood and dabbed his nose gingerly against his sleeve, then lifted his chin. A look of slyness combined with the same body stance telegraphed his next move. He lunged forward, exactly like the first time. Blue took a couple of long steps back and turned to his left. He tucked his arms in close and swung his leg in a perfect arc. His heel caught the drunk on the jaw, bringing him down like a bag of wet cement.

The buddy who'd been squatting stood and after giving Blue a look of respect, waved him off. "He don't learn. We'll take it from here."

Delta kissed Blue's cheek and walked over to the prone man. She plunked gravel on his forehead before Blue pulled her away. "Let's go."

When they got in the car, Blue expelled a tight breath. That was the first time he'd had to use his skills outside a regulated match. He'd done all right.

A giddy Delta bounced on her seat. "That was awesome." She leaned over and nuzzled his neck. "You swung that leg pretty good. Ever think of swinging it over ...?"

Blue gently put his hand over her mouth.

She licked his palm.

He snatched his hand back. "Delta Louise."

Delta crossed her arms and sat back in a huff. "You promised to never say that in public."

"We aren't *in* public. Besides, stern measures were called for."

In the darkness of the car, Blue could almost hear her thoughts clicking.

"There are other ways you could get my attention," she said, coyly. "Or I could kiss your thigh better."

Blue groaned, a sharp-edged need emerging at her words. He put the heel of his hand against his forehead. The outline of those long legs in cowboy boots taunted him. He was truly afraid that if he responded to her challenge he would pull her astride his lap and make them both sorry. Well, he'd be sorry tomorrow, anyway.

She started playing with his jacket zipper. "What are you afraid of?"

A choke of laughter burst from him. "Me, you, us, the fact that you're going to hate life in the morning and I don't want to be added to the mix. Now, can we change the subject?"

"You weren't afraid a couple of days ago," she mocked. "But we'll revisit the subject when you're in the mood. Let's drive around. I'm not ready to go home, yet."

When *he* was in the mood?

They went down to the river and out into the hills for a while then back to the Jameson house. He turned to Delta. "You ready to tell me what's going on? What the hell was in that clause?"

# Chapter Fifteen

The cool air cleared her head and Delta knew Blue would not let up. She stared at him in the dim light from the house, glad that he couldn't discern her misery. She would deal with her shameful actions toward him later. "A person hates to admit they've been made a fool of. Twice."

"The clause," he prompted.

"Slayton not only talked me into a loveless marriage, he asked me to sign a pre-nup. Being an educated, independent woman and thinking he'd love me forever, I did."

Blue's sharp intake of breath added to the weight of her confession. "That's right. Stupid, huh? Slayton and I even laughed over it."

"And this clause was part of that," Blue said. "What are the particulars?"

Delta could hardly get the words out it hurt so much. "Basically, it says, 'If the marriage ends in the first five years, the husband or wife, for a period of three years after the dissolution has been granted, has the right to fifty percent of any business profits generated by the influence of the other spouse."

"Which applies to you, how?"

She clasped her hands until the knuckles ached. "Almost everything. A couple of women in Slayton's social circle hired me to design lake houses after our divorce. I think it started because they didn't like his mother, but they ended up so happy with the results that word spread to friends and business associates. I'm sure Slayton's attorney could find a link to all but a couple of my clients."

Blue gave a soft whistle. "The son of a bitch is taking half your company. No wonder you're going crazy. But I don't understand how he came up with something that specific. You didn't have your own business when you got married."

Delta sighed, a headache now camping behind her eyes. Punishment for the half dozen glasses of wine she'd consumed. "Slayton's uncle on his mother's side was taken to the cleaners when his second wife left him. She had a realtor license and used their set of friends to start a very lucrative business after the divorce. Made his family money look paltry beside her income. She laughed all the way to the bank and every time she saw him at a social event. Hence, the clause. I'm lucky enough to be a woman who dared to make something of herself after being shed of a man in Slayton's family. And I'm going to pay for that success."

She rubbed her temples. "Daddy read the whole agreement cover-to-cover and says there are no loopholes. As soon as arrangements can be made, *D. L. Jameson, LLC*, or its equivalent in cash, is half Slayton's."

Blue tapped his fingers on the steering wheel. "I don't understand why they waited until the three years were nearly up. And they can't get blood from a stone. Most of your money's already been put as a down payment on your new office so there's not a lot to gain."

"You don't know them," Delta said bitterly.

"There must be a way around it," Blue insisted. Maybe I could help."

She spoke past trembling lips. "Be my guest, but I think it's useless. I'm the sole proprietor and that means I'm out of business. Once the debts are paid, he'll get half the net."

"Does he own any businesses you could counter-sue for?"

Delta choked out a laugh. "Slayton doesn't work. The family's money comes from a manufacturing business in Florida."

"I still think it comes back to why he's suing now."

The thumping in her temples persisted. "What difference does it make? I've thought about it, too, but Slayton's too lazy to follow up on anything. I can't imagine him ... Oh my God," she said, cold awareness filling her.

"What is it?"

She closed her eyes and her head fell back. "A month ago I attended a garden luncheon at the home of a woman for whom I'd designed a sun room. My ex-mother-in-law was there, showing off Slayton's new fiancée. She must have won the battle of wills with Slayton because the poor thing was everything she wanted and I could never satisfy. Obvious pedigree, obedient, and hanging on every word Slayton's mother said. I felt sorry for the girl."

Delta rubbed her eyes, then looked at Blue. "I managed to avoid them and was getting ready to leave, when the evil one headed for me with her victim in tow. I had every intention of being polite and non-threatening."

Blue raised an eyebrow. "Non-threatening?"

She smiled weakly. "As my mother says, 'You have to experience childbirth to understand the pain.' It was the same thing with enduring Slayton's mother. She referred to me alternately as a husband-hunting social climber, or, my favorite, 'A little nobody gold digger'."

Blue shook his head, angling his gaze as if he didn't want to meet hers. "Geez, Delta. I can't see you letting that pass."

Delta nodded. "I came to take exception to her barbs. Especially since I was still her daughter-in-law at the time. After I left her shining offspring, she had the unmitigated gall to tell everyone that I tricked her son into marriage and they were glad to be rid of me.

"I'm not telling you this for sympathy," she said. "I've never told anyone in my family how I was treated. I'm just working up to the point where I screwed myself over and I think that was it."

"What happened?"

She sighed. "The girl really wasn't so bad. Sort of like a pretty plastic doll where you pull the string to hear the canned phrases. I know. I've had that glazed look myself. She studied me for signs of lunacy and social disease as they approached. I'm sure Slayton's mother painted a sordid picture of her son's impossible ex.

"Anyway, I stuck to my resolve to get away clean – until she brought up my work. She said it was a very nice addition. Too bad it was a copy of a design she'd seen in a magazine a number of years ago. Only not executed quite as well. She had told the hostess as much."

Delta pulled up her knees and rested her chin on them. "I wanted that contract so bad I didn't bill for half the hours I spent on the design. It was completely original and suited that house perfectly." She sighed deeply. "I truly contemplated slapping her but instead called her a liar. She was livid and the girl was horrified. I gave her my sympathies on her upcoming wedding and walked away."

Blue didn't speak, just put his arms around her and lay his cheek on her head.

Delta opened her eyes to squint out the windshield. "How could I have been so stupid as to get involved with Slayton? Well, never again. No weak-willed, self-hating cowards for me." She pulled at the door handle. "I'm ready to go in."

Blue walked her to the Jameson's front door. He tipped her head up and kissed her lightly.

Delta felt drained by her confession. She wanted desperately to feel whole and wanted. Before he could move away, she slipped her arms around Blue's neck and pressed tightly against him. There was only an instant's hesitation before his heat enveloped them both and he gave her what she wanted.

When she finally pulled away, she saw need wash into his eyes, the same as it had by the path. It lingered before clearing. Overtaken, she was sure, by his self-doubt.

She would not be deterred and smiled. "Told you we might learn something. See you tomorrow."

# Chapter Sixteen

Delta lay in her bed swallowing slowly. Her tongue felt like a particularly nasty growth trapped inside a Petrie dish. The breakfast smells, wafting from the kitchen took their toll too, especially the coffee. Without opening her eyes, a task she dreaded, she began to recall the events of last night.

Please God. If I ever feel that sorry for myself again, let me just throw myself in front of the wine distributor's truck; the results would be the same.

It's not going to happen again, though, she promised herself. That would be a victory Slayton and his family weren't getting.

Her brain sorted through its fuzzy state to Blue's promise to help. He'd sounded like there was an actual possibility the lawsuit could be gotten around.

Blue! Her eyes snapped open and the diffused morning light caused immediate, piercing pain. She closed them, gently. Not only had she jumped him, she'd bared her soul about the sham that had been her life with Slayton. Blue must think she was pathetic. Delta groaned from the dual realization. The groaning only encouraged the cat trying to scratch its way out through her eyeballs.

"Delta," her mother called. "Weren't you going to join some friends this morning? It's nearly nine."

"Thanks," Delta croaked. "I'm up." She had sixty short minutes to get herself to the walking wounded, undead stage. She heard a soft chuckle. At least her mother's sense of humor was returning since Gran's passing. Her own lay buried miles away from the cotton clogging her throat.

An hour later, she still walked carefully so as not to jar her head. The worst of the prickly-edged hangover had worn off with a cool shower, but since the weather was hot, she attempted to pull her hair into a ponytail. Bad idea. The tug on her scalp produced watery eyes and a sucking of air through her teeth. In the end, she went with the heavy curls her shower had created. She held her breath as she passed through the kitchen on her way out. Her sense of smell seemed directly connected to her wobbly stomach.

The sunshine proved Dewey's prediction of nice weather accurate, unfortunately. Delta kept to the path by the river because it was quiet and afforded dappled shade. It also gave her a few minutes to think about how she should act around Blue. You'd think she was Charlotte the way she'd almost crawled into his lap. And had she really offered to kiss his thigh? The scene on her front porch brought an instant of pleasure before regret. Blue wouldn't bring up the subject, but Delta still felt shame at the way she'd acted.

When she cleared the woods and started across the parking area, Patience drove in and honked, waving her over.

Delta felt a smile form, despite the noisy greeting. "You could have gone all day without honking," she said, wincing.

Patience grinned as she reached into the back seat. "Thought you'd be feeling poorly." She held out two thermoses. "Here, these'll help."

Delta took them. "How'd you know?"

"Honey, you called to tell me about the lawn jockey's lawsuit before you went out last night. You were already swimming in wine."

Delta nodded carefully, remembering Patience's older brother was big into beer and wine. "So, what's in these?"

"The brown one has half beer and half tomato juice. It works best for a beer hangover, but will probably help. The red one has ice water."

"You're kidding. On an empty stomach?" Delta swallowed in self-defense.

Patience held out a plastic baggie with a couple of pills. "Just go slow. These are vitamin B and C tablets."

A piercing whistle interrupted them and Delta shrank away, squinting. It came from a guy in the park who was waving.

"Who's that?" Patience asked.

Delta cupped her hands around her sunglasses. "Trouble. I think."

# Chapter Seventeen

"Oh, goodie," said Patience. "Trouble for who?"

"Just a feeling I've got," Delta answered. "His name's Harlan Braxton and he's new in town. Showed up at Tinker's last night and made himself comfortable at our table. Especially with Charlotte. Who didn't seem to mind at all."

"Charlotte's a fool," Patience said, grinning. "A fact that I will be taking full advantage of."

Delta looked at her friend's long slender legs encased in form-fitting jeans and her midriff-baring pink t-shirt. She also wore a tiny silver bellybutton ring with pale pink stones that matched her shirt. "Dewey'll never know what hit him."

Patience nodded. "He'll grow to love the unexpected. Starting today."

"Speaking of the man whose future is not his own to decide." Delta nodded as Dewey drove into the lot. She sighed when he cut the engine, killing the loud rumbling that threatened to make her head explode.

When Charlotte exited his big grey Tundra, she blew Dewey a kiss and walked toward the field where Brax stood.

Dewey shrugged and started shifting a large ice chest from the truck bed. "She's anxious to get in the shade. It's warmer than she thought it was going to get."

He smiled at Delta, then recognized who stood next to her. "Hey, Patience."

Dewey's hands stilled as he realized the implications of Patience's presence. "Uh, you the one brought the picnic?"

Patience smiled shyly.

Dead man, thought Delta. He's hog-tied and doesn't even know it.

"Ladies."

Delta jumped at Blue's quiet word. His fresh, alert appearance didn't help her mood, either. His sunglasses, unlike hers, probably did not hide bloodshot eyes and puffy eyelids. Neither did he tense at every little sound. Well, that was just wrong. A man who had spent an evening in a crowded, loud roadhouse and fought a drunk in the parking lot should not look this good.

He glanced at the thermoses she held. "A little hair of the dog?"

Her face warmed. "Patience fixed me a tonic."

Dewey eyed the food Patience had deposited on the ground by her car. "I can take this ice chest over to the shade, then come back to help carry the rest." As his gaze traveled upward again he spotted her belly ring and Delta swore he stopped breathing for a second. Yes, indeed, Charlotte's going away party was already scheduled.

"I can help," Blue said.

Dewey tore his gaze away from the sparkly pink stones and swung the big ice chest into Blue's arms. "Thanks."

Blue staggered back a step. "Sure."

Patience closed her car door and pulled her curly red hair into a ponytail before bending over to pick up a round container. "I don't want this fresh chocolate pie to spoil, so I'll carry it first."

Dewey hefted the large picnic basket. "After you."

That left Delta to bring up the rear with her two thermoses. She felt better already.

As they put the food under a tree, she noticed Brax and Charlotte with their heads together, talking in low tones. Delta's gaze cut to Dewey.

He was busy helping with the food and she didn't know if he saw or not. Hopefully, it wouldn't be a problem, soon.

Brax and Charlotte walked over, arm in arm. "Here's the man I said I'd bring to even out the teams." Charlotte said.

Patience took in Charlotte's tight t-shirt, electric blue tap shorts, and short-heeled backless sandals. "Speaking of teams. You going to be able to move fast in that outfit? I thought we were playing flag football, not Broadway."

Charlotte flipped her hair. "It's too hot to wear jeans. Besides, I don't do well at sweaty, athletic things."

Patience lifted a shoulder. "That's too bad. I do everything well. *Especially* sweaty, athletic things."

Charlotte rolled her eyes and Delta sucked in her cheeks and bit down. Blue choked out a laugh and Dewey emitted a short whine reminiscent of a hound dog in pursuit.

"It is kind of hot," Dewey managed. "We should probably take on some water, then set the rules."

Brax offered his hand to Patience. "Harlan Braxton. I'm new to the area. And I gotta say this town has some very pretty women."

Dewey ducked his head. "Sorry. I forget not everyone knows Patience." He straightened his shoulders. "Patience owns Mackie's Café in town. Best cook around."

Patience leaned over and kissed his cheek. "Why thank you, Deputy."

Charlotte paid no attention, but Dewey's face reddened. "Welcome. Any of you ladies played flag football before?"

Patience looked him directly in the eye. "Played flag with my brother and his friends all the time. I love football."

Right into the end zone, Delta thought as she took a sip of the beer and tomato juice and puckered.

Blue laughed at her and spoke softly. "Glad to see you're feeling better. I want to take you up on your offer from last night."

Delta swallowed too fast and choked. "What?"

"You okay?"

*Okay as in ready to jump him? Okay as in wanting him naked?* "Um, yes, I'm okay. What do you mean my offer?"

His expression showed nothing. "What did you think? I said I thought there could be a way around your lawsuit and offered to help. You said 'Be my guest.'"

Delta absently rubbed her temple. "That's right, I did. Do you have an idea already?"

Blue grinned. "I'd like to break Slayton's kneecaps, but failing that, I know a very savvy attorney."

"Oh," said Delta, disappointed. "Didn't I tell you Daddy said the agreement's solid? Besides, I already have a business attorney and I can't afford another one."

Blue shook his head. "You don't have to. He's a client I made a bundle for. He specializes in divorce cases and offered me a free consultation. He can't take a case in Georgia, but he's very good at coming up with strategy and ferreting out unattractive circumstances of his opponent's clients."

Delta felt hope flicker. "Really? That's so great. I don't want it *pro bono*, though. I could give him an office space redesign."

"Don't think that'll be necessary," Blue said. "But I'll tell him. First, let's see what he comes up with. When can I get copies of the paperwork so I can get him started?"

She tapped her chin. "I only have one set of originals. I'll go to Daddy's office after the game and scan a copy.

Send it to you in an email later today. I have to meet with
my business attorney tomorrow."

Blue nodded. "I'll forward it to Mark as soon as I get
it."

"You two ready?"

Delta brought her attention back to Dewey. "I am."

"Men against women?" Patience asked.

Dewey grinned. "That's the most fun, but hardly fair."

Patience shot a thumb at Brax. "Don't know him, but
if it was me against you and Blue, y'all'd leave shirtless."

Dewey goggled at her and laughed. "You're a real
sport, Patience."

"Men against women, it is then," she said. "Delta?"

Delta started pacing. Patience had coached her wo
days ago. "The rules as we, the women, understand them,
are; two flags apiece, one for each hip. Flags are to be worn
at an agreed-upon length on everyone and tight enough
so they don't fall out but not so tight that they can't be
pulled out easily. Barring pockets, wearer can use waistband. Once the ball is set in motion, everybody is eligible
to be a receiver. Three forward plays or completed passes
constitute a first down. Goals are to be clearly marked.
Running backwards is optional."

She swiveled her head to encompass the three men.
"That about it?"

Patience wasn't the only good sport, Blue thought as
he listened to Delta lay out the rules. He could see the
pain of her hangover clearly. She'd taken off her sunglasses and the lines around her eyes showed the effort.

Nevertheless, she was a graceful, beautiful woman and he regretted, for just a beat, not giving in and making love to her last night. Especially after the way she'd pulled him to her for that kiss on her porch.

And why had he brought up the offer to help her fight the legal hassle she was having? She'd forgotten all about it. Oh, well. One or two contacts with that sharp client of his and he could call his promise met. Yeah, he could do that.

"You playing?"

Blue realized Dewey was talking to him as the women walked downfield. Brax stepped over to them. "Man, you boys got it lucky 'round here. Did you see that bling hanging off the bellybutton of that redhead?"

Dewey frowned. "She's off limits."

This was news to Blue, but he didn't say anything as Brax glanced at Charlotte, then held up his hands. "Just remarking."

Patience brought out a dozen bright red handkerchiefs and each player put on two, then she carefully marked the goals with large white napkins held in place by rocks.

Dewey looked downfield as they huddled. "We're going to take it easy on them. No rough stuff, understand? Maybe even let 'em get away with a few mistakes."

Blue and Brax nodded, but Blue privately thought Dewey was in for a surprise. He didn't know or care about Charlotte's motives, but Delta was very competitive and Patience appeared equally competent. He was sure they were planning the demise of the men.

They didn't have long to wait.

The women won the toss and on the first play, Charlotte jumped up and down with her arms in the air, squealing, "Here, here, send it to me."

In the short time it took the men to refocus, Patience had run the field for a touchdown, unimpeded.

The look on Dewey's face was worth the embarrassment at having been had, Blue decided.

"Beginner's luck," Dewey said as the men huddled before the next play. "I'll keep an eye on Patience since she got lucky before."

Blue couldn't resist. "I'm faster. I'll go after her."

Dewey worked on that for a second. "But you've been sneezing and that slows you down. Besides, I'm the captain and what I say goes."

"Who died and made you captain?" Blue asked.

"Y'all gonna talk it to death or play?" Patience called. The women giggled.

"All right," Blue conceded. "You guard Patience and I'll take Delta." He looked at Brax, who wore a neutral expression. "You mind taking Charlotte?"

"Sure," he said. "I assume that means you're saving me for the big play."

Blue laughed. "Right."

The men had to work a little harder than they planned, but got a touchdown to even the score. When the women got the ball, they didn't try to distract the men with Charlotte again. Patience spun one eighty and faked a handoff to Delta before sprinting past them. She would have gotten away clean if Dewey hadn't been concentrating on her. His long reach saved the men from another humiliating touchdown by the women.

"Too close," Blue said in the huddle. "And pretty slick. I thought she might've been kidding about having played a lot, but she has some good moves."

Dewey watched Patience walk to Delta and Charlotte. "Yeah, great moves."

The women were closing in on a second goal when they surprised the men by handing off to Charlotte. She ran a few steps, then tripped in her kitten heels. Brax couldn't stop, and fell on top of her. Charlotte's squeal wasn't exactly one of pain as Brax rolled her over. Dewey stood with his arms hanging loose, looking uncertain.

Patience walked over and stopped right in front of him, breathing hard. "That's not the way that play was supposed to work."

Dewey blinked.

Blue started forward when he felt one of his flags being pulled from his pocket. He turned to see Delta tilt her head away from Dewey and Patience, so he followed her to the shade.

"I need water," she announced. "And you've been sneezing. Want to join me in a break?"

He folded his arms and leaned against the tree. "If you'll explain what's going on with Patience."

Soft gray eyes gazed over his shoulder at the other two couples. "Not sure she'd want that. You could always ask her yourself."

Blue glanced at Dewey and Patience deep in conversation. "She looks busy."

"Coward."

"Uh huh. How are you feeling?"

"Much better, thanks."

He decided to take a risk. "About that problem with your ex."

"What about it? I already said you could have your attorney friend look at it."

"Couple of other things," Blue said. "Thought about what triggered the suit and I agree. I think it was your run-in with his mother. I also think she knew before the marriage ever took place. You were independent-minded and very talented. If Slayton went ahead, against her strong wishes she would find a way to win in the end. So she had that clause inserted as your punishment for not being who she wanted you to be. If you realized the marriage was a mistake and left him, she'd have her revenge when you turned successful. So, she waited."

Delta looked paler than she had at the beginning of the game. She swallowed. "I am so stupid."

"Not stupid," he said. "You were in love and vulnerable. The good part is, even if they take half your business, you're still a brilliant, independent architect. It might take a little longer, but in the end, you win."

Her shoulders sagged, but a ghost of a smile spread. "Let's hope so. You said a couple of things?"

She'd already turned him down once, but that was before the lawsuit. Blue wanted her to know help was available. He huffed out a breath. "If you need some cash to float your expenses until you get back on your feet, I could bail you out."

He saw her struggle with her frustration.

She sighed. "Thanks, but no."

He knew that would be her answer. "Delta ..."

"Break's over."

They turned toward Dewey's voice. The others were standing where Charlotte and Brax had fallen, looking at them expectantly. Dewey no longer seemed upset and Patience was smiling.

"Can we at least talk about this some more?" Blue asked, pushing away from the tree.

"Talk all you want," she said. "I pulled myself out of a place where I'd allowed people to use me because I wanted to repay them for accepting me into their family. I'm never going there again."

*What the hell?* How could she compare his offer with the way she was treated by her ex-husband's family? He took her arm to stop her progress. "Wait a minute. You think I'm capable of hurting you like that?"

Delta held up her chin and spoke slowly. "No, you aren't." She shook her head. "No."

# Chapter Eighteen

Blue saw the anguish in her eyes and let it go. That son-of-a-bitch really did a number on her. Somebody would have to be willing to invest a lot of time and patience to gain her complete trust. He found himself wanting to be that someone, then checked his impulse. Last night she had said she would never be involved with a weak-willed, self-hating man again. He knew she wasn't talking about him. What he didn't know was if he could overcome his own ghosts in order to be with her.

The teams played for another hour before giving in to a tie game. The men's only advantage was Charlotte. If she'd been any kind of threat, they'd have lost for sure.

Everyone leaned back groaning after eating the lunch. Patience had outdone herself and if Blue wasn't mistaken, most of the dishes were Dewey's favorites.

The couples were paired differently than at the start of the day. Charlotte announced she would keep the new-comer company, so she sat by Brax. Dewey sat by the food, which put him next to Patience. Blue caught his friend grinning at the redhead repeatedly, and he didn't think it was due to the excellent food.

As everyone started to clean up, Charlotte whispered in Brax's ear. His gaze slid around the group before he shook his head. Charlotte whispered more urgently and he mouthed the word "no". Again, Blue got the distinct feeling they weren't new acquaintances.

Charlotte moved away from Brax and pinned Blue with a stubborn look of intent. "Brax is the one I told you about who might be interested in taking Brisco's Folly off your hands."

Blue flicked a glance past Charlotte to Brax. The guy didn't change expression, but a muscle worked in his jaw.

Delta stopped stacking plates and looked at Blue. His instincts jangled a big alarm where Brax was concerned. "It's not for sale," he said.

"Blue?" Delta looked shocked at his answer.

Brax slipped a card from his pocket, his expression neutral. "I'm prepared to offer above the fair market value. Here's the amount and where I'm staying. Think it over."

"Nothing to think about," Blue responded. "It's not for sale."

Delta reached for the card. "We haven't made a final decision, yet. Thanks for the interest. We'll get back to you."

She slid the card into her jeans pocket and continued to clean, her fury escalating. What on earth gave Blue the right to make a unilateral decision? Hadn't she just told him she would make it on her own? Selling Brisco's Folly could be her chance to start over. After all, the property was half hers and Gran was her flesh and blood, not his.

She sucked in a breath, her thought shaming her as her glance moved to Blue. He was probably only reacting to his dislike of Brax. She didn't particularly like the man herself, but Blue's behavior was too strong for the circumstances.

When the group broke up, Charlotte made a show of leaving arm in arm with Dewey as Brax walked, seemingly unconcerned, to a shiny red truck.

Delta stood talking to Patience. She saw Blue waiting and felt at odds with her reactions of last night and this afternoon. As a result, she avoided him.

"How long you gonna stay mad at him?" Patience asked.

"I don't know what you're talking about."

"And butter wouldn't melt in your mouth, as my Mama used to say."

"Don't start with me," Delta said. "Blue was selfish and rude. He may not need that money, but I do."

Patience held her hands up. "Tell him. Not me." Her gaze followed Dewey's truck out of the parking lot. "You think he noticed me today?"

Delta laughed outright. "You know he did. He couldn't stop looking at you." She cast around for another topic. "When did you get your bellybutton pierced?"

"'Bout the same time the Tarot cards confirmed Mr. Dewey Harcourt's the man for me." Patience grinned and fisted her hands on her hips. "You stretching this conversation out the rest of the day?"

Delta made a face and picked up the two thermoses and a sack holding garbage. When Patience hefted the picnic basket, Blue came over.

"Let me help with that."

"Believe it or not, and you should after today," Delta said. "We're perfectly capable of getting this stuff to her car. *And* making our own decisions."

Patience raised her eyebrows. "Ouch." She glanced at Blue. "I'm fine with this, but thanks. The food's gone so it's pretty light. Besides, you got a big enough job cut out for you, already."

Blue followed them across the parking lot and stood by, hands in his pockets.

When Patience drove away, he turned to Delta. "Are you going to let me explain?"

She narrowed her eyes at him. "I imagine you don't like the looks or the actions of Brax. Neither do I, but most of what we don't like is Charlotte's fault. However, that didn't give you the right to speak for me. Especially since offers for a piece of land like Brisco's Folly don't come around every day."

"Guilty, as charged," Blue said. "But I think Braxton is more than a temporary distraction for Charlotte. For all we know, he wants to pave over Brisco's Folly and turn it into a junkyard."

Delta folded her arms. "Well, that's what *I* figured. But I'm greedy, so I didn't think you or the town would mind."

Blue sighed. "Look, I'm sorry. It ticked me off at the way he and Charlotte were treating Dewey and I didn't think it was a big deal. If you really want to sell, your father's got that legitimate offer ... So are we okay?"

Delta calmed down. If she were honest with herself, she'd admit her new relationship with Blue had, for some reason, made her take it out on him extra hard. Did she feel the hurt more? "I guess we're okay, but a back-up offer's always good to have."

Blue shook his head. "I can't believe you're really thinking of dealing with this guy."

"And I can't believe you're being stubborn to the point that you won't even consider his offer as a back-up."

Blue rubbed the center of his forehead. "What's the offer?"

Delta blinked. She hadn't even looked. She pulled the card out of her pocket, read the amount and gasped, then handed the card to Blue. "It's over $500,000. I hope the offer Daddy has lined up is this high."

Blue frowned at the card, flipping it over and back. "How do we know this is good?"

She took it back with trembling fingers, her throat tight. "I guess we don't, but if both offers are legitimate and close in amount, Gran's bequest could save my business."

He pulled her into his arms, and Delta realized how much she needed holding. What would that be like? Going to your husband or lover when you were feeling frustrated or out-of-sorts? And what if Blue were that person?

The thought filled her with unexpected warmth. Where was the anger of a few minutes ago? When she'd been truly pissed off at Slayton, which happened more and more often in their last year together, there was never any give from him. He'd just hold up a hand and walk away. Being emotional with Blue was different. He cared enough to work it out.

She stepped back reluctantly. "I have to get to Daddy's office to scan those papers, then go home and pack."

He ran the backs of his fingers across her cheek and smiled. "In the meantime, I'll engage the cavalry."

Another emotion flickered briefly in Delta's heart. "I'll keep my fingers crossed and see you when I get back."

"It'll work out. We'll make it."

Did he mean they, he and she, would make it? Or did he mean they would find a solution to her lawsuit?

"Walk you home?"

An aching tiredness crept into her bones and Delta longed to take refuge in her childhood room and sleep her anxieties away. She laced her fingers with Blue and nodded.

"Skin on outta that bed!" Dewey boomed through Blue's bedroom door. "S'almost daylight and you wanted me to wake you before I left for the station."

Blue cracked the one eye not buried in his pillow and uttered a sound that made Dewey laugh.

Why on God's earth had he chosen an evil exercise like running, he thought, as Dewey's laugh receded. And it was his turn to do the laundry. Blue staggered to a standing position, stripped the bed and left everything in a pile on the floor.

"Laundry when I get back," he mumbled to no one in particular as he pulled on his shorts, sweatshirt, and running shoes.

Shorter fall days and a sky heavy with the threat of rain made the path along the river barely discernible, but Blue had walked or run it thousands of times. He ran slowly, warming up, behind the houses of people he'd known forever. Some he liked for their small town sense of community. Others he barely tolerated because the same mentality bred locked-down, shuttered biases. There was one particular bias he needed to overcome and decided he should be here to do it. It didn't hurt that Delta was here, too. Once he broke that boundary, he might talk himself into working on the one between himself and Delta.

Happy with his decision, he hit his stride as usual at a half mile. The crisp air filled his lungs and cleared his muddled head. He wasn't even bothered by whatever made his allergies act up.

An occasional light flickered through the trees and he glanced quickly at the back porch of the Jameson house as he passed. Thoughts of Delta and the changes in their relationship occupied his mind and he had to concentrate as he approached a thickly treed slope. It was darker here and the leaves underfoot had turned to soft, slippery mulch.

An angled shadow at the edge of the trees caught his eye. In the split second before his stride propelled him forward, his mind imagined it moved into his path. Whatever tripped him, he hit the ground hard, his arm thrown out at an awkward angle. His head struck something hard-edged, then he slid a foot or two and rolled off the sharp bank into the water.

The southern branch of the Patchet River was never warm, even in the midst of a Georgia summer. At the end of September, it presented a frigid, dark welcome. Blue automatically brought his arms up to push for the surface, but overwhelming pain weighted down the left one and it was useless. Words rang through his pounding head as he fought against the numbing cold and fear; why now, and Delta ...

The undercurrents sucked him away from the bank and dry land. A strong will and strong legs overcame the threatening lethargy and he kicked upward. Too little, too late.

The bank seemed an unreachable island. He slipped under again and came up disoriented. Something in his high school swimming class pushed itself to the front of his brain and he took a gulp of air then curled in a dead man's float to save energy. He repeated the technique several more times and eventually the current carried him to a gentler slope of the riverbank where his numbed feet found solid ground before he blacked out.

Damn. He hadn't made it after all.

No feeling in his arms or legs and he couldn't move. These must be his last thoughts. Well, it sucked going out with so much pain. His lungs and throat hurt like hell, but that was nothing compared to the screaming pain in his arm and head.

Something warm floated onto his shoulders. Wings? Yeah, Richmond, you got wings. Whatever it was smelled so good. Delta. It smelled like Delta. He smiled. Dying wasn't so bad after all. He even heard her. Soft words coming from the darkness.

"Come on, sugar. Help me out here. You weigh a ton. Get out of the water or you'll freeze. Please. I'll promise you anything. Stop smiling now, and say something so I know your brain's still working."

"Cold," he said. "So cold."

"I know, sugar. But you'll be warm, I promise."

An awareness that he was being tugged at made its way into Blue's consciousness. He tried to move in the direction the voice wanted and felt something slimy against his cheek. "Not good," he protested.

The tugging changed to the injured arm. Pain spiraled to his stomach. He groaned and hauled himself to his good elbow, then threw up.

# Chapter Nineteen

Delta had laid her jacket across Blue's back. She reached gingerly over him and pulled some clean tissues out of the pocket to dab his mouth. "I called Dewey. He's on the way. I'm sorry about your arm. I dropped my penlight and didn't see it was hurt. Did that happen when you fell in?"

"Damnit, Blue," she sniffed. "I'm babbling and I used all my tissues on you. Now that I know you're not dead, I'm going to cry."

She rolled him onto his back. New, misty sunlight showed her his teeth were chattering.

"Tripped over something," he said hoarsely.

Delta found her penlight and pulled the sleeve of her jacket, now mashed partway under him, up to wipe at his face where some leaves stuck. She gasped at the gash and swelling above his temple. It turned garish when red and blue emergency lights filtered down from the road.

"Dewey's here," she said. "Stay quiet while I get him."

She slipped twice as she scrambled up the leaf-slick-ened slope to the car. Tears and panic choked her words as she met Dewey. "Please hurry, he almost drowned. And he's not very coherent. His head and left arm look bad."

Dewey nodded and stuck a square package under his arm as he followed her toward the river. "How in the hell did he fall in? He's lived with that path his whole life."

"He said he tripped over something," Delta said absently.

Dewey cast her a questioning look and scanned the path when they reached Blue. The deputy spread a ther-mal blanket on the bank and slid his arms under Blue's body, being careful to jolt him as little as possible. Blue grimaced anyway and squeezed his eyes shut when Dewey slipped him out of the water and onto the blanket.

"I'm not going to wait for a county ambulance," Dewey said to Delta. "I'll carry him to the cruiser and you help me lay him across the back seat."

Delta nodded and stroked Blue's cheek. "He looks so helpless. I've never seen him like this." She stared at Dewey's face while he pressed gently on Blue's torso and limbs, asking questions.

"You've seen a lot worse, right? Promise me he'll be okay?"

Dewey didn't meet her gaze. He carefully lifted Blue and started to walk. "His physical condition's good to start with. That counts for a lot."

Even though it sounded reassuring, Delta couldn't stop the tears spilling over.

As they reached the car and were positioning Blue on the back seat, he winced and opened his eyes. "Now I know I haven't died. You've handed out too many speed trap tickets to be going the same place as me."

Dewey laughed low. "Hell, that's just 'cause the SEC ain't caught up with you yet, boy."

Blue's gaze found Delta and he smiled with blue lips. "You called me sugar."

Delta's heart gladdened that he recognized her and Dewey, but she couldn't stop petting on him. "I was under a great deal of stress. It won't happen again."

Dewey interrupted. "Flirting later. Blue, can you bring your knees up? I want to close the door so we can get underway."

Blue moved his feet and raised his head." If I don't survive your manhandling, take care of Delta."

Delta drew a sharp breath and felt the blood drain from her face. Had they missed some critical wound?

Dewey rolled his eyes. "That must've been some hit on the head, you thinking Delta can't take care of herself. She seems pretty capable to me."

She recognized the light banter for the distraction is was, but her hands still trembled as she tucked the blanket around Blue. "Dewey's right. You're the only one I can see that can't take care of himself. Now try to relax, but keep talking."

She backed away to shut the door. "Watch your head."

Dewey spoke over the top of the cruiser. "It's not exactly SOP, but since we'll be there in less than five minutes, you want to ride along?"

"Yes," she said, reaching for the passenger door.

Peck's Bluff supported only a small hospital/clinic with a dozen beds. When Dewey pulled up there was an attendant ready with a gurney.

"I can walk," Blue said as he clutched at the blanket, trying to sit up.

"Don't make me come back there," Delta threatened.

"Listen to her," Dewey warned. "Besides, we gotta follow department rules here or I get my ass chewed. Anyway, I can press your weight, easy."

Blue's head slumped. No color had returned to his face. "Braggart."

"Ain't braggin' if it's true. Now, lay still 'til I come around there."

Delta got out and waited while Dewey spoke to the attendant. "Hey, Sam. My friend hasn't got any ID on him, but I can take care of enough paperwork for the doctor to start checking him out."

The young man nodded. He and Dewey gently slid Blue out of the cruiser and onto the gurney.

"I'll call Aunt Caroline," Delta said as they rushed inside. Blue's skin looked even more ashen under the fluorescent lights.

Blue pulled his hand from under the blanket, his cold fingers encircling her wrist. "Don't upset her."

"Your mother's the calmest person on the planet," she teased. "But I promise not to upset her."

He tipped his head, then flinched from the movement. "Stay for a while?"

He needn't have asked. "As long as it takes," she said.

# Chapter Twenty

Delta held Blue's hand until Dewey and the attendant wheeled him through double doors labeled *Patients and Emergency Personnel Only*. She looked to her left and was mildly reassured that the small waiting area looked the same as it had the last time she was here; about eight years ago when Van had fallen and broken his leg water skiing.

She sat down, shivers and light-headedness settling in. Her body hunched forward, and she rubbed her arms. The next thing she knew, Dewey had thrown a blanket across her shoulders and handed her a cup of hot chocolate.

"Thanks," she said. "I can't get warm."

"Mild shock, probably. When you feel better, I need to ask you some questions."

Fatigue fought for her attention. "First, I have to call Aunt Caroline."

"Already done," Dewey said. "I filled out the basics of the paperwork and talked to the doctor on call. I told Mrs.

Richmond there'd been an accident and I thought Blue'd be okay. She's coming down with some of his things."

Delta regarded him thoughtfully. She knew he wasn't one of those good ol' boy deputies, but she'd also never stopped to consider him closely. He'd been in Blue's class in high school, and very sports oriented. Now she saw what Patience did. Beyond the short, blond, military haircut and large frame, was a very conscientious man. One good at his job and a true friend. He took the hand that wasn't holding the hot chocolate, rubbing it between his large ones.

"Better?" he asked.

"Yes, thanks." She took a deep breath. "I don't mind telling you I was terrified when I saw him lying there, still as death."

Dewey nodded. "I know Blue was running. Why were you on the path?"

Delta swirled the hot chocolate, staring at the watery brown liquid. "Blue has a client who's a sharp divorce attorney. He might be able to help with my lawsuit. I was supposed to scan and email my paperwork to Blue, but the scanner in Daddy's office was broken. I wasted most of the afternoon waiting for the repair guy to show and finally gave up. Had dinner with my folks and then over to see Patience.

"I was on my way to drop off the paperwork at Aunt Caroline's, hoping Blue could get a copy scanned and emailed today." She slipped her hand from between Dewey's and picked up a plastic file covered in dirty smears.

She didn't even remember bringing it. "Guess it will have to wait."

"Didn't know about the lawsuit," Dewey said. "Sorry to hear it."

"Not something I'm proud of," she said. "You saw me *celebrating* night before last."

He nodded. "Oh, that thing you said about your ex to Charlotte."

Delta shivered. "Anyway, if I hadn't been on the path, or he hadn't drifted to the shallow place I found him – he might not have been seen ..." Tears burned the back of her throat and her voice cracked. "Sorry."

"It's a natural reaction," he said, pressing some tissues into her hands. "You be okay while I go see if there's any word? They're more likely to give me information."

"Thanks. I'll be fine."

She watched Dewey's retreating back and saw the look of surprise on the faces of passers-by coming toward her. Not only were the file and her jacket spotted with mud, so were her knees. And now that warmth was returning, her right knee throbbed. She had gone down hard trying to pull Blue farther from the water.

The pain wasn't the worst of it. The situation with the lawsuit and now Blue's close call threatened to swamp her. She started to cover her face with her hands and realized dirt and blood smudged her palms. Blue's blood. The shaking started again, harder than before. She scrubbed her hands against her pants, tears blurring the smears even more. Nothing Slayton or his parents had ever done to her had torn this kind of reaction from her. As fast as they had come, Delta forced her tumbling emotions to still. *Get ahold of yourself, Jameson.*

She rose stiffly and went to the ladies' room, returning to the reception area in time to see Aunt Caroline hurry down the hall carrying a tote. She was pale, but appeared composed.

"Delta, honey, are you all right? Were you in the accident, too?"

Delta looked down at her stained khakis, and clay-smeared shoes. She knew her eyes and nose were red and swollen from crying. "No, no. I'm okay. It wasn't that kind of accident. Blue tripped on the path and hurt his head and arm before falling into the river. I found him partway up the bank and tried to drag him out."

Aunt Caroline nodded. "Thank goodness you came across him. Where is he now?"

"He's still being evaluated," Delta said.

As she spoke, a pretty young doctor came past the doorway followed by Dewey. "Are y'all here for Blue Richmond?" she asked.

Delta twisted her fingers together. "Is he going to be okay?"

The doctor gave a wry smile. "If he'll cooperate."

"That means he's all right," Aunt Caroline said, blowing out a breath in relief.

Delta wanted to see for herself. "Can he have visitors?"

"He's groggy and cranky and his head looks worse than it is," the doctor said. "His arm's been x-rayed and isn't broken. He must have flexed his deltoid before he hit whatever banged up that area. My guess is a tree root or rock. I wanted to keep him overnight for observation, but he's vetoed that."

"Thank you, doctor," Blue's mother said. She handed the tote to Delta. "Why don't you go on? Dewey and I'll be there in a minute."

"Are you sure?" Delta asked.

"I'm sure. Now that I know he's okay, I can wait a bit."

The doctor escorted Delta to the room. "Don't take more than five minutes. "He's on pain medication and needs rest."

Delta opened the door and went in quietly. Blue lay on the only bed in the room, his eyes closed. She walked over and sat the tote down.

Blue blinked slowly, then smiled. "Hey."

"You scared ten years off me."

"They took my clothes and gave me a shot, but I made them let me brush my teeth. Want to fool around?"

She was so glad to have him back, nothing else mattered. She choked out a laugh. "That's the pain medication talking. Besides, you mother's outside and she'll be in here in a minute."

He grinned. "Then you're thinking about it?"

Part of her was so relieved he was going to be okay, and another part of her wanted to kiss him silly. "I most certainly am not."

"Right, so give me a chaste kiss, and I'll change the subject."

She looked over her shoulder, then leaned over to give him a peck. Unfortunately, she was standing on his right side. His arm snaked out and pulled her down for a thorough kiss just as his mother and Dewey walked in.

Delta pulled away from the bed, her face hot.

"Guess I shouldn't have worried about you being on your deathbed," his mother said.

Blue gave a loopy grin. "Delta was checking to see if I had any loose teeth."

"Blue!" Delta was mortified.

A twinkle lit his mother's eyes as she walked over to the bed and bent to kiss his cheek. "I see. I wasn't told your mouth was injured, but I hope that was a kiss of gratitude. Dewey tells me Delta probably saved your life. I know I'm grateful."

She hesitated as she fussed with his hair. "We can only stay a few minutes. Please do what the doctor says while you're here. And you'll be spending the night at Gran's. The doctor said you need to be checked for signs of concussion every few hours." She brushed at his cheek. "I told her you're too hardheaded."

Blue yawned. "Yes, ma'am."

Exhaustion weighed on Delta. Had she been allowed, she would have gladly crawled under the clean white sheets and pale green blanket of Blue's bed, curled up in his good arm and snuggled in. She blinked hard. Associating herself in such an intimate manner with Blue didn't shock her as it might have even a week ago. Was feeling that safe with a man you had known all your life a sign that you were falling in love? Or had it been there for a long time, waiting for the circumstances in their lives to change and find them?

Delta stepped back. "I, um have some calls to make and an appointment to reschedule. I'll come back and visit later."

"They're releasing him this afternoon," Dewey said, grinning. "They need these beds for sick people."

Blue looked at Dewey. "This shot's supposed to last a couple of hours, but I wanted to talk to you about something today anyway. Can you come over this evening?"

Dewey nodded, then turned toward Delta as Blue's eyelids dipped against the numbing shot.

# Chapter Twenty-One

Pain pulled Blue out of sleep to the edge of awareness. His arm and head were sore, but he was warm and dry, so it couldn't be that bad. Had he lost a kickboxing match?

"Hey, darlin'."

His head jerked toward the voice and Blue immediately regretted the movement. He peered out of eyes that refused to open all the way. Charlotte stood close to his bed. Why was he in bed? And why did Charlotte look like she'd been crying?

She patted his shoulder. "They said you'd be okay. I just wanted to, you know, check on you myself." She bent to kiss his forehead, lightly. "You take care, now."

He nodded in agreement before an overwhelming force dragged him back into oblivion.

Sharper pain pulled him out of sleep a second time. He lay in the hospital bed, now remembering his accident. He felt stupid for tripping over something on the path.

With that thought, the vague memory that the object had moved, swam in, then out of his consciousness. He shook his head, grimacing at how much it hurt. His grimace turned to a grin at the memory of Delta's kiss. He felt a little bad that he'd tricked her. He'd been medicated just enough to be reckless, though not so out of it that he'd been unaware of what he wanted. He'd wanted to feel alive and kissing Delta had accomplished that.

Yesterday at the park, he hadn't brought up her attempt to knock his gentlemanly kiss of the previous night right out of the park and into a very hot, heart-pounding trip to the nearest motel. Blue figured she'd be embarrassed enough. Which left him wondering what Delta did want.

The bag she'd brought in sat on a wheeled tray at the foot of his bed. With some wincing and maneuvering, he shifted it to his lap, then raised the head of the bed. His mother had obviously packed it. On top, were toiletries in a plastic bag, next, his wallet and watch, then, underwear, clothes and shoes. His happiness at having everything he needed to escape was short-lived. According to his watch, he'd missed most of the action on the Chicago Exchange. He'd also have to type one-handed now, thanks to the injury to his arm.

Maybe his mother could bring his laptop to the hospital. He reached for the phone by his bed. "Ow." Not a good move. They'd immobilized his arm, so his attempt only shifted the injured muscle. He pushed the nurse call button, and a few minutes later the doctor walked in.

She raised her eyebrows at the items spread in front of him. "You have a high tolerance for pain medication, Mr. Richmond. That shot would have felled an ox for at least another hour. How are you feeling?"

"Better than when I came in, thanks." He tipped his head toward the sling binding his arm. "How long do I have to wear this?"

The doctor moved to his bedside, placed her fingers on his wrist and took his pulse. Next, she pulled a disposable thermometer out of her pocket. "Put this under your tongue." She wrote on his chart then clicked on a small light to test his pupil responses. Then she read the thermometer and wrote some more before looking at him.

"To answer your question, I have to ask you a few. Deputy Harcourt's attempt at filling out your health history left some holes. He answered negative to everything and we're so short-handed, everybody, including me, forgot to ask your mother when she was here. Anything you want to add?"

Blue shrugged his good shoulder. "Nothing in my father's family. Don't have a clue on my mother's paternal side."

The doctor studied him for a moment. "Sounds like that bothers you."

"Let's just say it's had its moments, lately."

"You know," she said. "The average person's background is rarely perfect."

The pain was now a constant wave in his head and shoulder. He was in no mood to explain his recently discovered relations. "Guess that makes me average," he griped, then sighed. "When can I get out of here?"

She shrugged and smiled. "Leave the sling on about three days, then limit the use of that arm for another week. The muscle needs ice packs, and I'll give you a prescription for pain medication – you'll need that to sleep. I'll write instructions for whoever gets the lovely job of watching over you. I'm also giving you some antibiotics. Open wounds and river water are not a good mix."

To answer your second question, this afternoon. You'll have to come back to get the stitches on your head removed in about ten days. Or have your own doctor do it."

Blue nodded and started to gather the items on his lap, but the doctor beat him to it. "Enough chatting. You're awake because you're hurting. I'll leave these within reach and be right back."

She returned in a few minutes with a hypodermic and swabbed his arm. "Who would you like me to call to pick you up?"

"My mother, I guess." He tipped his head toward the syringe. "And thanks."

He started to relax before she even left the room.

The next thing he knew, he heard the doctor talking quietly to his mother.

"You were right. He's a stubborn, hard-headed man."

Blue's mother laughed and glanced in his direction. "Ready to take you home," she said. "Do you need help dressing?"

He swung his legs over the side of the bed, trying to blink away the grogginess. "Just leave my bag in the bathroom. I'll try it alone. Disregard the growls of frustration."

Blue thought he'd never get out. For less than a day's stay, the paperwork at the hospital had been staggering. At least it seemed that way. Between the pain and pain medication, most of the afternoon had been a blur.

Luckily, the Exchange was slow, but he had some stocks and funds to monitor, so he spent a torturous hour hunting and pecking one-handed on his laptop. Dewey showed up as he'd transferred his last entries to his spreadsheets.

"Hey, man. How're you feeling?"

"Lopsided," said Blue. "And my butt's asleep. When I try to stand up after taking a pill, the room spins. Other than those minor things, I'm doing great."

Dewey laughed. "You forgot sarcastic *and* pissy."

Blue rolled his neck, and the feeling of being kicked in the head by a mule settled over his right eye. He closed his eyes and let out a slow breath. "Sorry. It's almost time for the next pill."

Dewey grimaced at the head wound. "Haven't seen one that bad since Tommy Myers face guard broke and he took a cleat in the cheekbone."

"Thanks," Blue said. "I have deformity to look forward to."

A half-laugh, half-cough, erupted from Dewey. "By the way, I found the reason you fell. Some kid left his wagon on the path. Looks like you tripped over the handle. You were going at a pretty good clip, too. The wagon slid most of the way down the bank and stuck in the bushes."

Blue squinted and tried to bring up the shadowy form right before the moment of impact. He feared he would lose it entirely after a couple more pills. "It moved into the path," he said slowly.

After a pause, Blue opened his eyes. Dewey studied him. "You mean it slipped free of the wet leaves by the tree and rolled down?"

"I mean it more than likely had help."

"You sure?"

Blue nodded, closed the laptop, and held up a hand. "Hold it a minute."

His mother appeared at the entryway, eyed the laptop, and sighed. "Time for your pill. Do you have food in your stomach?"

He pointed to a plate where a lone cookie remained amidst crumbs. "Yes. Can we make it a half tablet?"

She walked to him and slid her cool hand over his forehead. "You can try that, but if it doesn't do the job, promise me you'll take the other half?"

"Promise."

His mother turned to Dewey. "The pill will let him sleep for about an hour. You can read the newspaper or watch television, then we'd like you to stay for dinner."

Delight sprang into Dewey's face so fast, Blue laughed through his pain.

"Yes, thanks."

Blue took the pill, then stood to roll his shoulders and pace the room a couple of times before sitting back down.

"So, how'd you know your mom was coming? Dewey asked as soon as Blue's mother left.

"Board in the floor creaks at the entrance to the hall,"

Blue replied. "Gran asked grandpa to fix it a hundred times, but he never did. It was our secret so we'd know when someone was on the way."

Dewey nodded. "Dad and I always went out to the garage." He glanced toward the front door. "I could walk down to the path before dinner."

The pill warmed Blue's thoughts. "Any footprints'll still be there later. I got other stuff to talk about."

Dewey leaned back. "Me, too. You first."

Blue nodded. "Thanks. Other thing I wanted to talk about is Brisco's Folly." He glanced toward the hallway. "Why do you think Braxton's interested?"

"Been thinking about getting a piece of land myself," Dewey said, glancing toward the parlor windows. "And I got to tell you Brisco's Folly is about as worthless as it comes. Maybe twenty good acres out of a hundred and sixty. The rest is a breeding ground for all kinds of bugs and stuff. Can't see as how anyone would spend good money on it. Unless he knows something nobody else does."

He shrugged and shifted to look directly at Blue. "I gave up a long time ago trying to figure out why some people do what they do." A look that passed for sly lit his face. "I can find out a little more about him."

Blue nodded carefully, the pain meds making him wool-headed. "That'd be good."

Dewey grinned. "You wouldn't mind returning the favor by telling me what you think of Patience, would you?"

Blue wasn't so far gone that he didn't know fishing when he heard it. "Not sure what I think counts for much," he said. "But for what it's worth, I think you could do a lot worse. She isn't a bouncy, blonde cheerleader type - but that hasn't worked for you so far. What she is, is hardworking, nice, straightforward and has a good sense of humor. Not to mention a knockout in jeans. Oh, and she's a great cook."

"Yeah," Dewey said, his eyebrows drawing together. "I never noticed that stuff about her before. Except for the great cook part. She's a couple years younger than us and never, you know, hung out. She spent a lot of time working at Mackie's." He nodded as if making a decision. "Guess I'll be spending more time there."

Blue's eyes were trying to drift closed, but he fought it. "I asked Delta about her at the park yesterday," he said. "I thought Patience showed interest in you."

Dewey scooted to the edge of his chair. "You thought so, too?"

Blue tried for serious, although he wanted to laugh. "Pretty brassy of her since you've got this thing with Charlotte, right?"

The frown returned. "Uh, well, Charlotte's not the serious type, you know? Anyway, what did Delta say?"

Blue's laugh sounded loud to his own ears. "Real subtle, Harcourt. Sounds like we never left the eighth grade. Delta told me to ask Patience myself, but I think that was her way of telling me that it's between you and Patience."

Dewey looked at him earnestly. "What's between me and Patience?"

"Hopefully, it'll get down to bare skin if you're smart," Blue said, with an exaggerated wink.

His friend's eyebrows rose in comprehension and Blue swore he blushed.

"Looks like I need to have a conversation with Charlotte, Dewey admitted. "I don't think she'll be real upset."

"Nope. I think Charlotte has already moved on," Blue said, leaning back to close his eyes. "Let me know what you find on the path. Maybe tomorrow around lunchtime. You could place a take-out order at Mackie's for burgers, fries, and milkshakes, to go."

Blue smiled at the enthusiasm he heard in Dewey's agreement.

Delta glanced at the phone again, murmuring, "He's okay. No need to call."

She'd felt humiliated this morning when Dewey and Aunt Caroline came in to find her bent over Blue's bed in a kiss. Never mind that it was his idea and that the strain of finding him so cold and hurt brought her to the brink of shock. When they had all laughed, she knew rationally that it was in fun and broke some of the tension surrounding his situation. But it had reminded her too much of times when Slayton and his parents laughed with the sole intention of hurting her.

She'd called the hospital this afternoon to learn Blue had been released and talked herself out of checking on him.

When the phone rang, Delta nearly jumped out of her skin. "Hello?"

"Expecting a call?" Blue asked.

Delta felt her shoulders relax. He sounded good. "No. I'm sitting near the phone. How are you?"

"Tired, but it beats the alternative."

She shuddered. "I'm tired, too, and I didn't nearly drown this morning."

"Are you going to Atlanta tomorrow?"

"Yes. I was able to change my appointments."

"Can you come over and keep me company a while?"

Delta glanced at her watch. "All right. Are you sure you're up to it?"

"Yeah. See you soon."

A few minutes later, she came through the back door of Gran's house and saw neatly labeled boxes on the counters. It made her sad. She had moved comfortably through these rooms where the people had loved and protected her. Now, it would be her brother and sister-in-law's home, and she couldn't walk in any time she pleased.

Blue sat in a large chair facing away from her but when she thought to enter the room quietly, he spoke. "Come on in."

His long legs stretched before him, his laptop balanced on his thighs, the cursor blinking.

"How's the world of high finance?"

He smiled. "Tokyo market's slow."

Delta sat in a chair to one side and looked at him. Other than the sling and the bruising around the neat black stitches at his hairline, he looked good. She shook her head. "I can't believe you're actually working after what happened this morning. And that Aunt Caroline is letting you."

Blue's gaze cut to the hallway. "Mother's at home picking up some of my things."

"So, you're sneaking in a few minute's work?"

"My clients count on me," he said, matter-of-factly.

She nodded. "And since you work for yourself, there's no one to take up the slack. Does that mean you never get a vacation?"

Blue shook his head. "I can maintain my accounts by reviewing a spreadsheet I set up to auto-populate once a day."

"I'm impressed."

He closed the laptop and reached for her hand, playing with her fingers. "I have an ulterior motive for asking you over. I'd like to discuss Braxton and his offer."

Delta stiffened and he hurried on. "I don't think you get it. There's a chance that because I've opposed him in his attempt to get Brisco's Folly, my *accident* was intentional. I don't have any proof and I know this sounds crazy, but he may be dangerous. Stay in Atlanta for a while."

Delta slipped her hand from Blue's. Damn him for short-changing her, the way Slayton had. "You probably forgot, so I'll remind you. In the past five days, I've lost Gran, inherited marshland, gotten sued by my ex, and nearly lost you. Even so, I'm in full control of my life and my faculties. That means I can take information in and make an informed decision without help."

Blue leaned back and looked at her with tired eyes. "Help me out, here. Are you seriously this stubborn when it comes to your own welfare, or are you putting yourself out there because of some misplaced need to overcome your treatment at the hands of your ex and his parents?"

Delta stood, the hurt in her chest pressing upward and making it hard to swallow. She looked down at Blue, disliking him very much at this moment. "Oh, I can be agreeable. It depends on what's being asked, and more importantly, who's doing the asking."

She turned toward the door to the hallway. "Take care. I'll be in Atlanta for a couple of days. As planned."

# Chapter Twenty-Two

Delta strode out of Gran's, right past her parents' house to the park and back again. The chilly air hit her skin, but didn't cool her off. How dare Blue accuse her of making decisions based on weakness. Did he really think she was some indecisive, simpering idiot? He was one to talk. Feeling sorry for himself because he would never know about his natural grandfather. So what? There were countless people in the world who never knew their biological roots. They functioned fine.

She ran out of steam and took a deep breath. There were also countless women who had lived with not only psychological, but physical abuse, which they'd managed to overcome, more easily than she.

Blue's claim that Harlan Braxton might be dangerous or even responsible for his accident on the path didn't make sense. There had to be something more than an unsubstantiated guess and dislike behind his accusations.

Nothing, however, gave him the right to say what he'd said to her.

Delta rolled her shoulders and put on a calm face to head back to her parents' house. She'd walked a few yards when a low engine rumble caught her attention. A vehicle paced her from behind. She stopped and turned to see a red truck slowly following. It seemed vaguely familiar, but not to the point where she felt comfortable.

A quick look around confirmed the safe distance to one or two lighted porches. Delta relaxed. The truck might not be pacing her at all. The driver might be lost or looking for an address. Even so, her anxiety spiked when the vehicle stopped beside her. The window slid down and she released a foggy breath, recognizing Harlan Braxton. Speak of the devil.

"Can I give you a lift?"

She still had enough mad left to want to prove Blue wrong. *What if a little time in Braxton's company accomplished that?* "I could use a cup of coffee."

His eyes widened in surprise. "Great. There's an all-night coffee shop at the motel where I'm staying. Hop in."

He had to be staying at Peck's Bluff Inn, the only motel in town that had a coffee shop. It qualified as a very public place just down the road from the County Sheriff. How safe was that? She walked the few steps to the truck, but didn't open the door. "Were you following me?"

Braxton shrugged and grinned. "Not at first. Charlotte had something to do tonight, so I got bored and was checking out the town when I saw you. Nice coincidence, though."

Peck's Bluff *was* a typically small, boring town if you only knew a couple of people. She climbed in the truck and admired the upscale interior; burl wood dash, glove leather seats, and an expensive sound system playing a soft country song by Martina McBride. Delta fastened her seatbelt. "This is very nice."

He nodded. "Been wanting one of these special editions for years, so I treated myself after I delivered on my last deal."

"Delivered?"

"Sure," he said. "Didn't Charlotte tell you? I do the research and legwork, then put real estate deals together for people who have the money, but not the time, and who want to remain anonymous."

Delta was skeptical. "And one of these wealthy, anonymous people wants a hundred sixty acres of swampland?"

Braxton nodded again. "Yes, ma'am, they do. How about I give you my pitch during that cup of coffee?"

She cocked her head. "You've been hanging around town to get an opportunity to present your case? Why didn't you contact us through an attorney or broker?"

He shrugged, seeming to make a decision. "Truck payments and other overhead. As I said, I do all the work. It's more profitable if I don't have to cut anyone else in. Besides, your boyfriend seemed against the idea without hearing me out. I hope you'll be more open."

Delta thought about Blue's negative attitude and decided it would be stupid to not at least listen to what Braxton had to say. She didn't want to seem too eager, however. "Before you go to the trouble of giving me a sales pitch, what do the people you represent want to do with Brisco's Folly?"

Braxton grinned. "That's the best part. They're willing to pay top dollar and want to build a camp for disabled kids. I always research my clients, and this guy not only has the bucks, he has an asthmatic grandson."

He took his gaze off the road for a second. "Not that I believe it's purely altruistic – I've never run into that. He'll get big tax breaks. But you have to admit it's a great idea."

She agreed; taken aback at the memories his words evoked. "Van had misdiagnosed strep throat when he was ten. Before we knew it, he got rheumatic fever. One chance in a million. There was some damage to his heart valve, but not nearly as much as there could have been. So, I've always been in favor of organizations that benefit children."

"Who's Van?"

"Sorry, you wouldn't know. He's my younger brother."

"Oh, that must have been rough."

They arrived at the coffee shop and were shown to a table. Delta found she'd relaxed completely. "Where do you call home?"

Braxton grinned. "My roots are in a little town north of Lake Charles, Louisiana called Ponchatoula. I don't live there, but lots of my relatives still do. Ever heard of it?"

Delta nodded. "I've never seen it, but I had a client who loved to shop for antiques there."

She lost track of time as they chatted about growing up in small towns. When she finished her coffee, Braxton brought out a letter of credit attesting to his ability to draw against a very large sum of money. Delta held a look of what she hoped was polite interest, even if her insides were doing the Macarena. She handed the letter back. "Um, how did you happen to hear about Brisco's Folly and know it might be for sale?"

"Good question," he said. "There are only a few dozen private holdings of that size in the state. It's my business to track their availability." He sighed. "Unfortunately, when I last checked, I heard your grandmother wasn't expected to live out the week. That's when I came into town and settled on the bank I'd be doing business with."

That made sense to Delta, but she had one more question.

"If the purpose is to build a camp, why do you need such a large parcel of land?"

Braxton leaned back, his gaze assessing. "If your boyfriend had asked the questions you're asking, we'd already be under contract."

*That was the second time he'd called Blue her boyfriend. Was that how others saw her and Blue when they were together? Patience saw them as a couple. Dewey did too, yet neither she nor Blue had spoken about any kind of relationship exclusivity.*

"... but to answer you, I was told by my client that he planned to reclaim part of the land to add a rehabilitation center and housing for family members. Kind of like a *Ronald McDonald House*. Only on a smaller scale and with peaceful trails included. I've walked the area and it looks doable."

Delta locked down her thoughts about Blue and focused on Braxton's reply. His description of his client's plans for Brisco's Folly would be a wonderful use of Gran's legacy. Then she had a reality check. It was maybe too wonderful. Braxton was giving her answers that anyone in her position would love to hear.

A few things still bothered her. He'd showed up within a matter of hours after Gran's death and immediately hooked up with Charlotte, who had apparently filled him in on the family goings-on. Secondly, he said he represented an anonymous client.

What exactly did that mean? A client that could paint a beautiful picture, then use the land for something entirely different? She supposed those were the risks you took, but it still made her uneasy.

"... Sorry, I was daydreaming," she answered.

"Perfectly okay. I've had a long day, too. Ready to leave?"

She nodded, deciding she could tell Blue that Braxton's offer was at least worth looking into.

It had been two days since Delta had gone to Atlanta and Blue felt better, physically, each morning. He'd spent the first night under his mother's watchful eye at Gran's, but the next day moved back into his old room.

His attitude about Braxton hadn't changed, but he did examine his dislike of the man and concluded it was a gut-deep feeling the guy was a phony. He'd had enough experience in the financial world to depend on his hunches, but had nothing tangible to convince Delta. It bummed him out.

The look on Delta's face the other night when he'd challenged her decision-making abilities bummed him, too. It had been his lame attempt to get her away from some unknown danger, and he owed her a big apology – if she consented to speak to him again.

Blue sighed. Things weren't going well for Dewey, either.

He'd gotten called out that night and didn't get to check the area where Blue had tripped until yesterday afternoon. Unfortunately, he couldn't find any solid proof that the wagon had help rolling into Blue's path.

Dewey had also suddenly become unsure about approaching Patience, although Charlotte had clearly changed camps, not even making herself available for his heart-to-heart chat.

The morning of his third day of recuperation, Blue woke up restless. He walked over to Gran's and found his mother in the pantry sorting canned goods. She smiled and gently touched his temple. "How're you feeling, besides bored?"

"Like I should head back to Chicago and think some things over," he admitted.

Her expression stilled. "You mentioned this last spring that you were considering moving back here permanently. Are you still thinking about it?"

Blue nodded cautiously. "The logistics of the move aren't a problem. The personal issues need work, though."

"You know what?" she said. "I made a mistake twelve years ago. I knew something else was involved in your decision to go to college so far away, but you'd always been so self-sufficient. I thought you'd realize whatever was making you unhappy here, would stay with you until you let it go."

This was something entirely unexpected. First Gran, now his mother. And they were right.

"I think you're avoiding a change that would be good for you," she continued. "Besides, don't you have to wait for the people who want to present that offer Fuller told you about?"

Blue shrugged with his good shoulder. "Yes, and I'd prefer if the proceeds from the sale went to Delta alone, but she's, um, ..."

"A little more stubborn and defensive about her independence than she used to be?"

Blue nodded. "I can't seem to say the things I want to about helping her without getting her back up."

His mother's calm expression frayed at the edges, threatening to break into a grin. "Hmmm. She's a very bright business woman. Have you tried offering a straight-up business loan instead of one based on friendship?"

He searched his recent conversations with Delta. "Not really."

"Well, you stick around and keep trying," she said, patting his cheek. "She's pretty wonderful."

He laughed. His mother was right. Delta was worth his patience. He could only hope she would be as patient with him.

Blue lifted his arm carefully. "This sling comes off today. Is there anything I can do to help around here?"

"As a matter of fact, there is. Gran stored some of your school things in the attic. Van brought the boxes down yesterday, but they need going through by you since I already took what I want."

"Boxes? As in more than one?"

"Only two left," she said.

"Okay. Where are the garbage bags?"

She lifted an eyebrow. "Don't be too hasty."

Blue shook his head. "I can't imagine there'll be much worth saving."

Halfway through his task, he was proven wrong.

# Chapter Twenty-Three

Exhaustion overcame Delta after meeting with her attorney. Slayton's suit looked like a done deal. She didn't like the thought of starting over, but she had a good name and reputation. That meant something.

Plus, she refused to spend as much time feeling sorry for herself as she had after her divorce. What a waste.

Then there was Blue.

His flash of temper and her own of the other night ran through her mind on the drive back to Peck's Bluff. Something had definitely changed between them, and if it had been anyone else who'd spoken to her like that, she'd have walked for good. Yes, he'd said some really unkind things. Partly, she thought, in his effort to convince her he was afraid for her, and partly because he was a little loopy on pain meds.

Her subsequent meeting with Brax had bolstered her opinion that they didn't have to depend solely on the mystery offer her father was mediating. She even gloated a little. Mr. Blue Richmond might change his mind when he heard what Brax's backer planned to do with Brisco's Folly.

Delta fell into a sleep of pure emotional exhaustion when she got to her parents' house. The next morning she showed up at Mackie's early. Patience opened the door with a big grin.

"That fool Charlotte's cut my Dewey loose."

"Best news I've had in days," Delta said.

"Oh, chickapea, I'm sorry," Patience said. "Those nasty people taking your dream apart. I feel bad."

"Good Lord, it's been ages since I've heard the name chickapea. Gran used to call me that all the time. No sense you feeling bad, either. All those high-society divorcees need somewhere to spend their alimony. What better way than having one of their own design a gorgeous space for them?"

Patience hooted. "That's my girl. Now, let me tell you I been thinking Dewey got my message the other day. He's been in here mooning around every morning 'til the coffee pot's dry."

"Do tell," said Delta.

"I figure today's the day," the redhead nodded. "'cause I'm not getting any younger, and waiting on a man's like watching paint dry."

Delta cheered considerably. "So what are you going to do?"

Patience bobbed her eyebrows. "I'm gonna come right out and tell him how I feel."

Jealousy bubbled in Delta at her friend's level of confidence. "Go for it."

Sure enough, Dewey was waiting outside when Patience opened the door. Blue came in with him, and they walked to Delta's booth.

"So," Blue said, as he slid in next to her, "how was your trip?"

Her happiness at having his warmth next to her cancelled Delta's original intention of making him squirm. But he was not to be let completely off the hook. "As expected," she said. "Has *your* mood improved? And did you find out what caused your accident?"

He looked at her, grinning. "Better all around. Nobody has to cut my meat for me anymore. As for my near-death experience, it was caused by a little dark green wagon sitting on the side of the path. I tripped over the handle."

Delta broke eye contact. The remembered vision of him lying half-submerged and bleeding brought on a shiver.

She started to chuckle, when she caught Dewey's look of surprise at Blue's explanation.

Blue nudged her with his good arm. "I reserve the right, however, to make it more sinister when I tell my kids."

Her chuckle was forgotten. Delta had never heard him refer to having children before. Never. It turned her stomach upside down, but she was saved from making an inane remark when Patience came out of the kitchen bringing them coffee cups.

She held out her order pad and spoke to Blue, first. "Hey, Blue, glad to see you're better." Then she turned to Dewey. "Hungry today?"

Delta bit her lip at the look of invitation on her friend's face. Dewey swallowed and nodded.

Patience never took her gaze off Dewey as she flipped her pad closed and sauntered toward the kitchen. "Then I'll just bring y'all your favorites."

Delta couldn't help herself. "You okay, Dewey? You look a tad flushed."

He refocused. "Uh, yeah. I been feeling kind of off-center. Like being tagged hard. You know?"

Delta knew his confusion would end soon, but shook her head.

Dewey frowned. "Oh, well. It's hard to explain."

The conversation changed to the weather, Atlanta's business growth, and a high school friend's third baby, until Patience returned with their plates.

"Let me know if there's anything else you need. At all," she said, directly to Dewey.

When she went to help her other customers, Dewey glanced at Delta. "Uh, would you know ..."

"Not getting involved," she said, loading her fork with hash browns. "You're a big boy and you've almost got it figured out."

When they finished eating, Dewey laid some money on the table and reached for the last of his coffee. Patience walked over, and put her hands on her hips. "Breakfast is on me, Deputy, and so's the tip. Here it is. I'm twenty-eight years old, in good health and not too sore on the eyes. I own this café and bought my folks' house and forty acres. I expect you might already know that."

Delta watched in fascination as Patience proceeded to slide on her knees across the seat to Dewey. His gaze darted around the room and settled on Patience's face as she cornered him. His own face was scarlet.

A glance at Blue showed he was also enjoying the show.

"Here's something you don't know," Patience continued. "We are kindred spirits, Dewey Harcourt. I got my heart and mind set on having you and it's now or never. I'd make a good, faithful mate, and I figure we've already wasted time we could've been warming up my big bed."

Dewey managed an inarticulate sound.

Patience nodded. "I've said what I wanted and the choice is yours. If you decide I'm not for you, well, I tried."

She started to back out of the booth, then stopped. "Oh, what the heck," she said softly.

Dewey still had his head back with his lips slightly parted in surprise, or fear. It was hard to tell.

Patience took full advantage. She put a hand on either side of his face, lowered her head and started kissing him.

The deputy's big hand came up to grip the edge of the table until his knuckles turned white.

Blue sucked in a breath and a hush fell over the café.

When the kiss ended, Patience put a tendril of hair behind her ear before pinning Dewey with a look hot enough to melt chocolate. "Think about it," she said, then backed out of the booth, squared her shoulders, and strolled to the swinging kitchen doors. Hearty applause from the other patrons followed. She didn't look back.

Blue produced a megawatt smile. "Now, there's a woman to be reckoned with."

Dewey licked his lips and his gaze stayed trained on the doors through which Patience had disappeared. "Do you think she was kidding?"

"I'll take that one," Delta said. "She was serious as a heart attack, Dewey Harcourt. You'd better think long and hard about what she offered, because if you trifle with her after this, I'll hurt you myself."

Beside her, Blue reached in his pocket and threw a twenty on the table, grabbed Delta's hand and started tugging. "Come on. Let's leave Dewey to his pain."

Delta jerked her hand back. "Why should he be in pain? Patience is the one who stripped emotionally in front of all these people."

Blue winced. "You're making it worse for him, talking about long and hard, and Patience stripping. Dewey's a very elemental guy and I'm referring to his physical pain."

It dawned on her then, what Blue was talking about and she felt her face grow warm. "Oh, that."

"Yes, that," he said as he pulled at her. She scooted out, noticing Dewey hadn't budged, or looked away from the swinging doors.

She allowed herself to be walked outside, but Blue surprised her when he turned away from their respective homes. At the corner of the café, he guided them into the alley and maneuvered her up against the building.

"What's this all about?" she asked. Any other questions fell right out of her brain when she caught the look in his eyes. Her earlier speculation that she was falling in love with Blue hiked a notch.

"I wanted some privacy to apologize," he said, leaning close to kiss her cheekbone. "I was out of line the other night. *And* a little zonked." He kissed her other cheekbone. "I've known you long enough to realize that self-doubt didn't enter into your decision. Stubbornness, yes, but not otherwise motivated. Forgive me?"

She nodded slowly. "Guilty on the stubbornness. But you didn't mention that Braxton's offer is still open for discussion."

He studied her face, looking for what, she didn't know.

"Well?" she asked.

Blue shoved away from the building and huffed out a breath. "It's not a matter of trusting your judgment. Or that I don't care because I don't need the money. It's that Braxton sets off every alarm I have. Delta, this guy is the poster boy for crooked. He ..."

Delta narrowed her eyes. "Braxton's backer wants to build a camp for disabled kids on the property. And I've seen the bank papers verifying he has the cash to back it up."

Blue's eyes didn't even flicker.

Her earlier warmth toward him dissipated. "You don't believe it," she said. "You haven't even checked it out and you don't believe it."

He folded his arms and cocked his head. "Even if Braxton's backer exists, I seriously doubt his plans are as benevolent as he claims. So, here's the deal. Let's see what your father's buyer has to offer, and if the money or the use of the property doesn't make you happy, we'll contact Braxton. Fair?"

After all the legalese used to invoke the pre-nup clause that took her business, Delta was sick of negotiating. Besides, she couldn't think of an objection to the offer. She nodded.

"Great," he said, lifting his hand to trail a finger down the side of her neck. "Now, forgive me?"

Her heart pounded and her hands, seemingly of their own volition, now rested on his waist, fingers curling inward. "Let me think," she smiled. "Will you make it worth my while?"

"That, I can promise," he said, lowering his mouth to cover hers in a seductive kiss that spun warmth to her core.

When Blue lifted his head, she lay her cheek on his shoulder, afraid too much feeling showed in her eyes.

He smoothed her hair. "That was nice."

"Yes," she agreed. "Very. I'm trying to think of something else you need to apologize for."

His low laughter pleased her. "I'll work on it."

Instead, he stepped back and took her hand. "Come on. I have a surprise to show you, I think you'll like it."

Delta smiled. "Does that line really get results?"

He burst out laughing. "Not yet, although now that I think about it, that's a better idea."

Better, indeed. But she shook her head and let him lead her down the street. He carried his left shoulder a little higher than the right due to his injury, and she felt an overwhelming gentleness toward him. If she wasn't careful, she would end up giving everything, as she had with Slayton. Her stomach dropped. Had it already happened? This wanting to be with him? Had fondness for Blue grown in to love somewhere along the way?

Blue turned his head and wiggled his eyebrows. "Aren't you curious to see if you're going to like what I've got?"

Delta smiled and swallowed. *I already do; maybe too much.* "Depends," she said, enjoying the warmth of his fingers as he tugged her along. *But only until I can see how much control I have.* That thought brought her conjectures up short. Did she fear going into a relationship, even with Blue, unless she had control? Had her determination to be strong after the divorce led to this overbalance? This fear?

Blue took them into Gran's and opened a box in the corner of the living room. Reaching inside, he pulled out a sheet of paper and handed it to her. "Here's the surprise."

# Chapter Twenty-Four

It took her a minute to recognize the paper. "It's the sales contract we signed when that professor of business law visited our Future Business Leaders of America workshop the summer after I graduated. You were home, and audited the workshop to get pointers for the business you were starting."

Blue smiled. "He was a notary, too. See the seal at the bottom?"

"This can't be legal," she said. "He did this to illustrate how a contract works."

"Money changed hands."

She continued to stare at the paper. "I remember. A dollar. If this were really legal, though, you'd own half my company."

"Right."

She saw where Blue was going with this, but couldn't summon any enthusiasm for his game. "So, in theory, Slayton only gets a quarter of my company, not half."

"Here's where it gets interesting," Blue nodded. "Based on this, I can threaten to sue. It could take a long time and cost a certain family a lot of money."

Reality chased hope from Delta's chest. "It'd just be dismissed as a frivolous lawsuit. I hadn't even started a company, yet."

"All true. But we'd be able to mess with them. Who knows, it might be aggravating enough for them to walk away or negotiate a smaller settlement."

He took the paper back and leaned in for a kiss. "I've spoken to the attorney friend I sent your paperwork to. He loves a challenge and is going to send a very nasty letter to Slayton's lawyer."

Delta sighed. "But your friend doesn't have a license to practice law in Georgia. Something I didn't think of the other day when you mentioned he might be able to help."

"True again," Blue said. "But he's representing me, a resident of Illinois." He held up a finger when she started to speak. "And, he's allowed to operate in conjunction with an attorney who does. Your father."

That hadn't occurred to her. She looked at Blue's confident smile. "Thanks, even if it doesn't work, thanks." She glanced back to the paper in Blue's hand. "Did you tell your friend I wouldn't be able to pay him right away?"

"Already taken care of," he said. "I agreed to be his partner in a match next month."

Her heartbeat tripped. "A kickboxing match? Will you be okay by then? I mean, the bag work and training you have to do. I hope you didn't sign on for ..."

"For you?"

"Something like that."

He ran the backs of his fingers across her cheek. "Yeah, I did. But you can return the favor."

Happiness spiraled through her at his words. He didn't have to do any of this, but he had and that meant a lot to her. She swallowed. "Two dollars?"

He shook his head. "No. Kiss it better."

"Kiss what better?"

His gaze added heat to his words. "Whatever takes the most punishment during the match."

"We'll see," she managed.

He groaned. "That means no."

She laughed outright. "It means we'll see, depending on the body part affected." In reality, she could think of very few areas of Blue's body she wouldn't want to kiss. On the other hand, it sounded like the match would take place in Chicago, so the offer was pretty non-committal.

"That's fair."

"Hmmmm?"

"Earth to Delta. I said I'm perfectly willing to negoti-ate." He curved a hand around her neck and pulled her to him for a kiss.

She was still thinking about the discovery of the contract and his offer to help when she got back to her parents' house.

Her mother came out of the kitchen. "Your father wants you to call him. It's regarding Brisco's Folly."

Delta's father answered on the second ring. "Jameson."

"Hi, Daddy."

"Hey, girl. I've got good news. That party interested in Brisco's Folly wants to meet you and Blue in my office tomorrow morning at ten."

Delta did a little dance. Things were definitely looking up. "I'll be there. Did you tell Blue?"

Her father laughed. "He's next."


The first thing Blue noticed when he walked into Fuller Jameson's outer office the next morning was a pretty woman holding a baby. She looked vaguely familiar, but Blue couldn't place her. He smiled and nodded.

A few minutes later, Delta came in and walked over to her.

"Sue Ann. Oh, my gosh. I heard about your baby. Congratulations, she's beautiful. Is Bobby here?"

The woman blushed, her eyes sparkling. "Thank you. How are you? Bobby's in with your daddy, waiting for you and Blue.

That's who she was, Blue thought. Bobby Dean Tyler's high school girlfriend, apparently now his wife.

The conversation he'd had with Dewey about the theme park Bobby wanted to build came back to him.

Could the country western star be interested in Brisco's Folly for that?

Delta's father stepped to the door. "We're ready for y'all."

Blue stood aside as Delta and Sue Ann went into the office. Sure enough, Bobby Tyler waited beside one of the chairs.

He grinned and extended his hand, first to Delta, then Blue. "Good to see you two. Thanks for coming to hear us out."

"Why don't you pitch your project?" Delta's father asked, after they were all seated.

Bobby nodded. "Sue Ann and I have been talking for a few years about how we'd like to preserve some of the beautiful country hereabouts. We used to enjoy walking the trails in Brisco's Folly. I'd practice while Sue Ann kept me company."

The look Bobby gave his wife was wide-open adoration. When Delta reached for the baby and held her, Blue had a hard time concentrating on what Bobby was saying. A feeling between possessiveness and something Blue couldn't describe spread through him.

Bobby continued. "Anyway, we made several visits here to talk to Miss Molly 'bout buying her land for the Center." He looked expectantly at them.

Blue cut his gaze to Delta and saw a blank stare. He shrugged.

"Miss Molly never told you?" Bobby asked.

"No." Blue said. "What Center?"

The country singer leaned forward. "Sue Ann and I would like to fund a non-profit organization for the preservation of a natural marshland. A place for trails, tours, exhibits, speakers, and wildlife study. We think Brisco's Folly would be the perfect location."

He turned his attention to Delta. "Your grandma spoke about your work as a green architect, and since we want it to be a green structure, we'd like you to submit a proposal."

Blue was blown away, and Delta looked clearly pleased.

"I love the idea," she said. "And I'd very much like to propose a concept, although I've only done one commercial building, so far."

Sue Ann smiled. "We've seen it and were very impressed."

"Thank you," Delta said. "You might also want to know that Blue has recently received his national certification as a green contractor. He's worked with the most highly regarded man in the mid-west."

Bobby looked at Blue. "I thought y'all were a big successful financial type."

Blue felt a warm thrill at Delta's compliment. He shrugged. "I still manage a limited number of portfolios," he said. "Green contracting is a field I've become interested in."

The singer nodded. "If it all comes together as we hope it will, I've asked your father to join Sue Ann and me on the Board of Directors. We'd also like the two of you to be board members."

"Sounds like you've given this a lot of thought," Blue said. "Will you be involved to this extent for the whole project?"

Bobby shook his head. "Can't spare the time. Too many bookings and travel. My business manager will handle most of the details once the big decisions have been made." He grinned. "But we wanted to be the ones to make the offer."

Blue glanced at Delta. If it was up to him, the answer would be yes, today, but he'd promised her a choice. "What do you think? Want a couple of days to look it over?"

Delta nodded.

"Can we get back to you next week?" he asked the Tylers.

"That works great for us," Bobby said. "I have a concert this weekend in Missouri, then we're taking a breather."

The baby started fussing and Delta kissed her head before returning her to her mother.

When they stood to leave, Sue Ann gently bounced the baby against her shoulder. "I sure hope y'all accept our offer. It would allow us to give something back to everyone in the area."

After they left, Fuller Jameson rocked back, smiling ear to ear. "So, what do y'all think?"

Delta started to speak when the office door opened again. Bobby stuck his head in. "Just to sweeten the pot, we plan on namin' it the Molly Brisco Memorial Center."

# Chapter Twenty-Five

The door clicked softly behind the country western star and Blue laughed. "Why does he need a business manager? If there were any question about accepting their offer, that would be the clincher."

Delta's eyes shone. "Unless the offer is insulting, which I doubt, I'm in."

Her father handed Delta the document on his desk, and Blue leaned over.

"Wow," Delta said. "It really is worth a lot of money."

"It's based on the last county evaluation plus ten percent," Fuller Jameson said. "You might be able to get more, but this project will be healthy for the area. And likely as not, any other offers would be for industrial purposes. Not many parcels of this size and make up could be used for anything else."

Delta passed the papers to Blue, a frown stealing the joyous expression of only a few seconds ago.

She turned to her father. "Daddy, we have another offer."

Blue saw genuine surprise on the lawyer's face.

"From whom?"

"We were approached a few days ago," Delta said. "By the representative of a buyer who wants to remain anonymous. The amount's in the same range as Bobby and Sue Ann's."

Blue knew what his choice would be, hands down. But he'd promised Delta he'd wait for her decision. He didn't think it possible, but if she chose to go with Braxton, he'd pursue the option to buy her out. His thought that there was something shady about the man still held.

Fuller Jameson lifted an eyebrow. "That's quite a coincidence. Did the representative say what they wanted the land for?"

"They want to build a camp for disabled children and eventually, housing for other family members," she said.

Delta's father nodded. "Well, that sounds like a fine idea. The two of you have a big decision to make."

Blue thought she'd want time to weigh their options, so he started to stand. Until warm fingers tugged at him. He looked down at happiness blooming on her face.

"I choose Bobby and Sue Ann's offer. Gran would have wanted it that way."

Blue heard her father's release of breath and swallowed past a new lump in his throat. "That has my vote. I think if everything's clean, we should go for it right away."

"Clean?" Delta asked.

"Free of liens or legal attachments that would delay or compromise the sale," her father said. "There aren't any. I checked. Molly's estate was through a trust but this will still take a few weeks. The state's pretty slow."

"I'll make some calls and see if I can find someone who can walk it through the process for us," Blue said.

He took Delta's hand. "In the meantime, why don't you let me loan you an advance against the final net? You'd be able to offset some of the damage the lawsuit is causing."

Delta's demeanor changed in the space of a few seconds. "The land might be free of legal restraints, but I'm not. How is this sale going to affect the lawsuit?"

"Has a date been set for the split of your company assets?" her father asked.

Delta hesitated. "Everything's listed and in the hands of their family attorney. We're supposed to wait for them to review and accept the amount."

"Don't push them," Blue said. "We can work our way around the furniture and lease deposits for your new space."

She slid her hand from his and rubbed her fingers together. "How? There's a waiting list for offices in that building."

Blue grinned. "Ask for an extension in writing. Attach a copy of Bobby and Sue Ann's bid for your half of Brisco's Folly. Sweeten the deal by offering to extend the term of the lease for the space and the furniture an additional year. In this economy nobody's going to turn that down."

"I wouldn't do that," Delta's father said. "Any new money spent toward your business has to be after the date the suit is settled. Even though Slayton can't claim money you inherited after the divorce, they might take you back to court to try and prove you intended to invest a large sum after the settlement date."

Delta stood and glanced between him and her father, a weary set to her shoulders. It saddened Blue that the utter happiness she experienced a few minutes ago had vanished. He bit back a swear word.

"Thanks for the advice," she said. "It's really a Catch-22 isn't it? Slayton and his parents can afford to go after me if they hear of even the slightest hint that I'm preparing to stay in business, especially at an exclusive address, after they take half my assets." She lifted her mouth in a wry smile. "Guess I'll have to weigh my options, then do whatever it takes."

Fuller Jameson raised an eyebrow. "What exactly, does that mean?"

She raised a mirrored eyebrow. "It means Daddy, that I have my share of Captain Sinclair Brisco blood and I intend to hold off the enemy, *without* getting caught."

With that, she gave a shallow curtsy. "I'm leaving for Atlanta and an appointment with my business attorney. Blue, I told Daddy about your idea. Why don't the two of you discuss it?"

After she left, Blue turned to her father. The older man held up his hands. "As I said before, she comes by her stubbornness honestly. Her mother can wear a body down."

Blue nodded, although he worried about Delta's assertion of doing whatever it took. Gran's death, the lawsuit, her business losses. She was taking hit after hit and seemed determined to do it all alone. He hoped the stress didn't cause her to make a bad decision in the name of winning.

His attention refocused as her father picked up a pencil and rolled it between his fingers. "Speaking of wearing a body down, my wife thinks you've got intentions toward our little girl so I'm gonna say this once. That bastard she was married to and his family broke her spirit, and she's just now getting it back. I think very highly of you, Blue, always have, but not so high I wouldn't come after you if she got hurt again. Understand?"

The fact that Delta's parents were seeing them as a couple warmed Blue. "Absolutely, sir," he said, "I wouldn't hurt her for anything."

Fuller Jameson's gaze went to the door. "She's a level-headed, hard-working young woman. This lawsuit's thrown her off-kilter is all."

"In that regard, sir," Blue said. "What do you think the chances are of my idea succeeding?"

"Truthfully, son, I don't think it'll hold up in a court of law. The paper y'all signed wasn't intended as a binding contract. Original purpose holds a lot of sway in matters of this kind. It'll lighten your pocket and give Slayton's lawyers a good laugh, though. Not that I'm for giving them any pleasure."

Blue smiled. "A good laugh is what I'm aiming for. Got an email from my attorney friend in Chicago who's representing Delta. He's hoping the paper acts as a distraction a little longer. As long as they're looking the other way, the laugh will be ours."

A glint shone in the attorney's eyes. "Got something up your sleeve, 'sides your arm?"

"Maybe, sir. Just maybe."

Blue left shortly after Delta and had about decided to head for Mackie's for lunch when a horn sounded behind him. Dewey pulled to the curb in his Tundra. He held up some papers as the window slid down. "Got some information back on Braxton. Want to have lunch and I'll fill you in?"

"Sounds good," Blue said. "Mackie's okay?"

Dewey bobbed his head enthusiastically. "Meet you there."

They had to wait ten minutes for a booth to open, and Blue noticed Dewey tracked Patience's every move. "Interested?"

His friend cut his gaze to Blue. "She's way different than I thought she'd be, you know?"

"Not in a bad way, though."

Dewey shook his head. "Not even."

Patience set down their plates and left. Both men made short work of their respective sandwiches, then Dewey pulled out the papers in his jacket. "Like you thought. Braxton is not a nice guy. He came onto legal radar about three years ago. He and an older man billed themselves as real estate brokers. They read obituaries and within a month of a man's death, charmed their way into the widow's house. They had a good run, taking 20% as a *down payment* for just listing the house. Braxton made some connections through the older guy until they had a falling out. The other man landed in the hospital and Braxton landed in Fulton County lockup."

Dewey looked up at Blue. "He's not above using his fists on women, either."

That point made Blue's stomach churn. "He wanted for anything, now?"

"No," Dewey said. "You gonna tell Delta?"

"Yes," he answered. "And Charlotte."

"Think either one will listen?"

The roiling in Blue's stomach moved to tighten in his chest. "If I tell her the source, Delta will. Not so sure about Charlotte."

"Yeah, she's pretty unhappy," Dewey said. He cocked his head. "Speaking of Delta. The other day you told Delta you'd tripped over the wagon handle. Nothing about the wagon in motion or somebody moving it onto the path. How come?"

"Self-preservation," Blue said. "We hadn't found out about the new proposed use of the land yet and Delta was desperate to keep Braxton's offer as a back-up. I said I didn't think my fall was an accident and that I thought he was dangerous. I told her to stay a little longer in Atlanta."

"You *told* her?" Dewey goggled.

Blue grimaced. "Yeah. She didn't take it well."

Dewey shuddered, then brightened when Patience came back for their plates.

"Chocolate pie for dessert, Deputy?"

Blue grinned as his big friend nodded at the cute redhead.

When she left again, Blue leaned back. "Going to ask her out?"

"Went to her place for dinner last night," Dewey admitted. "Had a great time. We have a lot in common."

"Glad to hear it," Blue said. "Speaking of local successes, you know that rumor about Bobby Dean Tyler and the theme park?"

Dewey nodded.

"Well, it's half true. He's buying Brisco's Folly. Going to build a non-profit center for the study and preservation of natural marshlands. A place for trails, tours, exhibits, stuff like that. Calling it the Molly Brisco Memorial Center."

"Oh," Dewey said, a kaleidoscope of expressions crossing his face.

Blue laughed and pointed. "You wanted that theme park, Harcourt. You are such a twelve-year-old."

Dewey ducked his head. "A study center will be nice, too."

Delta walked away from her father's office, her thoughts whirling. She took some deep breaths and made a few decisions. First, she would stay in business and re-build. Second, she would let Blue grow her inheritance so she could invest it in Delta Jameson, LLC, in small amounts. Her shoulders slumped. She'd just have to sac-rifice the beautiful office space and new furniture for a few years.

Her thoughts of Blue made her smile. He hadn't changed much in the past twelve years. Still putting oth-ers' happiness before his own. The smile turned wry. That wasn't necessarily a good thing, but she didn't have much of a personal life, either. She got into her car and tapped the wheel with her thumbs, her smile turning to a grin. Maybe they could help each other. Hands on.

Only one person she could discuss *that* with. Hope-fully Patience would be home this evening.

Having made up her mind, Delta's time in Atlanta was short. She met with her attorney to learn he had been forewarned of another matter concerning Delta of damag-ing significance. Since her ex whined nonstop about most things, neither Delta nor her attorney had a clue what it could be. Then she notified the realtor she wouldn't be taking the office space, and cancelled the suite of fur-niture she'd ordered. With Atlanta in her rearview mir-ror, Delta realized she looked forward to Peck's Bluff a lot more than she used to.

She greeted her mother, grabbed a bottle of water, and called her friend. "Hey. Heard from Dewey?"

A soft chuckle came over the phone. "Heard, saw, and experienced."

Delta squealed. "I am officially inviting myself over to get the details."

"You better get a hurry on. He's coming over tonight, again. Guess I unleashed me a tiger."

"You deserve every minute of happiness you get." Delta said. "Especially since you went out and grabbed it with both hands."

"Nothing to stop you from doing the same," Patience replied.

*I know. I'm my own worst enemy.* "Working on it. See you in a few."

"Well, this is probably more than I wanted to know, and she hasn't said a word," Delta thought when Patience opened the door looking totally satisfied with herself.

"Come on in," the redhead said. "What'd you do, tempt fate and law enforcement by speeding?"

Delta laughed. "Now that you're practically related to one of the county's finest, I'm not telling."

They got comfortable and started drinking tea.

Patience stared at Delta over the rim of her cup. "I'm not the only one with something going on. What's been happening with you?"

It all came pouring out. The offer on Brisco's Folly and her decision to tough it out.

Her friend responded slowly. "Sounds safe."

Delta lifted a shoulder. "I boasted to Daddy and Blue that I had Captain Sinclair Brisco blood and would win, no matter what. On my way to Atlanta, I considered trying to put one over on Slayton and his parents, but I couldn't get past the ugly situation I would be in if they found out. I can rebuild my business, but I'm not sure my ego could stand another slapdown."

"Besides," she nodded, "This way, I get to maintain control."

Patience narrowed her gaze. "There's times when control isn't all it's cracked up to be."

Delta swallowed the bait. "Like when?"

Patience smiled. "Like when you're warming the sheets with someone you're crazy about."

Delta lifted a shoulder, her earlier intent to discuss Blue with Patience wavering. "Speaking of warming the sheets, I'm dying to hear what happened between you and Dewey. Give."

Her friend let her know by a direct stare that she realized she was being sidetracked. "Well, he came into the kitchen after you and Blue left the other day and asked me to dinner. He apologized and said as how it wouldn't be as good as my cooking. I wasn't sure if it was a compliment or he was wanting me to offer to cook for him. I've come to the decision that he hasn't got an insincere bone in his body, but at the time, I figured my place would be a good chance to get him alone, so I invited him over. Worked pretty smartly, too."

Delta couldn't have stopped the stupid grin on her face for anything. "So, what happened?"

Patience sighed and blushed beneath her freckles. "He showed up early with a bouquet of wildflowers, nervous as a hound dog that's lost the scent. When I saw those flow-ers sprouting out of that big fist, I 'bout melted."

A snort of laughter escaped from Delta. "You'd have melted if he showed with a fistful of scallions."

"Nevertheless," Patience retorted. "He was very sweet and said nice things about the house. I served dinner right away while we chatted. Mostly about things we had in common. Did you know Dewey likes to garden?"

"Yeah, yeah, I get the picture." Delta said. "Small talk and eating. Get to the good stuff."

Patience leaned back, her hands resting on her knees. "For a woman who's not interested in having a relation-ship of her own, you're sure fascinated by mine."

Delta stuck out her lower lip. "Pleeease. You know I'm a sucker for happy endings. Besides, I'd tell you if it was me living the dream."

An eyebrow punctuated Patience's nod. "I'll hold you to that. Anyway, as I started to cut the dessert, a triple layer chocolate cake, Dewey complimented my dress."

Pink flooded her cheeks again. "That's when I told him I was naked underneath it."

# *Chapter Twenty-Six*

Delta choked on her tea until tears ran down her face. "Hurry," she croaked.

Patience got up to smack her friend on the back, then sat down again. "He stood and walked around the table, took my hand, pulled me to my feet, and gave me the sweetest kiss I ever had."

"Let me get this straight," Delta said, past a gritty throat. "Dewey Harcourt actually stopped eating, before chocolate dessert?"

"Guess he found something more to his liking."

Delta held up her hands in surrender. "I can't take any more. All I know is you seem to have made the perfect choice and I'm extremely happy for the two of you."

Patience grinned. "Thank you. He's gentle and patient and maybe a little naïve, but all I'll ever want."

Delta felt a rush of longing and the need to give herself permission to feel again, even at the risk of failure.

Looking at how things turned out for Patience, she knew that kind of happiness would definitely be worth it.

They talked about her plans for starting her business again, and how her attorney thought she could take on new clients not associated with her former life.

"Take some time off in the middle of December," Patience said.

"What for?"

"I mean to have a short courtship."

Delta was stunned. "You're that sure?"

Patience nodded.

"Time for a hug," Delta said, standing and bringing her friend to her feet. "I think that's wonderful."

The screen door rattled with a knock and Delta saw Dewey's blurred outline on the other side. "I'll be in town until we meet with the Tylers next week," she said. "After I get things sorted out in Atlanta, you and I need to spend a whole weekend shopping. Promise?"

Patience nodded and walked her to the door, already intent on seeing Dewey. "It's a deal."

Delta might have been the doorjamb for as much attention as Dewey paid her. He gripped another bouquet of flowers, looking, she was sure, at Patience for approval. He couldn't even tear his gaze away long enough to glance at her. "Hey, Delta."

Delta sighed and stepped around the two of them. "Deputy."

The drive back to town imposed a sobering thought. She had promised herself she would bring to mind the hurt, betrayal, and pain she had suffered at Slayton's hands if she ever gave up control of her emotions again. But the right man could help her forget all that, couldn't he?

Blue! She'd gotten so engrossed with the Patience and Dewey update, she'd forgotten to bring up Blue. She rolled her eyes. *You have time*, she told herself. *Plenty of time.*

The flashy silver sports car driving away from her parents' house had belonged to Charlotte's ex. Before the divorce.

She went inside and found her mother in the kitchen drinking tea.

"How did your visit with Patience go?" she asked.

Delta grinned. "Great. She is so totally focused it's amazing. Said to expect a wedding before Christmas."

Her mother smiled. "Good for them. Tell Patience congratulations from me the next time you see her."

"I will. Speaking of focused women, was that Charlotte I saw driving away?"

"Yes. You just missed her."

Delta felt a spidery prickling at her neck. "Did she want anything special?"

"She came to pick up her mother. Winnie, Caroline and I have been piecing a wedding quilt for Van and Merrilee. We needed more binding."

"Double wedding ring? Those are so gorgeous."

Her mother laughed. "I'm glad someone in your age group thinks so. Charlotte was underwhelmed."

"Charlotte discussed quilt patterns?"

"Not really. She made the comment that she wouldn't have one of those old-fashioned things on *her* bed. Then we chatted for a few minutes about Brisco's Folly. She said she'd heard about the offer."

The prickling spread down Delta's spine. "Really? What'd she say?"

Her mother sat up straighter. "Why? Did I let the cat out of the bag when I shouldn't have? She seemed to be very happy and said to congratulate you and Blue."

Suzanne Jameson loved to share good news. Especially about her family.

"No," Delta said, assuring her mother. "I was just curious."

Curious as to which offer Charlotte meant. It sounded like Suzanne Jameson hadn't brought up the news, Charlotte had. Which probably meant she thought it was Braxton's offer they were excited about. Charlotte would be very unhappy when she found out it wasn't. She glanced at her watch. "Where's Daddy? It's after six."

Her mother concentrated on her tea cup. "Oh, he went back to the office for a while."

The subject of their conversation walked in the door. "How're my two best girls?"

"Fine," they said in unison.

He looked at Delta. "You're back early. How'd things go with your attorney?"

She sat on the arm of her mother's chair. "About as expected. I made some decisions that aren't quite as 'in

your face' as I'd like." She grinned. "But I told myself that
in a couple of years, Slayton and his parents will be sorry
they ever messed with Delta Jameson, LLC."

He put his arm around her. "That's my girl. Now,
Delta Louise, do you know what tomorrow is?"

She tried to look perplexed. "Hopefully, it's your thir-
tieth wedding anniversary. Otherwise I wasted the money
I spent on that present I hid upstairs."

Her father squeezed her shoulder. "You've been so
busy I wasn't sure you'd remember. I'm taking your mother to Atlanta for the whole day and night. Shopping, a
nice hotel, dancing, then, dinner for two in our suite. The
whole messy thing."

Delta's mother beamed. She stood and hugged her
husband.

"Nice going, Dad," Delta said. "You get my vote for
husband of the year."

"We're leaving early," her mother said. "I wrote the
number of the hotel by the phone."

Delta gave each of them a kiss. "Have fun."

She left them in the kitchen with their arms around
each other and went upstairs to her room. *It can happen
and it can last if you work at it,* she thought. *This thing called
love or passion or whatever. Patience knew it and her parents
were proof.*

A few minutes later her mother knocked on her door
and poked her head through the opening. "I meant to
tell you earlier. A man named Porter Buchanan, I think,
wants you to call him before nine tomorrow morning

regarding some work on the Averill place. His number's next to the one I left of the hotel."

Delta's brain immediately released happy endorphins at the mention of the Averill House, then she frowned. "Uh, you *think* his name was Porter Buchanan?"

"Oh, he had a terrible cold, or maybe allergies, so that's as close as I can come. He said he bought it to use as a summer home, but there are lots of changes he and his wife want to make first."

The details of the pre-nup that disallowed her from using any of her former husband or his family's acquaintances to further her business loomed in Delta's mind. "Did he say how he heard about me?"

Suzanne Jameson frowned. "Oh, honey. I forgot to ask."

Delta nodded. "That's okay. I'll find out in the morning."

# Chapter Twenty-Seven

The half-started drawings she intended to use as a basis for the Molly Brisco Memorial Center were spread across the desk in her father's home office, the morning light brightening the pages. Delta hadn't been able to concentrate on them at all. Eight-thirty is good, she thought, dialing the number for Porter Buchanan. Not too anxious, not too late. A husky, nasal voice answered.

"Mr. Buchanan?"

"Yes."

"This is Delta Jameson. You asked me to call you regarding the Averill House."

"Yes, Ms. Jameson. Your service indicated you weren't accepting new clients due to a family matter, but I persuaded them to give me the number where you could be reached, anyway. I've checked and found you're the best in the area. I make it a point to deal only with the best. Can I ask if your family matter will be resolved soon?"

Delta resisted the urge to giggle. Mr. Buchanan certainly got to the point, but all his m's sounded like b's due to his cold. Instead, she focused on the flattery. "Thank you, Mr. Buchanan but I need to ask you a question first, please. How did you hear about my work?"

"My wife," he answered. "She subscribes to *Atlanta Architecture* and read an article about you. Talked non-stop for weeks. I have a few contacts in the construction field and found out you're talented, hardworking, and honest. As I said before, I like to work with the best. That answer your question?"

She released a held breath. It sounded like the Buchanans weren't influenced by, or had connections with, Slayton's family. "Yes, thank you. What timeframe did you have in mind?"

"Good, good. We were hoping to have the work done over the winter and occupy the house next spring. Generous budget, too."

Delta's heart beat faster and her palm holding the receiver sweated. This sounded better and better. "My personal constraints will be resolved soon and I could fit your project into my schedule if we come to an agreement on terms. In the meantime, I could give you an evaluation, no charge. I'm familiar with the property."

"That's encouraging," he said. "Do you have time to check out the house today and get back to me? I'm stuck here with a bad cold, but my contractor has another job in your area and I can send him to meet you and show you around about noon. He has keys to the place."

"That would be fine," Delta replied. "And thanks again for the opportunity."

She decided to answer her ringing cell phone on her way to the appointment. "Hello?"

"Hey," Blue said. "I got some good news on Gran's probate. Can I take you to lunch?"

"Maybe dinner. I have a chance to do some design work on the Averill House, down at the end of River Road. I've been in love with that property for years. It's secluded, right on the water, and the view is spectacular. I'm on my way out there now to meet the client's contractor."

She heard the smile in his voice. "No connections to your ex's family?"

"Not even a little," she declared.

"Good news all around, then. I'll call you later to see how the meeting went."

Delta did the math in her head as she drove out River Road.

She hadn't seen the house since a night before high school graduation party more than ten years ago. The original owners had it commissioned by an architect that fancied himself the next Frank Lloyd Wright. He was very good, but had never achieved the worldwide fame he sought. The Averill House was deemed his best.

Pulling up, Delta was disappointed, but not surprised, to see that the acreage had become overgrown and all but a few of the windows in the house were boarded up. She'd gone online to discover the house hadn't been occupied for five years. The contractor hadn't shown yet, so she decided to look around.

When she opened the car door, she was glad she'd worn a heavier coat and muffler. The Georgia weather had changed drastically from the mild temperatures of just a few days ago. Out here, the breeze off the river added to the chill.

Delta walked around the outside of the house, taking notes, her cold fingers cramping around the pen. She frowned when she reached the back door. It stood ajar. Maybe the contractor had had someone drop him off. The door creaked as she swung it inward. "Hello?" she called.

No answer. Delta laid her notepad and purse next to a galvanized bucket and pulled a small flashlight from her pocket. The kitchen was as expected, rust-stained sink, dirty walls, and a lot of cobwebs. Still, there were no water stains and no outward signs of wood rot or termites. She smiled. The "bones" of the house were as beautiful as she remembered.

A sound of something heavy smashing in the living room drew her attention. As she rounded a dividing wall, she saw the source of the noise. A figure of a man in filthy clothes kicked at a large piece of wood, then squatted on his calves, running a wooden match across the bricks at the base of the old fireplace.

Panic spread in her chest.

A fireplace unused for as many years as this one would surely have a clogged chimney.

"Please don't do that," she said softly, so as not to startle him. "It's not safe."

He ignored her.

She took a step closer as the match caught, then held. She leaned forward and touched his shoulder.

His response was immediate. A hoarse yell, dropped match, and his other arm, holding another chunk of wood swung in an upward arc. Delta had no time to move as the wood caught her on the side of the head. The last she remembered was recognizing terror, not anger, on his face.

Something hot covered her mouth and she had trouble breathing. Her head pounded. Delta reached to push aside the muffler that had fallen across her face, then squinted into the dark. The man was gone and dense black smoke rolled out of the fireplace, a telltale crackling of fire behind the choking curtain. Delta rolled to her knees.

She swayed on her feet, coughing, and made her way into the kitchen. The back door stood wide open. Delta grabbed her purse, fumbling for her cell phone as she staggered down the steps. Although the old wood structure would most certainly be engulfed by the time anyone got here, she called 9-1-1 to report the fire. Standing out back, her heart sank as smoke and heat ate their way up and out. She held the muffler across her mouth and reached inside the back door for the bucket. She took it and hurried toward the river. She would not give up without a fight.

# Chapter Twenty-Eight

Blue saw Dewey's cruiser pull up to Mackie's and walked over. "Eating lunch here every day?"

"Got me a special girl and damned if she can't cook, too," Dewey said, blushing.

Humor suffused Blue's voice. "I might argue that she got you, but it's a moot point. Want some company?"

Dewey reached for his radio. "Sure. Let me code out for lunch."

The radio crackled to life. "All units. A fire has been reported at an abandoned house on River Road."

The air left Blue's lungs and he scrabbled for the car's door handle. "Delta's out there. That could be her."

Dewey stared at him and responded to the radio. "Unit 4. I'm five minutes out." After clearing the main street, he got back on the radio. "You got a name for the person that reported the fire?"

"Jameson, I think. She was coughing pretty hard."

Foreboding clutched at Blue's chest as Dewey filled in the dispatcher and cut off the radio.

"If she had time to call it in, she's okay," he said.

"What the hell happened?" Blue rasped, still trying to get a full breath. "She went out there to meet a contractor and the next thing we know, the house is on fire."

They saw it then, black smoke thickening the gray sky ahead. Blue opened his seatbelt even though they were still moving fast down the gravel road.

"Side pocket," Dewey said, indicating Blue's door. "Insulated gloves and a cloth to hold over your mouth and nose."

Blue pulled them out. When Dewey was close to the house, he slowed the car. That's when they heard the wailing of fire engines behind them.

"... Deputy Harcourt?"

Dewey flipped a switch and sound filled the car as he skidded into the head of the drive.

"I'm at the location now."

"ETA for fire and aid is two minutes. The woman who reported the fire said she would stay nearby."

Blue tugged on a glove and grasped the car door handle as he scanned the area for any sign of Delta. Nothing but her empty car. Where was the damned contractor? His stomach clenched. She wasn't anywhere in sight and the front of the house was fully involved. "I'll go around back."

"I'm right behind you," Dewey said. He grabbed Blue's arm in an iron grip. "Do not, under any circumstances, go in there. Delta wouldn't do anything that stupid."

Unreasoning fear crowded Blue's mind. "Okay," he managed.

Smoke drifted toward the car and partially obscured the house, but Blue jumped out and headed straight into the suffocating cloud. He tore around the side, the heat a palpable wall.

There were no flames yet, but Delta wasn't there, either. Fear bloomed into terror. What if she went in to get something and was overcome? He scanned the area for Delta one more time, then started toward the back door.

Dewey dragged him away just as a thunderous crack sounded and the wall erupted in flames. Heat drove them to the border of trees that lined the river.

The sirens wound down and Dewey shot him a pained look. "I have to go let them know ... to check in with them." His big hand clutched Blue's shoulder. "Stay right here."

Blue nodded and dropped the glove and cloth as he bent over to suck in air. A twisted, desperate sound clawed out of his throat. This couldn't be happening.

"Blue!"

He straightened and turned, nearly toppling over when Delta ran into his arms. He swallowed over and over as he held her tightly, tears from the smoke mixed with emotion blurring his vision. Inside, the part of him that had shrunk, filled again. His words came thick and loud over the roar of the fire. "I thought you were in there. That you were gone ..."

Delta kept patting and hugging him, her hair and clothes disheveled and damp in spots. "How did you know?" She looked over at the house, then coughed against her elbow. "Such a terrible waste. I tried. I know it was stupid, but I went to the river and got water in the bucket." Tears now streamed down her face, too. "It was an accident. He didn't mean to hit me. He only wanted to get warm."

"Who?" said Blue. "The contractor? He hit you and started the fire? Where is he?"

"Wahoo!" Dewey shouted before she could reply. He ran to wrap both of them in a bear hug as water arced over the house, soaking all three. Blue gripped Delta's hand and ran as the roof and most of the frame collapsed inward.

They reached the front to see an ambulance backed in behind the fire trucks. The technician handed out blankets.

"Anyone hurt?"

Blue urged Delta forward, his hand keeping contact with her blanket. "She was here when the fire started. Someone hit her and she's shaking pretty hard. Maybe shock." The EMT nodded at Blue and helped her up, out of the wind.

Delta sat in the ambulance and mourned the loss of the beautiful house. Nothing remained but smoldering blackened ribs and an ugly, dripping mess. She couldn't stop shivering, despite the blanket. From equal parts cold, she thought, and the dawning realization that had she remained unconscious a couple more minutes, she'd be dead.

The EMT dabbed antiseptic on the swollen cut near Delta's hairline. She winced, squeezing her eyes shut.

"Looks like you won't need stitches," he said. "But a concussion's a definite possibility."

Delta nodded gingerly as she took short, shallow breaths to try and ease the sting. Tears filled her eyes anyway, and when she blinked them away, she saw her torn pants, broken nails, and various shades of soot on her clothes. Realization that she had been in nearly the same state barely a week ago added to her distress. Two accidents? Maybe. Or did Blue's assertion that Braxton might be dangerous have substance?

Sitting here, safe and alive, Delta didn't want to examine the set of circumstances she and Blue had both recently endured. But it was a definite wake-up call. Blue's question about the contractor was valid. Where was he? And if she'd been meant to walk into some kind of trap, why lure her out here on the chance that she would be hurt by a terrified man who looked homeless?

The technician moved away and Delta closed her eyes, overwhelming sadness temporarily replacing her fearful thoughts.

Her reprieve lasted only a minute.

"You feeling better?"

She opened one eye to see Dewey standing anxiously, with a pen and pad. Blue stood behind him.

"Yes," she said.

"I have to get some information for my report," Dewey continued. "I'll make it fast so you can get home."

Delta tipped her head. "Thanks."

Dewey's lips were pale purple. "You told Blue the contractor you were meeting started the fire by accident. That right?"

She shook her head. An action she instantly regretted. "I got a call from a prospective client wanting a remodel of the house. I was to meet his contractor here at noon. I came early to take some notes." She went over the details of finding the man trying to start a fire in the fireplace and accidently hitting her with the wood.

"Wait." Dewey stopped her. "What did this guy look like?"

Delta considered. "Uh, filthy watch cap, wispy salt and pepper beard, about fifty. Oh, and a really dirty brown trench coat."

Dewey nodded and scribbled. "Gotta be Dirty Harry."

Delta straightened and the blanket slipped from her shoulders. "He didn't look anything like Clint Eastwood."

The deputy laughed. "No. Harry's a guy who shies away from any kind of soap and water. Nearly stone deaf and been wandering in these woods for as long as I can remember. That house's been empty for years. He probably thought it was time to move inside for the winter."

Delta pulled the blanket back onto her shoulders. "Dewey, I'm desperate for a hot bath and dry clothes. Not to mention something for this headache, and a nap. If you catch up with Harry, he can tell you the same thing I just did."

He closed his pad. "What'd the EMT say?"

"Mostly scratches and bruises from thrashing through the undergrowth to the river. And a possible concussion from this." She gingerly touched her temple.

Blue stepped toward her, a worried look in place as he slid the backs of his fingers up her cheek. "We're officially a matched set. I know the drill. One of your parents will have to wake you every few hours to check how you're doing tonight. I'll drive you home in your car and pass the instructions to your mother."

Delta didn't contradict him. She stayed quiet as Blue drove her car to the Jameson house. She wanted time to herself before her family found out about the fire and her injury. The niggling thought that it might not be the safest time to be alone was pushed aside. She'd be damned if she'd ruin her parents' anniversary celebration. It'd be easy to set her alarm to wake up every few hours.

"I'll take you in," Blue said as they pulled up.

"Not necessary," she told him. "Just drop me off."

Blue set his mouth as he turned off the engine. "I'm not dumping you at the curb. I can leave your car here and walk home."

Delta started edging toward her front door, but Blue caught up and took her elbow. "I'll make sure your mother understands about checking on you."

Delta stopped on her porch. "Look, I can handle this. Please? I promise you'll get a call if anything happens. I really hate being fussed over."

He studied her face. "You sure?"

She nodded once.

"Program Mother's number into your cell," he said. "Keep it close by."

Delta shrugged. "Is all this necessary? Besides, my phone's gone. I thought I tossed it in my purse after I called in the fire, but it's not there. I must've missed and it's somewhere behind the house, trampled in the mud or under the wall that came down."

Blue pulled his out of his pocket, brought up a screen and punched in some numbers. "Borrow mine and keep it close by. I'll use mother's emergency cell phone until tomorrow. Press three and it'll call her number. I can be here in minutes."

She took the phone. "Satisfied?"

Blue pushed out a breath, caving to her insistence.

Delta put her hand on his cheek. "Thanks for being there."

He pulled her hand to his mouth and kissed it. "Thanks for being here."

A soothing happiness percolated through Delta's exhaustion, but she clamped her still-chattering teeth. She needed to be by herself to think about her reaction to

Blue at the fire. The force of her feelings when she saw him had been overwhelming and a little scary. A reaction, she was sure, would not have been so intense had it been anyone else. Blue said something she missed. "I'm sorry. What did you say?"

"I said, if you begin to feel any worsening symptoms, will you have your parents take you to the clinic?"

Guilt seeped in. Heck, she took the cell phone. Why'd he have to make her feel bad about going into an empty house? "That won't happen," she said, by way of not lying to him. "I'm feeling better already."

"Okay, get some rest. Then we need to talk," he said, suddenly hugging her hard, molding her body to his. The kiss that followed spun warm waves through her cold body. When he stepped back she had to steady herself.

"See you tomorrow."

Delta stood there stupidly until she realized he was waiting for her to go in the house.

Inside, the quiet she'd been looking forward to, now creeped her out. First order of business, check for locked windows and doors.

Next, a hot bath, some soup, and ibuprofen. Delta expended the last of her energy rinsing the dishes. Then upstairs. She was more than ready for a nap, but sleep eluded her. Although she was sure she loved Blue, she'd already given up her dream of a successful career in architecture once, for Slayton. Blue could monitor the market from anywhere and his interest in green construction melded perfectly with her direction in designing.

Delta sighed. No sense speculating. They would work through their issues. Or not. A thought she didn't want to analyze too closely. With no real decision made, she pulled up her covers and drifted to sleep.

Sometime later, her dream shifted to incorporate loud knocking. "Coming," she answered, confident her dream visitor had heard. The knocking turned to pounding and she woke up. Disoriented, and the memory from her close encounter still fresh, Delta felt her heart hammer. She grabbed the phone off her nightstand and pressed three.

# Chapter Twenty-nine

Blue let out his frustration on the Jameson's back door. She'd better be all right in there because he was going to kill her. He lifted his fist to resume his attack on the door when the cell phone in his pocket went off. Snatching it, he read the text ID, RICHMOND. He pressed the off button. He'd scared her. Good. Maybe she needed a scare after pulling a stunt like this.

"Who's there?" He barely heard the question.

"It's me, Delta," Blue said, in a quieter tone than he felt.

She opened the door in her Falcon's t-shirt, bare legs, and sleep-mussed hair. Blue resisted hugging her and tried to hold onto his anger. "Are you coming with me, or am I staying here?"

Delta blinked and yawned, pushing back her hair. "What are you talking about?" Her eyes widened. "Why were you knocking so loud? Is everyone okay? Van? My parents?"

He saw the ugly mark on her temple but again, kept his hands to himself. "As far as I know, they're okay. I'm here, banging on your door, because I went over to Gran's to help sort the last of the furniture a little while ago and mother mentioned that your parents are in Atlanta celebrating their anniversary. I hope you've had enough 'alone' time because you're not spending tonight that way."

Awareness sparked in her eyes. "The last time I checked, how I spend my time was none of your business. Today was an accident, Blue. Pure and simple. I saw the look on that man's face before he hit me and he was terrified. It was totally unintentional and I'm fine."

Blue scrubbed his face with his hands. "True, your time is your own, but since I care about you, your welfare *is* my business." *He was skating on thin ice, but his gut said he had to get his way on this.* "Okay, say it was a coincidence that you were hurt, almost killed today. That doesn't mean it's safe for you to be here alone. There are too many unanswered questions. I saw Charlotte driving past on my way here. She was alone. That means Braxton could be anywhere."

She sighed, her gray eyes now calm. "I'm sorry Blue, but I don't share your concerns. Harlan Braxton hasn't done anything to make us doubt he is who and what he says he is." She rubbed her eyes. "I've had a really crummy day and I just needed the space. Let's leave it at that."

*Damn her stubborn hide.* "So, you lied to me."

"When, exactly, did I say my parents were home?"

He crossed him arms. "You implied as much."

She tugged at the hem of her oversized t-shirt. "You better come in. It's too cold to discuss this on the porch." She turned and walked into the dusk-dimmed kitchen. "Suppose I buy into your theory that Braxton is dangerous. Where did you have in mind for me to stay?"

Blue hadn't thought past the part where he was furious. He rubbed his forehead. "Van's still in town. When will he be home?"

"He's not here," Delta said. "He's with friends in Athens for the University of Georgia homecoming weekend."

"You could stay with Patience."

She shook her head. "Dewey's a permanent fixture there, when he gets off shift. Otherwise, it's Patience and me alone in the middle of nowhere. What about Gran's?"

Blue started to panic. "Mother's coming down with something. They've been working on the house non-stop. Anyway, there's only one bedroom with furniture."

Delta went to the hall closet and pulled out a heavy coat sweater, wrapping herself in it before returning to the kitchen. "Then it looks like I'll be staying here."

Blue shook his head. "Not by yourself, you're not."

She looked wide awake and exasperated. "What, then? My parents love and trust you, but they would definitely not like how it would look with us staying overnight under their roof."

Blue recalled his recent conversation with Fuller Jameson. Delta was right. He stepped over and took her hand, rubbing the back with his thumb. "Look, I'm sorry, but stick with me on this." He tried for a soothing smile. "Humor a crazy man who's convinced there's something behind our *accidents* besides bad luck."

Delta lifted a shoulder, nodding. "You're not the crazy man type, so ..."

"So, let's try this. We walk the river path to Mother's. If we come up with a better plan once we get there, great. Otherwise, you take my bed and I'll take Dewey's, then I'll walk you back here early tomorrow. It'll be dark both ways."

"All right for now," she said, her gaze pinning him. "And I still think you're worried for nothing, but your self-appointed guardianship comes at a price."

He started to make a flip remark about getting a cut rate, but the look on her face brought him up short. *She was asking him to make a decision about the two of them.* Something he'd been thinking about since he'd found her safe behind the burning house. "Uh, it's almost five. We could get some burgers at Tinker's for dinner."

Her frank study continued, the gray of her irises deepening. Then she smiled. "Okay."

Blue backed to the door, finding the doorknob behind him, he turned it without breaking eye contact. He could swear she planted an image of them making love in his mind. Either that, or his subconscious was working overtime to make him happy.

He made it to the top step of the porch. The heat of anger changing to an entirely different kind of heat. "I'll just wait out here while you put some things together."

They didn't see a soul on the path when they walked to his mother's house. Blue let them in the back door and switched on the light. Pronounced shadows he hadn't noticed before smudged Delta's eyes. "Hey, you all right?" he asked.

She nodded. "It's like a bad movie. Heroine tries to save the homestead and gets knocked flat for her effort."

Blue wrapped her in his arms. "I'm sorry about the house."

Delta tipped her face up to his. "Thank you."

He meant for the hug and kiss to be light, a gesture of comfort. Delta's response, however, derailed his intentions. She pressed against him, her slender body warming his torso, her mouth opening. This was the second time she'd ambushed him, only this time she wasn't half drunk. He tried to ease away. "Maybe this wasn't such a good idea."

She regarded him in her serene, serious way. "I'm a big girl, Blue. There's something between us, and you should know I've been thinking about this for a while."

So had he. It would be easy to pick her up and walk to his room. To make lazy pathways on every inch of her skin with his fingertips, followed by his mouth. But their mutual desires were based on different motivations. He wanted permanence and promise. Delta wasn't ready for that. She still felt the burn of humiliation at the hands of Slayton and his parents. Her independence was too fresh, so she was coming to him for validation. It might not be that simple, but he couldn't bring himself to take advantage.

There were two possible results if they made love. Delta would wake up thinking it was a spectacular mistake and their relationship would be irreparably ruined or ...? He couldn't allow himself the optimism.

"It's been a really long day," he said. "Why don't we eat and watch a little television?"

"Fine," she said. "Invitation rescinded. Just stay there."

For a couple of heartbeats he wanted to grab her wrists, and pull her arms around him. Instead, he sighed. "What does that mean?"

"It means," she waved her hand back and forth between them, "that we've been through a lot together and I thought we wanted the same thing. But you stay in that safety zone you've created for yourself. It wouldn't do for you to step outside for me. Oh, hell." She turned and started toward the hall.

Blue touched her shoulder. "You're not being fair."

She shrugged off his hand. "Screw fair."

Delta leaned against the door she'd slammed. Damn him. In the few relationships she'd allowed since Slayton, she'd never lost control, never let sex be anything but a thinking, realized outlet with a beginning, middle, and end. She'd certainly never begged.

She paced, then stopped. Damn him, again. Every time she neared his closet, she was reminded how he smelled when he held her close. The edge of the bed looked safe for sitting until she found herself rocking, arms wrapped tight, with tears burning her eyelids.

A soft knock interrupted her misery. Delta straightened and cleared her throat. "What do you want?"

"You hungry? We could call Tinker's and get burgers to go."

The image of a hot, juicy burger with a mound of crispy fries from Tinker's made her saliva pool, but Delta didn't feel like giving him the satisfaction of doing something nice for her. "No."

"Okay. I'll call an order in and pick it up. Do you want to drive over with me?"

She was acting juvenile, but couldn't help it. "You went to all this subterfuge to get me 'safe', and now you're leaving to get a hamburger?"

Heavy sigh from the other side of the door. "The house is locked up tight and Dewey's parked nearby, lights out, until I get back. See you in fifteen."

Well, she couldn't fault him for not thinking of everything. Her stomach growled in concert with the sound of his car engine turning over, then fading from the driveway.

Delta waited a few minutes and went into the kitchen. Maybe she could scrounge something before he got back. The contents of the fridge and cupboards made her laugh out loud. Two cans of baked beans and a jar of homemade asparagus in the cupboard, and a partial box of Ho Ho's in the fridge. She pushed out a huff of air. If she snuck over to her folk's to grab a snack and Blue caught her, there'd be hell to pay.

The devil on her right shoulder said, "Do whatever you want. He's not the boss of you." The devil on her left shoulder said, "He's being overprotective because he cares. Lighten up."

Delta opened the fridge, took out a couple of Ho Ho's, and sat to wait for Blue. And think.

# Chapter Thirty

Blue carried his order through Tinker's and out the door. He'd almost reached the anonymity of the dark parking lot, when he saw Charlotte. She walked toward him, arm-in-arm with Harlan Braxton, head bent toward his, speaking earnestly. At least he now knew where Braxton was. Blue turned aside, hoping Charlotte wouldn't spot him, but no such luck. When she did, strained anger followed by an instant grin morphed so quickly across her face, it was almost comical.

Charlotte released Braxton's arm to grab his. "Blue, darlin'. You've got some explaining to do." Her gaze took in the wide doors, people going in and out. "Let's step over here."

A faint whiff of gin floated upward and Blue pulled his arm from her grip. He cut a glance to Braxton, who gave him a tight nod.

Blue's entire concentration was on Delta and how he'd left their situation. He didn't want to deal with Charlotte and her selfish demands. "How about tomorrow? Lunch at Mackie's around noon?" He asked.

She dragged at his jacket, waving an unlit cigarette as she spoke over her shoulder. "Brax honey, get us a table and order me a drink. I'll just be a minute."

Maneuvering Blue against the wall, Charlotte fished in her purse and pulled out a lighter. She lit her cigarette and inhaled deeply. "Can't smoke in Mr. Braxton's fancy truck," she said in a high-pitched sing-song. "Now, what's this I hear about you and Delta accepting another offer for Brisco's Folly? Harlan and I were sure, considering what the land will be used for, that y'all would choose his generous proposal."

Blue studied Charlotte's face in the unflattering light of a neon beer sign. She wore her anger and bitterness hard. He held up the sack. "I'd be interested to know where you heard that. Tomorrow. Right now dinner's getting cold, Charlotte."

She ignored his escape attempt. "Have you signed on the deal, yet?"

"Not yet," he said. "But we're not changing our minds."

Her gaze shifted to coyness and she slid her hands around his waist, pressing herself against him. "I could sweeten the pot."

Blue eased her away with his free hand. "Charlotte, back up a minute. Supposing things went your way? What would you get out of it? Braxton says he's representing someone else. The money he says he's holding isn't even his. So, why are you pushing us to go with him?"

Charlotte slowly pulled the zipper of Blue's jacket down, then back up. "Why, first of all, I'd get out of here." She rolled her eyes. "Away from this dinky, boring, little do-nothing town."

Blue tipped his head. She was so unhappy. And convinced moving to Atlanta would solve her problems. "You know, Charlotte, big cities can be lonely places. Take it from someone who knows."

Her eyes sparked. "They can also be fun and exciting if you have money."

He glanced toward the door to Tinker's. "Braxton doesn't always come by his money legally. He's conned and abused women and been jailed for violence against a former partner. An old man."

Charlotte's gaze didn't follow his. "Harlan told me all about that. The old man came after him with a pipe wrench and Harlan was only defending himself. I believe him and we're partners, now," she said. "He's going to teach me all about finding the right properties, for the right people, for the right price."

Blue felt uneasy, like he'd stumbled on a nest of yellow jackets in tall grass, the full danger not evident until it was too late. He stood very still. "And in return for this tutoring, what would Braxton get?"

A hard glint, evident even in the poor light, shone deep in her eyes. "Why, me, darlin', and all my persuasive powers." She shot him a knowing look. "Which can be considerable. And since you haven't signed anything yet, let me confer with my new partner and get back to you. I can guarantee a little something personal's in it for you." She kissed the tip of her index finger, touched it to Blue's lips, and sauntered inside.

Blue released a held breath and shuddered. He could stand here all night trying to convince Charlotte to slow down and take stock of her life before running headlong to the next, possibly dangerous phase, but it wouldn't do any good. Her sense of entitlement was too strong.

Delta swung a leg over the end of the couch, picking at a frayed spot of denim on the knee of her jeans. The Ho Ho's hadn't satisfied her hunger and her headache had returned with a vengeance. It would be a few minutes for the aspirin to take effect, so she closed her eyes and dropped her shoulders. What was wrong with her? First, she'd thrown herself at Blue after getting drunk the day she got served. Then, he'd gotten all mad and protective after her close call today and she hit on him again. Blue was right. It had been a bad idea.

A key shifted in the lock and she opened her eyes to see Blue walk in carrying a food sack. Bad idea or not, need skittered through her and she knew she'd always feel this way about him.

"Did you ignore my snit and bring me a burger?" she asked.

Blue nodded.

"Thank you," Delta said. "And I apologize for, you know, earlier." She absently massaged her temple. "This change in our relationship has come at a tough time. For both of us."

Blue set down the sack without speaking.

"The thing is," she continued, twisting her fingers together, "I'm not sure if we're closer because it's a natural progression of our feelings, or, because of everything we've gone through together."

Delta waved away the words as soon as she spoke them. This was way more complicated than she'd thought it would be. "Cancel that. I know how I feel about you, and it's not due to crisis or circumstances. I've fallen in love with you." There, it was out and she never would have believed she'd be the one to say it first.

"I know," Blue said, his gaze confirming he was feeling the same vulnerability she was.

"You know." Skepticism colored her tone. "How?"

He smiled. "Because that's the same conclusion I came to days ago. Just hadn't admitted it out loud."

She stood and paced – putting the couch between her and Blue, every corpuscle filled with adrenalin-laced longing. He wasn't helping either. Standing there watching her with his *"I'm everything you want and need, only say the word,"* look.

"I've cared for you ever since I can remember," he continued, making her breath still. "And I can't tell you why we've changed from us to *us*. But I know not being with you is killing me."

Hope flared alongside the heat in her. "Then why...?"

"Because it would have to be forever."

There is was, she thought, her skin now twitching for him, the forever part. Blue was that kind of man and she didn't know if she could be that for him.

"I'm not Slayton," he said quietly.

"No, you're not," she agreed, dropping her gaze. "But taking us to the next level would come at a price."

"And that price is, we can't go back," he said.

A shudder tumbled through her. "If it didn't work out, things between us would never be the same. That scares me."

Blue nodded. "Me, too. Yet, you accuse me of running away from who I can be, and you're doing the same thing, only with us. Permanence doesn't have to mean changing who we are. I don't want change, I want you."

Delta could tell he meant everything he was saying. For the first time, she felt like she could have it all. Warmth spread over her skin as she walked into his personal space. If she was ever going to be free in a relationship, it would be with Blue. She put her arms around his waist and lay her head against his shoulder.

He held her tight. "You're going to love Chicago."

Her head snapped back to meet his gaze, her heart hammering.

"Kidding," Blue grinned. "My townhouse is leased as of yesterday."

Delta put her whole heart into the hug. "Pretty sure of yourself, aren't you?"

He paused before answering. "No. It took me a year to realize this is where I want to live. Being with you these past couple of weeks makes me sure it's the right decision."

"So, you're moving to Atlanta?"

He shook his head. "Nope. I'm done with big cities. Moving back here."

It was small of her, but Delta couldn't help testing his assertion that their new relationship wouldn't force changes on them. "I still have to work in Atlanta," she said. "And I need to keep a space for myself. At least for the time being. Besides, it's under an hour by car, if you push it."

He didn't even blink. "Looks like I'll be sending for my car. The one with plenty of horsepower."

She kissed his jaw, relief coursing through her. "I can live with that."

Delta's tenuous acceptance of this new stage gave Blue a heady rush. He slid an arm up to cup the back of her head and leaned in to kiss her fully. Her response was immediate and electric, sending a wave of physical craving into his very foundation and shattering his earlier resolve. Delta had admitted she loved him and wanted to be with him, permanently. It was all he needed to hear.

He pulled away a fraction. "Um, about my earlier reluctance to ..."

"Right," she said, taking his hand and leading him down the hall. "Let's not let that happen again."

She was his, he thought. And with patience, she would eventually marry him. He doubled his stride to stand in front of her. "Did you, by any chance, pack those red cow-boy boots?"

"Blue Richmond!" Delta slapped a hand across her mouth.

He shifted his gaze to the ceiling. "So, is that a deal breaker?"

She grabbed the waistband of his jeans and tugged him to her. "Absolutely not, but that'll have to wait. Neither of us is leaving this house until I have my way."

Blue lifted her hands to kiss the palms. "I hope there are a few condoms left in Dewey's stash, because my plans are exactly the same as yours."

Delta kissed him lightly. "I'll be in your bed."

A few minutes later he entered his room and put his clothes on the chair by the closet, then sat on the bed and tore open a condom package.

He had known Delta as a friend all his life. But this was Delta the unknown, the beautiful woman he was about to make love to, he had hoped to make love to for some time.

A rustling sound behind him preceded the scrape of teeth on his earlobe. Blue turned and caught Delta's open mouth with his. She trailed her fingers up the inside of his thigh and he nearly lost it. He tried the mental control he'd learned in kickboxing, but when they lay down skin-to-skin, all thought converted to sensation. He wanted every touch and taste of her. He wanted the sound she made when she came to stay in his mind forever.

Blue knew he was his own worst enemy. He had to get past the greed of wanting her so bad it consumed and threatened to blind him to her needs. It didn't help that she now slid her finger around the curve of his ear and half-hummed, half-moaned when he touched her. Heat spun around them as he dragged his mouth across her sweet-smelling, salty skin.

Delta curved into him, his name coming in rushes of breath, her fingers leaving memories in their wake. Blue stroked a hand to the small of her back, then around her hip to the top of her thigh, his thumb veering downward.

"Blue, sugar? Please," she whispered hoarsely, her hands gripping his arms, urging him on.

Blue moved to his elbows, his mouth inches from her pale face. She lifted her head and licked his lips. "Enough," he breathed. "I've waited long enough," and slipped inside her. Delta reacted immediately, rocking against him, her gasps coming closer. Her cry of release moments later, shocked him.

"Once more," he said, his teeth on edge. "Let go again, this time with me."

She smiled, eyes half-lidded, and brought her arms around him loosely. "I don't know if I can."

Blue sucked a shallow breath. "Sure you can, sugar. Don't make me lose respect for you, now."

Delta threw back her head and laughed, the sound turning into a moan as he moved faster. His senses leaped as she tightened around him, blotting out everything but her name, and his on her lips.

# Chapter Thirty-One

Delta woke to a muffled thumping on the bedroom door. She squinted at it, grateful to see that the lock was turned. The rest of her senses revealed themselves a layer at a time. First, the feeling of being thoroughly satisfied, if not thoroughly rested. Then, the warm presence of Blue, his arm slung across her waist, a puff of his breath tickling her neck. Whoever it was, she wanted them gone.

She turned her head. The crack between window and shade showed darkness. "Go away," she croaked.

Dewey's booming laugh met her words. "Patience hoped you were here, seeing as no one answered at your folks' house. She was worried, but I guess you're in safe hands."

Delta became aware of one of those hands trailing fingers up her arm. She rolled out of the near side of the bed clutching her pillow and backing toward the bathroom.

Blue lifted himself onto his elbow and winked at her. She pulled down her lower eyelid. "These bloodshot eyes are your fault. I expect coffee when I get out of the shower. Fifteen minutes."

He feigned innocence. "What? I had to wake you up every couple of hours to make sure you didn't have a concussion."

"Hunh," she said. "A concussion is usually found *above* the neck."

"But you were very grateful," he nodded. "At least the *sounds* you made seemed grateful."

Delta felt herself coloring. She narrowed her eyes as she backed through the bathroom door, then pointed at Blue, shaking her finger. "Coffee."

She closed the door to his laughter and sighed. What an amazing night. Blue had been tender, conscious of her needs, and every bit as hungry for her as she had been for him. She had arrived at the ripe old age of twenty-eight without ever truly having been made love to. She never wanted to be without the feeling again.

Last night in Blue's arms had thrown her thinking in a whole new direction. She accepted the fact that she loved him and knew he felt the same. They were a couple in every sense of the word, now, and as they had said, there was no going back.

Fifteen minutes later, she walked into the kitchen, her nose not mistaking the smell of Patience's cooking. The center of the table held a plate of honey cornbread chunks with thick bacon protruding from the wedges. A fragrant apple pie sat on the counter next to the travel thermos of coffee.

"Oh, my," Delta said. "This calls for naming my first-born after Patience."

"I agree," Blue mumbled, his mouth full. "Don't care if it's a boy, or not."

"My girl thought you might be here and hungry," Dewey said, grinning. "And since I needed to talk to you all about the fire anyway, I got pressed into service."

His cell rang, and Dewey smiled at the readout. "Speak of the prettiest cook around." He brought the phone to his ear. "Hey."

Excited female chatter greeted him.

"Yes," he said. "They were here. Yes, together. Yes, in the same room."

*Okay*, Delta thought. *It begins.* And it was going to take some getting used to. She had hated the sideways glances calculating how she was doing after her divorce. She'd felt like a failure but suspected being the topic of gossip, even if the subject was a happy one, would be about the same.

The chatter on Dewey's cell phone escalated to a giggled shriek, and he held out the phone to Delta. "She wants to say a few words."

"Hey," Delta said into the phone. "Thanks for the food and coffee."

"Are you happy, chickapea?"

It was as simple as that for Patience. Was she happy? Delta didn't have to think about it. "Yes," she said. "I am."

"'Bout time," Patience said. "I'll get details, later. I gotta go. Just landed me a gaggle of truckers." And with that, her friend hung up.

Delta handed the phone back to Dewey and picked up a chunk of cornbread. She bit in and hummed her appreciation.

Dewey waited a beat, then slid his cup in a small wet circle. "Something weird going on."

"How weird?" Blue asked.

"Dirty Harry got picked up on a BOLO. He was going through garbage behind the Peck's Bluff Inn. His story about yesterday's events was pretty strange."

Blue reached to scoot Delta's chair closer to his. A move that pleased her to no end.

"What did he say?" Blue asked.

"I didn't take the interview," Dewey said. "I read it this morning. He was mostly non-responsive. Except when it came to the fireman."

Delta sipped her coffee. "He watched them put out the fire?"

Dewey shook his head. "This is where the weird comes in. Harry said there was a fireman there earlier who saw him peeking in the windows of the house. When the fireman came toward the back door, Harry retreated to the trees and watched the guy pop the lock and go inside. He had something shiny in his hand."

"Do you think Harry made it up to try and blame the fire on someone else?" Delta asked.

"The interviewer said he was adamant." Dewey lifted a shoulder. "Anyway, the fireman came out and carried sticks into the house a couple of times before leaving. Harry said he looked angry."

Delta's rolling stomach had nothing to do with hunger. She needed to hear the rest of the story. "What next?"

"Harry said he waited and waited near the trees to see if the fireman would come back. When he didn't, Harry went inside and found a partially laid fire. He made a point of showing us he always carries matches wrapped in aluminum foil. So, he went out and got some bigger pieces of wood and was lighting the whole thing off when you tapped him on the shoulder."

Delta absently rubbed her forehead in front of the bruise.

"So, he didn't attack me. Just as I said, he was more frightened than aggressive."

"Looks that way," Dewey said. "Although the fireman story is hard to buy."

She ran her finger around the rim of her cup and shivered. Gran used to say when you shivered, a goose walked across your grave. "Not if it wasn't really a fireman," she said. "But a man who drove a red truck."

Blue leaned forward. "Braxton?"

Delta reached for another piece of cornbread. "Yeah. I hate how it plays into your conspiracy theory, but it's something to think about."

The men exchanged glances.

"It may be more than a theory," Blue said, taking Delta's hand. "I asked Dewey to check into Braxton's background and it's not pleasant."

She slid a glance to Dewey and back to Blue. "How bad? Is Charlotte in danger?"

"Bad enough," Blue said. "But she won't listen. I already told her and she said she knew what she was getting into."

"Sounds like Charlotte," Dewey volunteered. "Once she has her head set on doing something, she's hard to turn around." He sighed. "You really think Harry saw a red truck and pegged the driver as a fireman? I guess that could be a connection for him and I'll follow up, but there must be hundreds of red pickups in the county. Besides, how would Braxton know Harry would be there yesterday? Or mistake him for a fireman?" He shook his head. "Hate to state the obvious, but you're seeing Braxton behind every tree."

Blue shrugged. "Then why is he still here in Peck's Bluff? He and Charlotte both know we're selling to someone else. And they've been told we're not going to change our minds. Well, Charlotte has at any rate."

Delta raised an eyebrow. "Charlotte contacted you about Brisco's Folly?"

"Not really. I ran into her and Braxton last night as I was leaving Tinker's," he said. "Braxton went on in, while Charlotte tried to persuade me to give their proposal another chance."

"*Their* proposal?" Delta asked. "And what kind of persuasion did she try?"

Blue held up his hands. "The way Charlotte explained it to me was she and Braxton are now partners. He's teaching her his business in return for her, um, skills. If we sold to them, she would get part of the cut, or a finder's fee, for her efforts."

Delta glanced at Dewey to see his reaction to the information about his former girlfriend. He didn't seem affected. As for herself, Delta was more than a little peeved at Charlotte and her *skills*. She could imagine what was offered to Blue in exchange for signing with her and Braxton.

Delta punctuated her words with her coffee spoon. "You can tell Ms. 'Finder's Fee' that the Molly Brisco Memorial Center is way more important than some extra spending money for her."

Silence greeted her pronouncement as she looked at the two wide-eyed men.

"Well, it is. And you can bet if I see her first, I'll tell her myself."

Blue coughed. "Okay. I think we're clear on that." He leaned forward. "But this is more than some extra spending money to Charlotte. Her desperation to get out of Peck's Bluff and this new partnership are not a good mix."

Her own growing happiness gave her pause as Delta felt a twist of compassion. "True," She nodded. "Charlotte's always gotten her way and now she seems to have teamed up with a guy who's convinced her that's going to continue." She put her hand on Blue's arm. "Maybe your financial genius brain can come up with something to give her a safer way out."

Dewey stood. "Hope you can help. Charlotte's real nice, but kinda focuses on money a lot." He drank the last of his coffee. "I guess the fireman story's a long shot. Poor Harry'll be at the mercy of the homeowner."

Delta rubbed her tired eyes. "The Buchanans are going to be so disappointed."

"They already know," Dewey said. "We had River Road blocked during the fire and Buchanan's contractor pulled over and identified himself. Said he'd picked up a nail at his last job site and got a flat, so he was running late. He'd tell the Buchanans about the fire."

Delta sighed. "It's all so depressing. Not just the loss of a possible green renovation, but that beautiful house is gone."

Blue reached to massage her shoulder muscle, then rub circles high on her back. "Can't help the fate of the house, but word's getting out about your talent. You're going to be one busy woman."

She looked at Blue. He could've commiserated with her and left it at that. Being Blue, however, he chose to also make her feel good about herself, despite the loss. The same was true of their lovemaking and she felt heat in her belly at the thought. "Thanks."

Dewey headed toward the door. "Catch you guys later."

"Wait a minute," Delta said, refocusing. "You should probably take the dishes and containers back to Patience."

"Uh, okay."

Delta stood and rummaged in the cabinets, then started transferring the coffee to a thermos she found.

"Why are we doing this, now?" Blue asked.

"Because Dewey has officially moved out and they're finished getting Gran's house ready for Van and Merrilee. That means your mother, since you said she's coming down with something will be much more comfortable moving back here. Besides, the wedding quilt for Van and Merrilee is getting too big to hide at Gran's, Uncle Joe doesn't want it at his and Winnie's house, and Van would see it if they moved it to our house. Aunt Caroline's house is the logical place to finish it."

Panic lit the eyes of the two men as they glanced around the kitchen.

"My suggestion is," Delta continued, "a cleaning service for at least four hours. Today."

"Done," they said in unison.

"Do we have a cleaning service here in Peck's Bluff?" Blue asked.

"Yes," Delta said. "They pull up in a covered wagon and as soon as the sun bonnets come off, they set to work."

Blue stood and kissed her. "Humor is not your strong suit in the morning, is it?"

Delta caught his shirtfront and pulled him to her for another kiss. She could get used to this.

"I'll make a couple of calls and leave messages," she said. "See if we can get a service to come on short notice."

"Thanks," Dewey said, and left with the kitchenware for Patience.

Blue took a drink of coffee. "Run that quilt-house-hopping thing by me again. Is there a point?"

"A very depressing one," Delta sighed. "Any day now, your mother will move back here and Merrilee will move into Gran's house. I know we haven't been a couple all that long, but when the moving around happens, where will we have any *privacy*?"

Blue blinked. "Oh, this is bad." Then he straightened. "I'll get an apartment."

Delta shook her head. "What would you tell your mother who has a house with two spare bedrooms?"

"Peck's Bluff Inn for a hot rendezvous?"

"Euww, motel linens and top story for the town gossips. No thanks."

Blue stood and took her hand, pulling her to her feet. "I'll figure it out without hurting my mother's feelings and insulting the woman I love."

She pinned him with a challenging look. "The woman you let believe Braxton was still on the loose when you came back last night. That woman?"

He squirmed like a worm for a second, then glanced down the hall behind her. "Any chance you could punish me with a cuddle? It's still dark outside, so it's still officially night."

Delta stepped closer, laughing. "It's officially fall. That's why it's dark outside, but I'll pretend that lame apology works."

Blue walked her home as pink rays of the rising sun painted the windows of the houses lining the path. "What are you up to today?" he asked.

Her heart hitched at memories of the fire. "I was going to start the renovation drawings for the Averill House, then check with my lawyer to see if he's heard from the Fourth Circle of Hell regarding the settlement."

Blue laughed. "Greed? I would've thought the Ninth Circle, Treachery."

"You know Dante's Inferno?" she asked, surprised.

"Intimately," he sighed. "I needed some lit credits to balance all the math classes I was taking in college. I foolishly thought poetry would be an easy A. Not so."

Delta stared at him for a second. The exact same thing had happened to her. Nice to know there were new things to learn about Blue. She yawned as they crossed her parents' yard. "Definitely Greed. That's where they live."

She glanced in the garage on their way. Her father's car was still gone. Good. She hoped to get in a couple hours nap before they returned.

Blue took the keys from her and opened the back door, then pulled her into his arms after he closed it behind them. "Dante's Inferno notwithstanding, I'll check with Mark, the attorney I sicced on them, too. I also need to work on that privacy issue. Very important."

Delta giggled. Standing here in Blue's arms after their night of lovemaking gave her an incredible feeling of satisfaction and tranquility. She kissed his cheek and stepped away. "Going to call the cleaning service people and leave your mother's cell phone number, then to bed."

He reached for her arm, putting the keys in her hand. "I'll do a quick walk-through while you call, then you can lock the door behind me."

Blue went back home and into his bedroom. He eyed his running clothes and shoes in the corner and laughed. After last night and this morning he had no energy left. God, too tired to run, his favorite thing in the whole world. His smile stayed in place. Now, his second favorite thing. He crashed face down into the pillow Delta had slept on and where her scent still lingered. A power nap and he'd be good to go.

He woke up forty-five minutes later to the cell phone ringing. He opened an eye and slid the phone off the nightstand. The cleaning service could be there by ten. Would that be okay?

"Sure," he said, and hung up.

His sleep-deprived brain tried to pull up a dream idea he'd had about helping Charlotte and after a minute, it came to him.

Blue called Fuller Jameson's office and got squeezed in right before lunch the next day.

At ten sharp a white van arrived. Dark pink lettering proclaimed *Marlo Makes it Sparkle* on the side door. Two small women who looked like a mother/daughter team got out and came up the drive. They did a walk-through and presented him with a very reasonable price.

When the women went to work, Blue decided to go
to Gran's, now Van and Merrilee's house, to see how his
mother was doing.

He found her in the kitchen, drinking tea and reading
the newspaper. Except for the table and a couple of chairs,
a steaming mug and a tea kettle, the kitchen looked empty.
"Where'd you get the paper?" he asked.

"I had the boy bring mine here this last month."

"How're you feeling? Need any help today?"

"A little better, and thanks, but no. The furniture
that's left is being turned over to Van and Merrilee. I'm
going to strip the bed and bring the linens home to clean."
Caroline Richmond gave him a tired smile. "Then I need
to take stock of my cupboards and refrigerator. Between
you and Dewey, there's no doubt some shopping to be
done."

"Tell you what," he said. "Finish your tea and paper,
then I'll take you to breakfast. Afterwards, we'll get grocer-
ies. Pretend the cupboards are bare."

One of his mother's delicate eyebrows rose. "Breakfast? It's almost eleven. Besides, I want to clean before I
put any food away."

Blue cleared his throat. "About that. Uh, Delta was
over and mentioned to Dewey and me a cleaning service
would be nice since you've been so busy here. She made
some calls."

His mother set down her mug, clearly delighted. "I
hope she called Marlo."

Blue nodded, surprised. He had expected some resistance from his neat-as-a-pin mother. "They've been there since ten. By the time we have brunch or whatever and shop, they should be done."

"How nice," his mother said, watching him closely. "Leave it to Delta to think of something sweet like that."

He hadn't intended to tell his mother of his and Delta's changed relationship, exactly. He'd wanted to let it develop naturally, but it looked like she was on to him. "Speaking of Delta," he started.

A smile flooded her face. "Finally."

His stomach lurched and anxiety slipped in. Was this how others would take this change? Did it show on his face how crazy he was about Delta? "No finally. No finally," he said. "Slowly. Takin' it easy. No change in living arrangements, no big announcements. Takin' it slow."

Caroline Richmond took off her reading glasses, still smiling. "Your secret's safe with me, honey. I just meant that it's taken the two of you a long time to realize something I've been thinking about for years. And that's all I'll say. Except it makes me very happy that you've decided to stick around."

"Good," Blue said, relieved. "Are you finished with the Real Estate section?"

She tipped her head. "You said no change in living arrangements. Is this an investment?"

He nodded. "I leased my townhouse and I'd like to put my new contractor skills to work. Thought I'd find a fixer upper and start checking out green materials suppliers."

Caroline Richmond beamed. "What a great idea." She turned to the next section of paper and stopped, her face paling. "Honey, you said you saw Delta. When?"

"Mother, you okay? I saw her again a little while ago."

His mother laid her hand flat against her chest. "Thank goodness. The paper says the Averill House on River Road burned down yesterday in the middle of the day. Suzanne Jameson called me from Atlanta to remind me the wallpaper samples Merrilee looked through had to be returned. She told me Delta called her all excited about a mid-day appointment out there."

Blue rubbed his eyes. "Wow. I must be more tired than I thought. Yes, she was there. Dewey got the call about the fire while I was with him and we found her. She accidently got a conk on the head, but she'll be okay."

He thought his mother would be relieved, but she looked more anxious. "First your accident, now Delta's. Is something going on?"

In truth Blue really didn't know, and didn't want to alarm his mother. He lifted a shoulder. "Did some checking and so far it's ended in nothing."

"Will you let me know if that changes?"

"Yes," Blue said. "Absolutely. Not to worry." He planned to do the worrying for all of them.

# Chapter Thirty-Two

Delta awoke to her mother's giggling in the kitchen. She rolled over and stifled a moan. Her lovemaking with Blue had awakened muscles not used in a long time. Oh, but it had been worth it.

"Delta," her mother called. "Are you upstairs?"

An involuntary hiss preceded her response. "Yes. Down in a sec." She sat on the edge of the bed and stretched in stages. Next, the bathroom to freshen up. A glance in the mirror nixed the thought that she could get away with hiding her head injury. The area was still dark red, with green tingeing the edges.

She took two aspirin and walked gingerly down the stairs into the kitchen.

Her mother turned with a smile that disappeared when she saw Delta. She walked over to gently touch below the bruise. "Honey, what happened?"

Delta sat in a chair. "Where's Daddy? I prefer to tell this only once."

Her father walked through the back door with a handful of shopping bags. "Hey, sweetheart."

"Fuller, something's happened to Delta."

He set the bags on the floor. "What is it?"

Delta pinched the bridge of her nose. "I'll be fine. Just a bump on the head. The sad part is the Averill House. It burned down." She told her parents about Dirty Harry, the earlier visit by the "fireman," and the prognosis made by the EMT.

"No wonder you were in bed in the middle of the day. Why didn't you call us at the hotel?" her mother asked. "We would have come right home."

"And ruin your anniversary celebration?" Delta made a face. "I don't think so."

"You could have suffered a concussion and you were here all alone. What were you thinking?"

Delta huffed out a breath, unprepared with a clever answer. "Actually, Blue stayed with me."

"Well, thank goodness one of you had a speck of sense," her mother said, hand to her throat.

Delta's gaze cut to her father. His expression indicated more questions, but she knew they would be asked in his own way.

"We had an early breakfast," her mother said. "Why don't we unpack, then I'll make us some tomato soup and grilled cheese sandwiches."

One of her father's favorite lunches, Delta noticed. "Sounds good to me," she said.

A half hour later they sat down to eat. "How was the trip?" Delta asked.

"Everything turned out marvelous. We dined and danced and shopped and ate breakfast in bed." Her mother blushed at the last detail, then waved her hand. "Oh, but that's so sad about the Averill House, honey. I know you were looking forward to working on it."

Delta nodded. "Always another old house in my future," she sighed.

Her father picked up the second half of his sandwich. "Has Blue decided when he's going back to Chicago?"

Wariness had her choosing words carefully. "He actually plans to stay here. We're going to, um, be seeing more of each other."

"That's wonderful," her mother said. "It's been three years, and I, for one, despaired of you ever coming out from behind your work."

Fuller Jameson put the sandwich back on his plate and smiled. "I guess your mother and I saw this coming. Blue's a fine man. He'll take good care of you."

Her parents saw them becoming a couple? Delta looked at one, then the other, her first instinct to proclaim that she could take care of herself, thank you. She lifted a shoulder. "He's only been back a few weeks. We'll see how things go."

After what she'd been through with Slayton, they still wanted someone to take care of her. She sighed. She loved her parents fiercely, but sometimes they had no clue.

Delta stood. "Good lunch. I'm going to change, then I need to buy a new phone. Mine was destroyed in the fire. I'm keeping my same number so you should be able to reach me if you need to. After that, I'm off to visit Patience for a while."

Five minutes later, Delta came back down to see her mother frowning as she replaced the phone receiver in the front hall. "What's the matter?" Delta asked.

Her mother shook her head. "Three messages from Slayton yesterday evening. Each ruder and more obscene than the last. Did you take the phone off the hook?"

*Well, crap times two.* What did Slayton-the-whiner want? And more important, she had to come up with a semi-truth for her parents. Because no way was Delta going to share the details of last night with them. "Uh, we didn't know Dirty Harry was harmless until this morning, so Blue thought it would be safer to stay at Aunt Caroline's. Dewey stopped and gave us the details on his way to work."

"Oh," her mother said. "Better safe than sorry they say." She wrinkled her nose. "Would you like to listen to Slayton's messages?"

"No. Erase them. I'll call him after I get the new phone." She pecked her mother on the cheek and left.

Mackie's was empty of customers and locked. Delta tapped on the door and Patience emerged from the kitchen with rubber-gloved hands. She grinned and let Delta in. "You packed a lot of adventure in since yesterday morning, chickapea. Spill, while I finish the dishes."

Delta followed Patience back to the kitchen and slid onto a stool. She sighed. "I'm crazy about Blue. Totally in love. But, and it's a big one, I'm already kinda feeling closed in."

Patience cocked a hip against the sink and crossed her arms. "Assumin' you and Blue let nature take its course last night, I'd say you're overthinking it. Any new tie-up is gonna be scary, but you and Blue knowing each other all your lives takes that scary up a notch."

"You're probably right," Delta said. "I should stick with the happy haze I woke up in this morning." She hugged herself. "Blue was ..." Her new phone rang. The display read Slayton's last name. *Great.* She glanced at Patience and rolled her eyes upward. "Hello."

"You bumpkin bitch!"

He was drunk, of course.

"Slayton, I'm going to hang up unless you can talk to me with some common courtesy. What do you want?"

"I want you to STOP. Right. Now."

"Stop what? I don't know what you're talking about."

He snorted in derision. "I'm talking about that damned effing Chicago lawyer you sicced on my family, you bitch."

Delta quietly clicked the phone closed and started counting. Her stomach quivered, but she mustered a half-smile for Patience. By seven, her phone rang again.

"Hello."

He spoke through gritted teeth. "Look, I don't know how you can afford this slick lawyer and his hyenas, but he says he's working for you. My attorney checked him out and says Mr. North Shore Chicago lawyer charges a thousand dollars an hour and right now he's up to his effing ass investigating my family's business. It's three weeks before my wedding and we will not tolerate this. Call. Him. Off. Or you will be sorry."

*Things were just getting better and better. Weren't they?*

Delta took a deep breath. She couldn't afford to totally antagonize Slayton, but neither would she allow him to browbeat her. "I'll look into it, but bear two things in mind. One, you will never leave obscene messages on my parents' phone or mine again, and two, if you threaten me one more time, I'll take out a restraining order. That would impress the judge reviewing your lawsuit, wouldn't it?"

She heard the click as bottle met crystal tumbler and saw Slayton in her mind's eye, swaying over the study wet bar in his latest golfing clothes.

"Who the hell do you think you are?" he slurred.

"I'm the bumpkin who got away," Delta said, and closed her phone.

Patience let out a giggle and did a little dance, throwing one of her gloves on the floor at the end.

Delta looked down at her shaking hand, the back of the cell phone slick from sweat. "I did pretty good, didn't I?"

"Damn straight," Patience said. "'Bout time you took the lawn jockey down a peg or two."

# Chapter Thirty-Three

Blue peered into the container of dried-up Spackle he'd found in the garage. His mother stood beside him, but his mind freewheeled in frustration. Aunt Suzanne had said Delta was out and should be home by late afternoon. Not soon enough for him. Since their lovemaking, he'd found his thoughts unable to focus on anything but wanting to be with her.

"I told the contractor to put anything worth keeping out here," his mother said. "But that was when they finished remodeling. I'm afraid most of it's unusable, now."

After she'd come home to a spotless house, his mother had mentioned she wanted to paint the hallway and update the pictures hanging there.

Blue glanced at his watch. He had time for a quick trip to the hardware store, then back to call Delta again.

"There's no rush," his mother said.

Blue tossed the container into the garbage. "That's okay. Besides, it'll give me a chance to see if the local hardware store has brought in any green materials."

"I don't want to be responsible for keeping you apart from your girl," she teased.

He laughed. "We'll be fine as long as you don't bring up grandchildren."

She brought her hand to her throat and sucked in a breath. "Oh. They'll be beautiful."

Blue rubbed the slightly crooked slope of his nose, warmth spreading through him at the thought. "As long as they have gray eyes and dark, curly hair."

His mother pushed him toward the door. "Go, before I start making baby blankets."

Peck's Bluff Hardware and Feed hadn't changed much in the dozen years Blue had lived in Chicago. Same brands and choices of tools. A new selection of bamboo rakes, handles down in a big plastic garbage can, sat just inside the front doors.

Blue grabbed a basket and picked up the Spackle and a new knife before heading to get a selection of paint chips in creams and ivories.

A familiar figure, except for the clothes, stood in front of the colorful display. *Twice in two days? Okay, Peck's Bluff was a small town.*

"Charlotte?"

The blonde turned, flipping at her hair. "Cuz! You're a sight for sore eyes. I was gonna call you today. Got a sec?"

Blue held back an exclamation. This was a Charlotte he'd never seen. She wore a baggy sweater, shapeless jeans, and minimal make-up. "Uh, sure. Surprised to see you here."

She waved a hand. "This? My parents think if they repaint my room, I'll change my mind about leaving. As, if. I promised to look at paint chips, just to get out of the house."

Blue nodded. He could've told his aunt and uncle to save their time and money. Charlotte would never be bought for a gallon or two of paint. "What did you want?"

Charlotte nervously clicked her bangle bracelets. "Brax and I have been thinking about a deal that'd make everyone happy. Since my portfolio and your half of Brisco's Folly are worth the same, as soon as you guys get the title, I'd sign over my portfolio to you. Seeing as Delta needs the money, I'd sell it to Brax's client and give her $5,000 from my commission in addition to her half of the sale. His client would give us good referrals to his friends looking for properties and you'd have more than the value of the land in two years. Everybody wins. What do you think?"

He knew from the desperation in her eyes she wouldn't like his answer, but he wouldn't be doing her any favors by holding out her hope, either. "Charlotte, you know that goes against the legal intent of Gran's Will. Even if it wasn't, our acceptance of the Tyler's offer is firm."

She patted her fingertips lightly against her eyelids, her disappointment tangible. "Right. Doesn't hurt to ask though, does it?"

No, it didn't. And Blue figured Charlotte didn't hear the word no, very often. He changed tactics. "You never told me how you found out we were going with another buyer."

"Not a big deal," she said. "I listen in on my parents and the rest of the oldsters all the time. Learn some interesting stuff. Anyway, I heard from Aunt Suzanne you were going to accept an offer and thought it was Brax." She stepped in close. "Too bad I won't get the chance to thank you, personally."

Blue sighed and inwardly thanked his lucky stars Charlotte was his first cousin. Otherwise he'd be the target of her attentions until he had to hurt her feelings.

He tried to recall the wording in the Will that bestowed Charlotte's inheritance. He couldn't do what she wanted, but he might be able to help another way. "Do you have the account number, managing firm, and access information to your portfolio? And would you allow me to look at it?"

She blinked, then opened her purse to pull out a folded slip of paper. "Carry it with me, darlin'. What did you have in mind?"

"Are you crazy?" he asked. "You could lose everything to somebody who knew what he was doing."

Charlotte shrugged. "I'm not stupid. Two of the account numbers are wrong, and no one would guess my ID or password in a million years." She talked while writing on a second slip of paper. "Here's the correct information. What're you thinking?"

Blue took it from her. "Let me take you to lunch tomorrow. Mackie's at 12:30?"

The old Charlotte smiled at him. "I'll be there."


Delta sounded tired when she answered the phone. "Hey."

"Hey," he said. "How're you feeling?

"My head still hurts, but not as much as yesterday."

"Good. Want to go for a drive?"

"I'd like that," Delta said. "Can we go to the Averill House property?"

Blue's stomach clenched. He wasn't sure he wanted to visit the place he'd almost lost her. "It's probably closed off as an unsafe area. Why do you want to go there?"

Delta sighed. "I want to sketch the footprint of the house.

Buchanan hasn't decided whether he's going to bulldoze it and rebuild, or take the insurance money and build elsewhere. For my own purposes, I want to get something down on paper that shows how the river stone open-sided fireplace and story-and-a-half observatory balanced the space beautifully."

He still thought of the house as a death trap, while Delta saw the amazing structure it used to be. He needed some of her vision if he was going to succeed in the construction business. "Okay. Fifteen minutes?"

She looked pale when she opened the Jameson's front door. Blue wanted to hold her in his arms under a cozy blanket until she fell asleep. Instead, he asked, "Ready?"

Delta nodded, handing him his phone. "Thanks. I got a new one."

They got in his car and headed toward River Road. Blue studied her profile as she leaned against the headrest. "You're pretty quiet. Everything okay?"

"Fine."

He hadn't been in many relationships, but Blue knew that one syllable was a challenge. He wanted to respond with full attention, so he drove in silence. When he parked as close to Averill House as the churned-up muddy road allowed, he turned in his seat. "Want to talk about it?"

"Slayton called me today."

If Blue had his way, he would simply drive to Atlanta, find the frigging country club golf course Slayton played, and knock the crap out of him until he agreed to leave Delta alone. He took a deep breath. "Oh. I found out what was going on by email this afternoon. I'm sorry he bothered you."

Delta pulled her jacket tighter and crossed her arms. "He didn't just bother *me*," she said. "He'd already left three obscene messages on my parents' phone last night. He was drunk and flipping out about some over-priced Chicago attorney investigating his family three weeks before he re-married."

Blue smacked the steering wheel with the side of his fist. "This is my fault. When I asked Mark for help,

I thought he'd send a strongly-worded letter or connect with a big-name Atlanta firm to get Slayton to settle sooner. Use the high school contract we signed just as an opening gambit. He took it way further than I thought."

He reached into the back seat of the car and brought some papers forward, handing them to Delta. "Read this and you'll see why Slayton's so ticked off."

# Chapter Thirty-Four

It took Delta several minutes to get through the entire document, outrage building with every paragraph. *Of all the grubbing, sanctimonious hypocrites.* Slayton and his parents had lorded it over her, making her believe they were better than she because of their place in Atlanta society.

According to this, their entire income came from subcontracting the manufacture of licensed products for the big theme parks in Florida. Her former in-laws ran a front operation with clean facilities and legal employees open to INS inspection at any time. In reality, the manufacturing space was unsanitary, employed illegal aliens from Cuba, and sat at the edge of a swamp. The workers were treated like indentured servants and several of the more vocal complainants had *disappeared.*

Blue reached for the pages. "I shouldn't have brought the rest. It's pretty ugly."

Delta held onto the papers, then sucked in a breath at the attached pictures. High chain link fence surrounded the huts where the workers lived, and signs in Spanish warning that the fence was electrified, hung in several places. Dirty, malnourished children wandered in the muddy enclosure.

Delta closed her eyes. This was how Slayton's family lived their lives - respectable and picture perfect on the outside, dirty and revolting on the inside. To know she'd been a part of that picture made her sick.

"Honey, are you okay?"

She jumped at Blue's soft words and opened her eyes. "No, I'm not. I'm angry and ashamed and ... and sad. I feel so stupid. I wasn't aware of any of this."

Blue nodded. "No one who knows you would believe you were. But this is trampling on several federal laws and all hell's going to break loose when the INS goes after them. It could bring Slayton and his parents down like a house of cards."

Delta thought about the time she'd spent in that luxurious viper's nest and shuddered. "They don't back down, Blue. You have no idea of their sphere of influence. Judges, politicians at all levels, power brokers. People who don't care if they use illegals or if my design contracts dry up." The enormity of the situation hit her and Delta whispered. "What am I going to do? I am so screwed."

Blue took her hand, brought it to his mouth, and kissed it. "Nope. This is *our* situation," he said. "I got you into this, and together we'll get you out."

Delta looked at him. He was strong and confident, and he loved her and wanted to help. What did she have to lose? So what if the cream of Atlanta society rejected her, she'd still design and she'd still have Blue. Delta took a deep breath. "Slayton doesn't know the extent of the damage, yet, and has been trying to intimidate me. That's going to stop."

"Good attitude," Blue said. "It doesn't say in this report, but your ex is probably in partnership with his parents. That's why he's harassing you."

Delta nodded. "When we were first dating, they asked their housekeeper and me to witness some paperwork. It had to do with their company. The three of them had already signed."

"Then the whole family could be looking at federal prison time."

A mini-video played in Delta's brain. Her ex-father-in-law in a small cell without his $100 smuggled-from-Cuba cigars and 15-year-old Dalmore Single Malt. The movie segued to her ex-mother-in-law walking into a federal prison dining facility without a single piece of jewelry and dressed in prison-issue gray clothing.

And finally, Slayton. No tumbler of scotch, no highlights in his hair, and no tee-time. The visions lifted the corners of Delta's mouth.

"Delta?"

She shook off her musings and was reminded her head hurt. "Sorry. Help me with my options. I can ignore any communication that hasn't been vetted by my attorney. Oh, I have to let him know what's going on before he gets blindsided. Then, ..." She held up empty hands. "Um, that's all I've got. Any ideas?"

Blue wiggled his eyebrows.

Delta laughed. "You are so sad, Richmond. Any ideas that would *help*?"

He sighed. "I think you've got it covered. Nothing else you can do except wait to be contacted by the authorities."

She hadn't thought of that. Her stomach sank. "Oh."

Blue rubbed the back of her neck. "My original instructions to Mark were to get some leverage so you could close the suit and get on with your life. I didn't realize he'd go all black ops and hire investigators to dig this deep."

"It's all good," Delta said. "Especially if those factory workers get helped. It might send a wake-up call to Slayton's fiancée, too. Added bonus if she smartens up and cancels the wedding. She has no idea how much misery awaits her if she goes through with it."

"She might not get the choice if the INS moves fast," Blue said.

Delta rolled her eyes. "You're talking about a government agency. There'll be plenty of time for Slayton and his parents to point a finger at their business manager and walk away."

"Maybe. Maybe not. In any case, they'd walk away broke. They'd have to pay for their defense, and bail bonds to stay free – plus, their only source of income would be shut down."

A hideous thought occurred to Delta. "Or they could drag me and the lawsuit into this. They haven't signed off, yet."

"Don't think so," Blue said. "Unless they're really stupid, they'll realize all their time and energy needs to be spent on the federal issue. They'll want to settle because they'll need every penny they can lay their hands on to pay their attorneys. Besides, here's where the pre-nup bites them on the butt."

Delta tried to push past her whirling thoughts and couldn't. "What does the pre-nup have to do with all this?"

Then the connection hit. "Oooh. They were careful to strip me of all rights or claims to anything Slayton owned."

Her HAPPY meter jumped from NOT SO HAPPY to BOY AM I HAPPY in an instant. The tension in her shoulders slid away and Delta squeezed Blue's hand. "Thanks for helping talk this out." She held up the paperwork. "And thanks for this."

His eyes sparkled. "Sure. Wanna fool around?"

Delta surveyed the interior of the small car, laughing. "Uh, I have a headache?"

She picked up her pad and pencil, glancing toward the remains of the house, now surrounded by yellow *Caution* tape. "The light's fading and I want to get this on paper." She held up her new smartphone. "I also want to take pictures."

A frisson of panic crossed his face. "You're not going to try and get inside?"

Delta pressed her lips together. *Control.* She sighed. No. This was genuine concern for her welfare. Not like Slayton's attempts to micro-manage her every move. Big difference. She raised an eyebrow. "Not planning to. Guess that conk on the head yesterday knocked some sense in."

Blue looked properly chagrined. "Okay, okay. Just sayin'. If you hurt yourself, it cuts into my fooling around time."

She socked his arm. "Nutcase."

They got out of the car and walked the perimeter of the house, careful to avoid the fallen debris. The roof was gone and the rest of the damage so extensive she could see through the remaining skeleton. At least it afforded her a view to the scale and locations of what she came to draw. After a few pencil strokes, Delta stopped and brought her hand to her mouth. Accident or not, the devastation of this beautiful house bruised her sense of fairness to the core.

She was filling out the details of her rough sketch when she glanced around and noticed Blue was gone. Lengthening shadows from the house's ravaged framework and chimney made finger inroads on the charred grass. She was about to shout his name when someone came thrashing through the trees lining the river. Her heart leapt to her throat before she saw it was Blue.

He hurried over, holding out his phone with a web page displayed. "Did you know this house is part of a fifteen acre plat and the only property with a structure?"

She frowned. *I need to get back, eat something, and take some pain meds.* "Yes. I did a background check after Buchanan called me. Why?"

He glanced at the page, closed out of it and pocketed his phone. "Nothing. Are you ready to go?"

Delta wondered at his lingering gaze on the screen, but her headache won over her curiosity. "Sure."

Blue drove less than a quarter of a mile and pulled over.

"Why are you stopping?"

He pointed to a large seventies rambler set back from the road. "It's for sale. Judging from the condition of the yard and the sign, it's been on the market a while. Let's take a look."

"Not me," Delta said. "It'll be locked, but you go." She leaned against her headrest and smiled foolishly, her headache receding. *He was looking for a house. Can't get more permanent than that.*

She heard him come back in a few minutes as he sneezed his way across the overgrown lawn. He got in the car with a flyer from the real estate display box. "Price has been lowered a couple of times. Family of the former owner wants to sell. I looked in the windows and it could really be something special."

# Chapter Thirty-Five

"You said what?"

Delta grinned, then sucked air, rubbing her forehead. "I told my parents we were an item. Had to."

He'd walked Delta to her front porch and kissed her soundly. She'd smiled and dropped the bomb. "What did they say?"

She wrinkled her nose. "My mother said, how wonderful it was, and my father said they saw this coming and how you would take care of me."

He laughed. "Have they met you?"

Delta grinned again. "I know. My thought exactly." She put her arms around his waist. "Glad to have you as a partner, though."

Blue hugged her back. "Partner sounds good. Um, my mother guessed this morning, too."

Delta leaned away without letting go of him. "What did she say?"

Blue shook his head. "Evidently, they've been ahead of us for a long time. She said 'Finally,' and she'd been thinking of us as a couple for years."

Delta's smile was wry. "That makes us a little slow on the uptake, doesn't it?"

He hugged her again. "Better late than never."

"Speaking of late," she said. "I really have to go into Atlanta tomorrow. I need to meet with the Buchanans and two other clients, and sort through my mail. I won't get done until late afternoon."

Blue nodded. "Forgot to tell you. I got an email confirming that our paperwork on Brisco's Folly is done. It's all ours. I'm meeting with your father around 11:00 to discuss the legality of an idea to help Charlotte and then meeting with her at lunch. I can pick up the paperwork in the afternoon, then take you to dinner. Shame to waste that empty apartment of yours."

Delta narrowed her eyes. "Congratulations on your sneakiness in mentioning my empty apartment – too bad you also brought up Charlotte."

Blue felt a twinge of happy at Delta's jealous reaction, but buried it. "I believe it was you who told me to use my financial genius to help her. She *is* my first cousin."

Delta sighed. "Busted. See you around six at my place?"

"Done," he said and pulled her in for one more kiss.


Blue slept great and got up early to run – only the second time since his accident. He looked forward to running year round now that he was moving back to Peck's

Bluff. There had been too many times in Chicago when the arctic winds in the dead of winter had made it impossible to be outside.

He walked into Fuller Jameson's reception area five minutes early. Nancy was on the phone, but smiled and waved him through. Blue made sure his step was confident. After Delta told him her father thought he could take care of her, he wanted to convey that impression. Even if he felt wobbly.

Delta's father stood, a calm smile on his face, and extended his hand. "I understand you and my little girl are seeing each other. Call me Fuller."

Blue shook his hand and let a held breath sigh away. He'd never called Delta's father anything but sir. And the label "my little girl" hadn't escaped his attention. He sat down. "Thank you for seeing me, Fuller. Actually, I wanted some of your time to discuss Gran's bequest to Charlotte."

A smile transformed Fuller Jameson's face and he laughed.

"When I saw you on my calendar, I put together this whole speech about taking care of Delta and not hurting her - giving you my permission to date her."

Blue saw how much Delta's father loved and cared about her and figured her divorce had hurt her parents as much as it did her. He wanted to make that kind of family for himself, for and with Delta. "I'd like to hear that speech, too."

The older man sat, smiling. "If I recall correctly, we already covered the part about not hurting her. And night before last you proved you can take care of her. That leaves my *permission*." He shook his head. "Not necessary in your case. Your mother's one of the finest people I know. She raised you right."

Even if Delta's father took Blue's mystery grandparent into consideration, he'd never bring it up. A knot of concern in Blue's chest eased. "Thank you, sir."

"Fuller."

*This would take some getting used to.* Blue nodded. "As for Charlotte, I have her permission to review her holdings to see if I can improve her income. I need to know a couple of things about the intent of her bequest. Could you lay out Joe's guardianship boundaries? For instance, if Charlotte wants, can she change the company managing her portfolio?"

Blue had never noticed before, but Delta had inherited her father's slow, easy smile. "The original intent was that he'd be a guardian only. But he was so upset that the portfolio wasn't coming directly to Winnie, he worked on his wife and Gran until they agreed that during his holding period, he and Charlotte would be joint tenants on the account." Delta's father held up his hand. "I know. I tried to talk Winnie out of it, but he pushed very hard to get his way."

Blue squelched an eye roll and shook his head. "I saw that when I logged in this morning to look at the account.

Not a good idea, and not in Charlotte's favor. Especially if Joe is second-guessing the funds manager."

Fuller nodded. "As far as your second question, yes. The portfolio is ultimately Charlotte's and she can change administrators if she wishes." He frowned. "You'll have a tough time convincing Joe, however. He fancies himself a true financial entrepreneur who has rapport with Charlotte's account manager and a special knowledge of the market. Unfortunately, he's never been a success. He's always ready to make a killing when the market falls apart on him. He ultimately blames Wall Street, or the political climate – anything but his own ineptitude."

Blue stared at the backs of his hands. "I know the type." He fidgeted in his chair, then straightened. "No other way to ask this, Fuller. Does Joe receive a monthly fee for holding Charlotte's portfolio?"

Fuller Jameson leaned forward, hands clasped on top of his desk. "Absolutely not. Joe said joint tenancy would give him access to study the balance of stocks and funds and make recommendations. But that's all." He pinned Blue with a direct gaze. "Why?"

*No way to back into this.* "Charlotte may already be aware of this, even agreed to it, but knowing her, I don't think so. Since the portfolio was turned over to him, Joe has been transferring $500 a month into a checking account at the bank where Charlotte works. Could be he's tapping the cash where the dividends are held; for her, but again, I don't think so."

Fuller Jameson's face showed his struggle with the information.

"Since it doesn't affect the principal amount of the portfolio," Blue said, "Could Charlotte be given a monthly allowance?"

Delta's father now tapped the center of his desk. "Let's talk about this $500 a month first. You're sure?"

"Yes."

The lawyer leaned back and sighed. "Looks like the dividends that were being reinvested all these years are now being transferred to the cash fund in the account. That about right?"

Blue nodded.

"What's the plan?"

The question made Blue smile. "My plan is to take over Charlotte's portfolio and make her some serious money over the next two years. If the intent of the Will allows, I'd also like to give her a monthly allowance of $1,200. It's not a lot, but it should ease her attitude about having to wait for the full amount."

Fuller tented his fingers. "Henry and Molly Brisco wanted to skip a generation so their *grandchildren* could enjoy life without worrying about mortgages or loans or such. In its purest intent, their original Will dispersed their assets as soon as the surviving spouse passed away. Neither intended for Joe to help himself to the cash in Charlotte's portfolio."

He smiled. "Since the topic of a monthly income that doesn't diminish the total of the holdings wasn't addressed in the Will, I'm going to say the decision is up to Charlotte."

"Thanks, Fuller."

"Unless Joe asks for my legal counsel, which he won't, I'm going to leave it up to you to see that the $3,000 is put back into Charlotte's account."

Blue grinned. "I won't even demand interest."

Fuller Jameson stood and held out his hand. "Nice talking to you, son."

*Son.* That single word was worth all the angry flack Blue was going to take from Joseph Tremont Canfield. Delta would be his wife and Fuller Jameson, a man he'd admired all his life would call him son. Blue's smile was heart deep.

# Chapter Thirty-Six

Charlotte came to lunch dressed for seduction. She wore skintight jeans, a low-cut green sweater that matched her eyes, waterfall earrings, and high platform heels.

Blue watched her bask in the gazes of day laborers and truckers as she made her way across Mackie's to his booth. Now that he and Delta were together, he hoped forever, maybe he could ease Charlotte's misery. "Hey, Charlotte. Looking good."

"Hey, darlin'. You know I try." She looked around. "Where's Delta?"

"In Atlanta on business."

Her smile widened. "Goodie. I have you all to myself."

Blue sighed. "I'm not here to talk about Brisco's Folly, Charlotte." He nodded toward the opposite seat when she started to slide in next to him. "I'm here to give you good news. And maybe some bad news."

She pulled her hair over the curve of one ear and sat down, an expression of disgust spoiling her pretty features.

"Well, I could sure use some good news. This," she waved to indicate the café, "is the highlight of my day."

Sitting in a warm, comfortable place with good food, and close to home rated very high with Blue, but he knew Charlotte didn't see it that way. He pulled a spreadsheet out of his jacket, laid it open, and flipped it around for her.

Charlotte cut a quick glance. "What's this?"

"A breakdown of your portfolio accounts as of today." He pointed to a figure at the bottom right. "This is the total."

Charlotte nodded. "I go in every other day and look at the summary page."

"The company that manages your portfolio is very reputable," Blue said. "Per Henry Brisco's wishes, they've invested in low risk and long term funds."

Green eyes squinted at the page. "That's good, right?"

"Good for you and good for them. They receive one percent for managing the portfolio."

She leaned against the banquette and crossed her arms. "I know. Nearly $3,000 a year. A big waste, but what can I do about it?"

"You can turn the portfolio over to me."

A frown marred the smooth skin between her brows. "That's your good news? You said you wouldn't trade it for Brisco's Folly."

"Not in trade," he said. "I'd manage the portfolio for you. No charge."

"Oh," she said, without enthusiasm. "Thanks. That would save me some money."

Blue had hoped for a more excited response, but Charlotte was all about the now. He tilted his head. "I'm very good at what I do. I earn my clients triple what you're getting now."

She leaned forward. "That's great, darlin'. It really is. I was just hoping the good news was about something I could use, you know, today."

Patience swung through the kitchen doors and glanced their way curiously. Her lunch waitress, Wanda, hurried over. "What can I get for y'all?"

"BLT and chocolate shake for me," Blue said.

"Unsweetened ice tea," Charlotte added, and Wanda nodded, leaving them alone.

At Blue's raised eyebrow, Charlotte giggled. "Girl's gotta watch her figure."

"Speaking of watching you, what's Braxton up to, now that Brisco's Folly is being sold to someone else?"

Charlotte immediately looked up and slightly to the left. A cue that she was at least partially making up her answer. "Oh. He's working to turn over a couple parcels in Florida." She lifted a shoulder. "They're more expensive, but when your offer doesn't work out, it doesn't work out, he says."

Blue didn't comment on his lack of faith in Brax's casual dismissal of his original target. "Well, good luck," he said.

After a few minutes of talking about Blue's plans to move back to Peck's Bluff, their drinks and his sandwich arrived. He ate and watched as her gaze traveled around the room. Blue suspected she was looking for the next step up, the next opportunity. He knew how it felt to be trapped and desperate. For him it had been a cruelty in his childhood, for Charlotte it was money.

He finished eating, then swirled his straw in the milkshake. "I have more good news, Charlotte, but first I have a question."

"Good news?"

She'd gone straight for the good news, but Blue ignored her.

"What are you planning to do with your inheritance?" he asked. "I mean, it's a sizeable amount. And it'll be even bigger after I manage it for two years."

Her eyes shone with the same light Blue had seen the day Gran's Will was read. Before Charlotte had learned she had to wait.

"Why, spend it, darlin'."

He pinned her with a look. "Does any of that spending include investing?"

The light hardened to a glint and she splayed her small hands on the table. "I'm investing it in me, darlin'. All of it. And hoping it pays off big."

Blue was taken aback by her vehemence. "What does that mean?"

"It means I'm going to look and act like I have money. Lots of it. Money attracts money. When it attracts the kind of man I'm looking for, I'll happily give up the fast life and settle down."

His fascination took over and Blue couldn't help himself. "Wow. Uh, what happens when he or his family finds out you're a small-town girl blowing through an inheritance?"

Charlotte's cat eyes narrowed. "How would they do that?"

"Well, wedding plans, meeting the folks. You know. That stuff."

She leaned back, her mouth a pout. "Sad thing is, I don't intend to be encumbered by family, so there's nothing to find out."

Blue started to protest. This was crazy. It may not have occurred to Charlotte that a rich man's family would have her investigated or insist on an airtight pre-nup. "Well, when you come back to ..."

She shook her head before he finished. "Not coming back."

"You don't mean *never*."

"Yes, darlin'. Never. There's nothin' and no one here I care to see again."

Blue thought that was one of the saddest declarations he'd ever heard. To leave her old life behind for good in search of a rich husband.

He pushed out a breath. "So your business deal with Braxton is only for two years? He okay with that? I mean when you come into the big money, he's just going to leave quietly?"

Charlotte tipped her head forward, a raptor hovering over a mouse in a field. "He knows I'll give it all I've got while it lasts and that's fine with him. As I said before, he understands me."

A lie about Blue being happy for her never found voice. He nodded. "Okay. Good news first. As one of Gran's executors and your new portfolio manager, I'm authorizing a monthly withdrawal to you of $1,200.

Charlotte's gaze rolled up and to the right, then her face lit with avarice. "Can I get the whole $28,800 up front?"

He was impressed with how quickly she'd come to the right amount. Too bad she was convinced her looks were the only thing she had. "You know the answer to that, Charlotte."

Her mouth turned down. "How soon can I get the first payment?"

"A week to ten days," Blue said. "But here's the bad news. Your father's on the account, too, and he has to be notified of the change in management. He's not going to be happy."

Charlotte gave him a blank look and lifted a shoulder. "What my father thinks isn't a problem. Unless this change is illegal, which I'm sure you've already checked on, we're going ahead with it. Right now."

Blue hadn't prepared himself for facing Joe so soon and his stomach clenched. Might as well get it over with. He glanced at the check, dropped some money and they left.

They found Joe at a small laptop in his office off the living room. He looked up with undisguised hostility when they entered. "What do you want?"

Charlotte didn't hesitate for a second. "I'm moving my portfolio management to Blue. Effective immediately."

She turned to Blue. "There. Done and done."

Nothing like ripping the duct tape off your eyebrows in one fell swoop, Blue thought as Joe Canfield's neck turned red, the color spreading upward.

"Don't be ridiculous," the older man said. "This is a con. He's trying to get back at me for some imagined slight. It's not only against the intent of the Will, as a joint tenant, I refuse."

"From now on," Charlotte snapped, "you're a deleted tenant."

Blue took an instant guilt trip, the blood pounding in his ears. Was Joe right? Was helping Charlotte secondary to getting even with the cruel taunts he'd suffered at the hands of his uncle as a small boy?

His conclusion came just as quickly.

No.

Even if the imagined slight Joe referred to was what Blue had overheard about his mother after Gran's funeral, he still believed he could and should, help Charlotte. Whether Joe liked it or not.

Father and daughter were glaring at each other and Blue thought again how alike they were. Both viewed money as a sign of success; Charlotte in catching a rich husband, Joe in proving he could master the stock market.

Neither would ever be happy, even if each gained their goal.

Blue didn't want to add to the tension. "Charlotte, could you please get all the paperwork that pertains to your inheritance so I can review it?"

Charlotte shot her father one more nasty look, then left the room as if dismissing him.

As her footsteps echoed up the stairs, Blue turned to Joe. "I'm taking over the portfolio – done deal. You will not ..."

Joe cut him off. "You're still a nobody."

The words caught Blue off guard and rocked him back twenty-one years to the summer between his ninth and tenth birthdays. Uncle Joe had taken every opportunity to belittle and harass him. Always in private, because somehow he knew Blue would not tell his mother. The misery lasted almost five years, until he had grown tall, filled out, and was more than a match for the older man. Blue now knew that Joe was a small man, not only in stature, but character.

He took a deep breath and shook off the insult, amazed at how easy it was. "That doesn't work anymore, Joe. As of today, you will not help yourself to any additional funds from the portfolio and you will replace the missing $3,000."

Joe's face turned apoplectic, his lips white. "I've spent a lot of time monitoring Charlotte's account. That gives me the right to a monthly administrative fee."

"No," Blue said, calmer than he felt. "It doesn't. The portfolio management company already gets a fee. The money you've been taking will be replaced, or, as an executor of Molly Brisco's estate, I'll take legal action."

Joe jumped up from his chair. "Get out! Get out of my house or I'll throw you out."

"What in the world is going on?"

Both men turned to the doorway where Winnie Canfield stood. Blue tamped down his mounting anger. He respected his aunt and didn't want her to find out about the money. It would only hurt her. Blue smiled, hoping he looked under control. "I've volunteered to manage Charlotte's portfolio. Uncle Joe misunderstood one of the legal responsibilities of being a signer on the account. Our discussion got a little heated. Sorry if we disturbed you."

Blue's aunt flicked an unhappy glance at her husband. "Joe. Is this true?"

The older man's mouth worked up a lie. "I outsmarted Charlotte's so-called expert manager on a company I'd been researching and told him to buy big at the IPO." Joe snorted. "I was right, so I took a small cut."

Winnie's lips pursed unhappily. "We'll discuss your going over the line again, later."

Blue was momentarily surprised, then realized maybe his aunt had seen this happen too often. Joe's type of market player never understood that by the time they acted on a tip, the stock price had already crested and they were too late to get in on the really big money. He'd had six months to put his stamp on the portfolio and it would take time to undo his work. Blue assessed Joe's combative stance and couldn't help throwing out a question. "Must be a heck of a producer for you to take the same amount every month. What's the name of the stock, Joe?"

His uncle took on the look of a cornered animal as he turned his attention to his open laptop and closed out the screen he'd been viewing. "Doesn't matter. It'll even out. No need for talk of replacing funds."

Winnie took a step toward her husband. "How much, this time?"

Before her husband could answer, another voice, tight with rage, came from behind Winnie. Charlotte stepped into the room. "Yes, Daddy, how much?"

# Chapter Thirty-Seven

Damn! True to character, Charlotte had snuck back to listen, and Blue's chances of keeping the theft quiet disappeared. His system took an adrenaline hit as he looked between the two. He had no idea what Charlotte was capable of where her money was concerned, so he stepped closer and attempted to smooth things over. "Hey Charlotte. It's only a bookkeeping item. We can work out the details, later."

Green eyes called him a liar, then she focused her temper on her father. She leaned toward him as her hand opened and closed into a shaking fist, fury etched on her face. "Grandmother Parker forgave you because Mother begged her to. Then you lost Mother's inheritance. Now, you have the nerve to steal from me. No more! This is where it ends."

Amazingly, Joe looked unrepentant. He stuck out the small Canfield chin. "Parker women don't know the first thing about investing. I'm on the verge of something big, and you're a sorry, ungrateful girl."

Charlotte straightened to her full five foot, three inches and flapped the folder in her other hand in Joe's face. "You're done screwing with my future, old man. The only thing sorry around here is you, and you are off the account. I'll leave it to Blue to collect whatever you stole, but any shred of respect I ever had for you is gone. You are no longer my father."

Winnie Canfield put a hand on her daughter's arm. "Charlotte, please."

Charlotte paid no attention to her mother, but held out the folder to Blue. "Get me the papers to sign removing him as joint tenant," she said. "If he balks, I'll prosecute."

Blue took the folder. He'd never thought of getting even with Joe. If he had, he certainly wouldn't have gone so far as to tear a family apart. He touched Charlotte's shoulder as she turned for the door.

When she looked back, Blue saw the same unrepentant stare as her father's, but hers had an edge of triumph.

"No need to worry about relatives poppin' up now, is there, cuz?" Then she left.

Blue's gaze remained on the empty doorway a moment before refocusing on his Aunt Winnie. His muscles stayed tense, a reaction to his part in the break-up. He felt no remorse for Joe, only his aunt, the lines in her face seeming to have multiplied in the last minute.

As he reached toward her, Blue's movement must have galvanized Joe. He stiffened, his voice taking on something between a wheedle and a threat. "I'll fight you and Charlotte on this. You hit your head on that jagged rock harder than I thought if you think I won't. I have friends in court who I can convince you're after the money for yourself. How much are you going to charge her? What happens when you lose the whole inheritance?"

Blue didn't answer, just took Winnie's arm and lead her down the hall toward the kitchen. Charlotte was nowhere in sight.

"Here, sit down. Can I make you some tea?" he asked.

Aunt Winnie shook her head, a wan smile in place. "No, thank you, dear. I'll be fine."

Blue squeezed her hand and started to turn toward the door.

"Blue?"

"Yes ma'am?"

"Can you do that? Can you take the account away from him?"

Blue nodded. "It's Charlotte's portfolio. If need be, she can go to a judge and prove Joe's been, uh, making unauthorized withdrawals. It would be best if he paid back the money and let it go."

He heard nothing from down the hall, so Blue relaxed. He waited for his Aunt to continue.

She looked distraught, her gaze not meeting his. "He wants to live up to the successful reputation he's built in his head. Can't let himself believe he's a failure. Never could."

Her insight was right on. Unfortunately, she'd had to learn that by living with Joe's anger and obstinacy for thirty years.

He shook his head. "Nobody can help him with that."

"He doesn't believe her, you know."

It was said so softly, Blue barely heard it. He knew she was talking about Charlotte and his jaw clenched. His aunt was grasping at straws; wanting to hear that Blue didn't believe it, either. "She seemed pretty serious."

Aunt Winnie nodded. "She's got the same short fuse as Joe. He's counting on her having no place else to go when she cools down. Like always."

Blue hadn't considered the ripple effect when he'd talked to Charlotte, but couldn't lie to his aunt. He sat down. "I've arranged to transfer a monthly sum to Charlotte. If she's careful with it, she can rent her own place. Either here or in Atlanta."

His aunt blinked. "I don't understand. How can you do that?"

Right. She didn't know about his offer. He rolled his shoulders. "I work in the market for a living, Aunt Winnie. Very successfully. I arranged to take over the management of Charlotte's portfolio for no fee. I can get her a much better return than she's getting now. She seemed so unhappy and so dependent on that Braxton character. I thought I could make the next two years easier for her. We came to notify Joe of the change."

Blue's aunt processed this information and started nodding. "When you looked at her account, you found money missing."

He tried to soften the telling. "Joe assumed, as a joint tenant monitoring the accounts, that gave him the right to assign himself a monthly salary."

Winnie colored pink. She patted his hand. "In other words, he stole it."

"That's how Charlotte chose to interpret it when she overheard." *And it sounded like this was not the first instance.*

Winnie's small smile came back. "Thank you for helping," she said. "Maybe this is all for the best."

Blue leaned to kiss his aunt's cheek. "Talk to you later."

Delta rubbed her uninjured temple. The meeting with her attorney had been expensive and a little scary. He'd had to answer multiple complaints from Slayton's family about Delta's "shameful attempt at inventing lies to blacken their honored name". Time, which of course, he charged to her growing bill.

Her meeting with the Buchanans didn't go much better. The husband wanted to sell the Averill House as a total loss. The wife dug in her heels, wanting to raise a summer house from the ashes because she loved the location. They didn't come to an agreement within the scheduled hour, so wanted another meeting. Delta hadn't taken sides and squirmed uncomfortably in the midst of their heated arguments. She managed to stay neutral, but came away exhausted.

She pulled into her apartment house parking lot and smiled. Blue had never eaten her shrimp scampi. She was looking forward to savoring an intimate dinner and an even more intimate night.

An hour later, she had changed into a comfortable long-sleeved t-shirt and jeans and had the kitchen running smoothly.

When the doorbell rang, Delta was momentarily surprised before remembering Blue not only didn't have a key, he'd never been to her Atlanta home. She padded to the door in stocking feet and peeked through the security viewer before opening the door. Blue stood waiting.

*Oh, my.* Her stomach did flip flops as she stepped back to let him in. He wore a leather bomber jacket with a dark green shirt underneath that emphasized the green in his hazel eyes. A couple of boxes of Blue's clothes had arrived from Chicago and she really liked his style.

When she opened the door, he handed her a bottle of wine.

Delta held it up. "White. How did you know I was cooking shellfish?

"Didn't" he said. "But red gives you a headache." He closed the door and picked her up, hugging her tightly. When he set her back down, she noticed his look of distraction.

"Hey, you okay?" she asked.

Blue took her hand and played with her fingers. "Sorry. Got caught in the middle of a Canfield meltdown this afternoon. It was my fault."

"Want to talk about it?"

"Later," he said, the cast of his eye having changed to something way more personal.

Her skin warmed. It was going to be a wonderful future having Blue look at her like this.

She pulled him further into the apartment. "That does it. I'm putting the shrimp back in the fridge, turning off the sauce and then I'm going to attack you."

Blue grinned. "I'll deal with the food while you deal with all those clothes you're wearing."

Delta laughed again and nipped his jaw before heading down the short hallway to her room.

She'd been so overwhelmed by Blue's generous and thorough lovemaking the first time, she felt she hadn't given enough of herself. That was going to change, tonight.

Dark rose light filtered through the west-facing window of her bedroom. Sunset, and it would be completely dark in a few minutes. She turned when Blue entered.

He dropped his clothes on the chair by the door, then his gaze connected with hers and the heat of sex flowed toward her, through her and returned to spool in her middle. He wore boxers to her bra and panties and that was still too much. She held up her hands, palms out, forestalling him as he stepped across the space, arms open.

"Been thinking about this all day," she said. "And I wasn't kidding about you first, then us. Got a problem with that?"

She felt him suck in air along his abdomen as she ran several fingers under the waist of his boxers. "Uh, no," he croaked. "So, I just stand here?"

"For the time being," Delta said, her hands busy. "Then I'll let you lie on the bed."

He strangled out a moan. "Delta, honey. You have no idea how much, um, *feeling* you're provoking."

She stopped in front of him, her bare toes softly kneading the tops of his. She bumped his hips with hers. "Sure I do, sugar. Our parts are different, but with the right person, those feelings flow both ways."

"Right," Blue said on a huff of air.

Delta had shed her bra when she was behind Blue and now hugged him, bringing his head down for a heated kiss. Her belly tightened, yet his growing reaction made her giggle. "I wanted to drive you to distraction, but I didn't realize how short the trip would be."

Blue leaned toward her ear as he slid the palm of his hand up her ribs. "We have years to go down that road. Right now, I need to be inside you."

Her first time with Blue had been a heated and desperate expedition to see if her physical feelings for him matched her emotional ones. They had. This time she'd expected a slow, knowing pace, but the urgency building in her banished that idea. "Yes," she said. "Slower later."

Blue stopped taking off his boxers mid-calf. "Honey, as long as it's you and me, I'll try, but slow might never be an option."

Delta laughed and stepped out of her panties, then put her foot between Blue's knees and stomped his boxers to the floor. There was enough light left to see the grin on his face. He picked her up and rolled her onto the bed, planting an elbow to keep his weight off her. His thumb moved to the V below her hip and her belly trembled with pent-up need. She'd thought to have him pleading, but lost total control as he slid into her.

"Sorry, honey. I'll make it up to you." His last word a rough sigh.

"Sugar ..." The endearment a rushed appeal and her remaining coherent thought as the ache building in her peaked in a blur of pleasure and release.

Blood roared in her ears and chest as she regained her breath. After a minute, Blue struggled to sit on the edge of the bed and put on another condom.

"Thought I was in good shape. Gimme a minute."

Delta giggled at his fractured self-deprecation. "Richmond, you are so pathetic. Here, let me help." She pulled him down and straddled his hips, then leaned close, her breasts brushing his chest. All thoughts that she had self-control fled as his hips jerked. "Ha. Still some life left," she teased, swallowing hard. "Spread out your arms and lie quiet."

Blue groaned. "Again?"

"Yes, again. This relationship is for partners and I get a turn, too."

"I didn't ask you to be quiet," he said between clenched teeth.

She lifted her mouth's bold exploration and slid down to pin his legs. "Hmm. True. Go ahead and make noise if y'all want."

His useless imprecations stopped when she took him inside her.

"Please?" The word exhaled on a hitched breath.

"That's what I wanted to hear," she said and carried them both to a very satisfying completion.

Blue chuckled a few minutes later. "Must be inbreeding." Delta turned. "What must be?"

"Slayton's family," he said, shaking his head. "I've said it before and I'll say it again—he is one stupid man."

She preened in the shadowy dark. "Oh?"

Blue grabbed her and gave her a smacking kiss. "Fishing for compliments?"

She wiggled against him until he groaned.

"Speaking of fish, I'm starved. Wait'll you taste my shrimp scampi."

He threw his arms open and Delta got dumped beside him.

"Cook away. I'll pour the wine."

Delta strolled toward the room's light switch, deciding to turn it on, buck naked. In the few seconds it took to get there, she changed her mind and made a U-turn, choosing instead the small nightstand lamp.

"Cheater," Blue said softly, pulling her close and kissing her belly.

"Can't help it, she said and kissed the top of his head. "Clothes, first, then dinner, then dessert."

Blue opened the door to the hall as they dressed, throwing the room into more definite shapes. He looked around at the furnishings. "You have great taste. Why so Spartan?"

She lifted a shoulder, a little embarrassed. "Money. I took nothing when I left Slayton and used Gramps's inheritance to start my design firm." She held her index fingers straight up with thumbs touching at ninety degrees, feigning a camera shot. "Someday I'm going to have this gorgeous shiny black Regency headboard - six feet high. It's at the Atlanta Decorative Arts Center at my favorite shop. The interior designer there and I have already designed a beautiful room around it."

"Sounds nice," Blue said and held out his hand.

They'd gotten halfway through dinner when she remembered to ask about his earlier statement. "So, the Canfield meltdown. I seriously doubt it was your fault. What happened?"

Blue pushed out a breath. "I talked to your father about taking over the management of Charlotte's portfolio. I'd looked at it and determined I could get her a much better rate of return, plus give her a monthly allowance."

Delta felt the tiny pitchfork of jealousy prick her, and ignored it. "Why would the family get upset at that? It sounds like good news."

"That part was," he said. "The part that upset the household had to do with some, uh, appropriated funds. When Charlotte and Aunt Winnie found out, Charlotte went ballistic and wanted Joe kicked off the account. She also disowned him as her father."

Delta propped her chin in hand and rolled her eyes. "You've probably forgotten the Canfield house is drama central. Charlotte and Uncle Joe go at it hammer and tongs on a regular basis. The whole circus has been going on since Charlotte was old enough to defy and get away with it. It's gotten much worse since she came home after her divorce. Did she also accuse him of losing all the Parker family money?"

Blue nodded. "Charlotte was so pissed. I think it was for real this time. I felt the worst for Aunt Winnie. If Charlotte leaves for good, she's stuck with that SOB."

Delta let him off the hook. "She's not stuck, sugar. Aunt Winnie can leave any time she wants. All the women in the family, except for Charlotte, have known it for years."

His face showed true surprise. "How?"

"Keep it a secret?"

Blue leaned forward, an eager expression in place. "Sure."

Delta laughed. "Grandmother Parker wasn't so stupid as to let Uncle Joe manage *all* her money. She quietly put a good deal of it aside, making Winnie swear not to tell anyone of its existence.

"Aunt Winnie was so used to doing as she was told, she agreed. She, my mother, and Aunt Caroline were very close in those early days and when they became concerned about Joe's financial instability, she told them in confidence. Over the years she's found having her own money means she has a way out. To everyone's amazement, she's never chosen to leave. She mentioned to mother once that she never wanted to grow old alone. Guess that means she's even willing to put up with Joe."

Blue sat shaking his head. "Seems Joe's been outsmarted by the Parker women he claims have no head for finance."

"Yep," said Delta. "And mum's the word."

"Let me do the dishes," Blue said, standing to arch his back.

"Have to say no thanks," Delta responded. "Quirky dishwasher needs loading just so, or only half the dishes get washed. Have a chair. I'll be ten minutes."

"Okay." He kissed Delta and was about to cross into the living room when the doorbell rang.

"Answer that, will you?" she called. "Don't sign me up for any Girl Scout cookies or Golf Magazine subscriptions."

"Got it." He opened the door to a stranger.

# Chapter Thirty-Eight

The guy stood in the dimly lit hall, blinking slowly, his mouth slightly open. He looked a little out-of-it, but something about him seemed familiar.

"Who is it?" Delta called from the kitchen.

Both men turned toward her voice.

"Don't know," Blue replied, then a whiff of alcohol as the tall blond used the door frame to prop himself upright triggered Blue's memory. It had been over six years since he had seen him, but it was Slayton.

Blue turned back to the man and stepped into a relaxed defense position, adrenaline mainlining. What the hell was Delta's ex-husband doing here? "I think you'd better clear out."

Slayton refocused on him as he held out a sheet of stationary. "Drove by two nights in a row. Not leaving 'til I show her this."

Delta stepped around the kitchen wall and drew back slightly, a shocked frown on her face. "Slayton. I told you

I'd take out a restraining order if you didn't' stop harassing me. I want you to leave."

Slayton looked her up and down. Not, Blue noticed, with hate or lust, or even interest, but in a disconnected anger. The kind people reserved for rude servers or cab drivers, only more intense. Blue's own anger escalated when Slayton just stood there, holding out the paper.

"You heard her. Take a hike," Blue said. He sensed Delta's tension and started to shut the door, but Slayton took a half step, his gaze on Delta.

Delta's stomach cartwheeled. Slayton had not bothered to come to court on the day of their marriage dissolution so his appearance on her doorstep unnerved her. The rigid set of Blue's shoulders confirmed he wasn't happy, either. She put a hand on his arm. "I'll handle this."

"You blew this for me," Slayton said, waving the paper. "Melissa and her family heard about your damned investigation. This is a letter canceling the engagement and the wedding."

It had been over three years since Delta had seen Slayton. Time had blurred his collegiate good looks and set him on the same path his father trod. One of alcohol and unhappiness. She realized she felt neither triumph nor distress about him and his situation.

"Melissa sounds like a smart girl," Blue interjected. "Now, back off."

Irritation sliced into Delta's musings. This was her home and however much Blue felt responsible for Slayton's appearance, it was hers to deal with.

She pulled on Blue's arm, trying to convey her insistence.

"You're wasting your time, Slayton," she said, not apologizing. "It was never intended to go this far, but it's out of my hands. If you were that concerned about your future, you and your parents should have run a legal business." Her voice rose. "And if you contact me directly again, I will have that restraining order issued."

Hate now infused Slayton's expression, but it cleared enough for her to see him take her measure. "Well, look who's grown a spine," he blurted.

"We're done here," Blue said and slammed the door.

They stood for a minute, listening, then Delta leaned forward and peered through the viewer. "He's gone."

"I don't like his coming here."

Delta turned. "Neither do I, but if it happens again, I'll take care of it."

A frown of hurt twisted across his face before it smoothed. "Sorry. Didn't mean to interfere."

She heaved an agitated sigh. "He's all talk and no threat. And he's finding out I'm no longer intimidated, which pisses him off. I'd rather be the one to deal with him, that's all."

Hurt changed to mild annoyance on Blue's face. "All right. You want to face your demons on your own. I get it. I was only trying to help."

Delta put a hand on her hip. "Do you think he would've tried to hurt me?"

"No," he shot back. "Except you can never tell with a drunk."

"Well, I lived with this particular drunk for almost three years," she said. "And if you'd paid attention to me instead of getting all worked up, that little scene would've been a lot shorter."

He reached to stroke her shoulder, but she hadn't let go of her mad and tucked her arm close to her body.

"What's this really about?" he asked, pinning her with a questioning look.

Delta closed her eyes and shook her head. Did she really know what her reaction was about or was it knee-jerk? She opened them and met his gaze. "I don't know if it was a response to the kind of day I had, or Slayton's unexpected appearance, or both, but I suddenly felt like nothing had changed. I had just traded Slayton's obvious control for another, more subtle kind."

Blue looked dumbfounded. A hard swallow preceded his words. "We're partners and you love me, but you think I'm trying to control you because I acted in your behalf?"

The living room offered more space, so Delta turned and strode in, crossing her arms. "It's not that simple. We *are* partners and I do love you." She sighed. "When you put it that way, it makes me sound immature. I guess I'm asking you to take my cue when it comes to things that affect me personally and that I'm more familiar with. I'm not the same Delta you used to know. I don't stand aside anymore and I'm not going to apologize for that."

"Understood," he said, but his eyes retained a fragment of uncertainty. "However, you need to know your ex is a very hot button of mine and I'm a slow learner where he's concerned."

Trust Blue to bring her down from her mad, unreasonable or not. Delta smiled and let her arms drop. "Fair enough," she said. "Thank you."

Blue took a step toward her. "Guess we have some speed bumps to overcome."

"All couples do," she said, going into his arms and relishing his hug.

They talked for a while, discussing the paperwork for Brisco's Folly and how soon they could realize the profit from the transaction.

"I almost didn't come away with this," he said, pointing at the envelope of documents. "The guy behind the counter wanted verification that I was who I said I was. When I brought out my Illinois Driver's License, he held it up to the light and asked for additional I.D. I had a Visa with my picture on it and a car insurance card with my name on it. He took them to another room and came back five minutes later, reluctantly handing them back along with the paperwork. Weird, hunh?"

"You do look kind of unsavory," Delta teased, then reached for his hand. "Gran wanted us to sell to the Tylers. This is what she meant when she said it would help the town." Her shoulders slumped and a wave of sadness washed over her. "Wow. I really miss her."

"Me, too," said Blue. He got up and walked around the kitchen table to massage her shoulders. "She was one heck of a woman." He bent and kissed the top of Delta's head. "And so is her granddaughter."

Delta smiled. "Thank you, sir." Patience had been right. Blue was definitely worth opening her heart for. She closed her eyes in pleasure as he worked his magic up her neck, then down again. "I need to catch up my backlog of work. Dealing with Slayton and the Buchanans has sucked away time I can't afford."

"Tomorrow," he said. "Let's crash."

They climbed into bed and snuggled. Delta took a cleansing breath, forcing her muscles to relax. Blue fell asleep almost immediately.

On reflection, Blue's interference, or help, or whatever you wanted to call it, had left her feeling stronger. Recognizing that she wanted to face her demons on her own, and wanting that for her; Blue had given her that strength.

She studied the ceiling, noticing the light fixture was a deeper shade of black, but the far corners of the small room were indistinguishable. This apartment was her post-divorce haven, a place where she'd forced herself to be calm and comfortable. Her parents had wanted her to move back with them for a while, but as tempting as that had been, she shied away from their overly helpful presence. The apartment had afforded her a measure of peace where she could let her years as Slayton's wife ebb away, snipping the strings of each bad memory, one at a time.

Seeing him on her doorstep tonight had felt intrusive, the feeling that she had returned to her old persona as an anxious new divorcee. It passed almost immediately, Slayton's whiny demand merely annoying. Now that it was over, she had to admit it was freeing, too. With Blue's help, maybe the last string had been severed.

# Chapter Thirty-nine

Cold rain painted the city grey. A harbinger of winter.

Blue carefully peeled the sheet from Delta's bare shoulder. She made protesting noises in her throat and, like a heat-seeking puppy, snuggled closer. As he had intended. "Staying in bed all day, Jameson? Because if you are, don't think you're going to get much rest."

Eyes closed, she responded to his threat. "Pfffttt."

He whipped the covers off them, jumped up, and stood at the foot of the bed. "Any breakfast food in the kitchen? I burned a lot of calories satisfying you last night and I think I deserve to be fed."

Growling, Delta launched herself at him, all pale limbs and wild, curly dark hair.

Blue caught her, pinned her arms, and carried her into the shower. "You'll thank me for this, later. Probably."

"Let's say I'll get even with you later and leave it at that," she grumbled. The sound turning into a hum as he soaped her in places guaranteed to make them both happy.

A mound of bacon, eggs, and toast were consumed as they chatted about their day. Blue realized, in moments of silence, that this feeling of peace and wholeness was the permanence he was looking for, what he needed. This was not a test relationship, and the only thing scaring him was that he wanted it so desperately and maybe Delta didn't, yet. He thought she was getting closer, though. She sat relaxed and make-up free, not bothering to hide the hiccups she got after drinking orange juice.

"Hope it's not raining this hard at Peck's Bluff," she said, munching away. "I want to walk Brisco's Folly to get location and layout ideas for the Center."

Blue stopped eating. "Hey. Remember that Sinclair Brisco blood? You've got the contract in the bag."

Pink crept into her face as Delta bobbled her eyebrows at him. "Keep it up. If my proposal is accepted, I could make choosing the green contractor part of the deal."

"It'd be nice to work together," he said. *Although kissing you would be a constant temptation.* "This is nice, too."

"Yes," Delta replied. "It is."

He watched her gaze wander their small space.

"Been my sanctum for almost three years. I worried that it might get awkward. You know, sharing." She lifted a shoulder. "But it's okay. Must be the person I chose to share it with."

Blue's insides did happy flip flops. "Good to know."

"So, what are you doing today?" she asked. "I figure I have a couple more hours here, then back to Peck's Bluff."

"Got an appointment."

Delta propped up her chin and waited, but Blue stood and gathered his dishes.

"Whoa, wait," she said. "Aren't you going to tell me what for?"

"Nope."

"But I'm nosy," she complained. "And a poor sport when I don't get my way."

"Good to know that, too," he said, turning and walking toward the kitchen. "Gotta leave in fifteen minutes. If you want help with the dishes, speak now."

Delta padded behind him. "There're only two reasons you won't tell me. It's a surprise for me, or you're being mean."

Blue laughed and faced her. She stood, dishes in hand and her lower lip sticking out.

His thoughts took a wild ride – the highway to Peck's Bluff washed out ‑ the two of them stuck here alone for days.

He shook off the daydream, moved the dishes to the counter, and took her in his arms. "Why would I be mean to a beautiful, sexy, paranoid?"

She bounced to tiptoe and kissed his nose, her grey eyes shining. "Then it's a surprise."

Maintaining a stern expression in the face of Delta's mood proved impossible. Blue shook his head, amazed that the happy warmth growing in his chest was his from now on. "Nothing to tell, yet, and I'm giving no hints."

He grinned as he made his way through the commuter-clogged freeways north toward the Atlanta Decorative Arts Center. He was getting ahead of himself, but he figured he knew just the place to put a six-foot tall, shiny black, Regency headboard.

Two hours later he pulled into the parking lot of *Peck's Bluff Realty and Insurance*. Lonnie Abbott, Blue's appointment, stood at the door with his best salesman smile, a new haircut, and a slightly wrinkled brown suit. He held up a set of house keys.

Blue's nose itched as they trudged the overgrown walk of the rambler he'd seen on River Road. The rain had dampened the grasses, but pollen was still thick in the air.

"This is a real diamond in the rough," Lonnie said. "Not many people can see that. Got an offer last spring, but it fell through. A little TLC and you'll be a contented homeowner. That's what I always say."

Blue had noticed the flyer box was empty and the banner proclaiming PRICE REDUCED TWICE, was missing from the real estate sign. Lonnie talked country, but was a shrewd agent.

The house's musty smell could be overcome by ripping out the carpet and dated drapes. A non-load-bearing wall moved or demolished in one or two areas would open the space to some really great light. The master was big and the one hall bathroom could be incorporated to en-suite.

Three more good-sized bedrooms. One could be split into a new bathroom and a his and hers office. That left two for family expansion. Close to perfect.

He stood in the center of the living room and took a deep breath. Would Delta like his preliminary plans? He'd move in alone, ask her for design input, and eventually, once she stood on more solid ground, maybe, just maybe....

An hour later, he and Lonnie drove back to the office and negotiated a price.

Blue's call to Delta, following the appointment, resulted in voicemail, so Blue called Dewey. "Hey. Want to meet at the café for lunch?"

"Sure," Dewey said. "Some stuff I need to talk to you about, anyway."

The lunch crowd had thinned and they got their favorite booth by the kitchen. When Patience saw them, she smiled ear-to-ear and came over. "Have you asked him, yet?"

Dewey glanced around quickly and gave her a peck on the cheek. "Just about to."

Blue couldn't help giving his friend a hard time as soon as Patience left with their orders. "She sure isn't a short, fluffy-headed blonde."

A grin spanned Dewey's face. "Man, I don't know what took me so long, but she's the whole package. Been right here in front of me."

Blue's own happiness prompted his response. "Congratulations. I think she's great. What did she want you to ask me?"

"Yeah. We want you and Delta to come over for dinner tonight. Got something to tell you."

"Tell me now."

"Can't."

Blue nodded. "Redhead?"

Dewey pulled his lips in and looked toward the kitchen. "Yep."

"Six okay?"

His friend leaned back against the banquette. "That's good."

"I've got some news, too. But I don't want Delta or Patience to know."

A frisson of panic crossed Dewey's face. "Not tell Patience?"

Blue rolled his eyes. "Suck it up, Harcourt. If Patience knows, it'll get back to Delta and it's a surprise."

Dewey hung his head. "Okay. I'm in."

"I bought a house," Blue said, leaning in, his voice low.

"Really? For you and Delta?"

"Haven't got that far, but I'm working on it."

Patience brought two plates and set them on the table. She spoke to Blue. "Can you pick Delta up? She said she'd be back at her folks' house."

"Sure," Blue said. "Can we bring anything?"

"Just your appetites," Patience said, smiling.

When she left, Blue continued. "That general contractor I used for my mother's reno still around?"

"Stanger? Yeah. His brother's part time on the force and says he's not busy right now."

"Good. I need some work done. Fast."

"On the new place?"

Blue nodded. "I hope Stanger's open to different ideas. I want to use green and recycled materials. Not much of that around here. Yet."

Dewey set down his burger. "That deal you're putting together for the flooring factory shaping up?"

"Got'em interested," Blue said. "The next few days could firm the details."

His friend beamed. "Sure could be the shot in the arm this area needs."


Delta made a face in the mirror as she stroked on some foundation. Her hands, and yes, as she looked down, her feet, needed professional care. She grinned at her image. *Especially if you plan on more appearances in the buff.*

While the number of her favorite day spa was ringing, Delta had a moment of panic. Her ex mother-in-law patronized the same place and under the circumstances, she did not want to encounter the woman. To hell with it, she thought, chances were slim and if it happened, it happened. Besides, the spa was exclusive and probably booked full.

"Hello. Thank you for calling *At Our Best in Atlanta.* How can I help you?"

"Oh, hi," Delta said. "I was wondering if you had any openings for a manicure, pedicure this morning?"

"I'm sorry. All our regular staff are booked today, but we have a trainee who might be available. Can you wait a moment?"

"Yes."

She held for about 15 seconds, then the receptionist came back on the line. "She can take you in 45 minutes. Would that be okay?"

Delta grinned. "That would be fine."

She had car keys in hand and was about to leave when her cell phone rang. The readout showed Patience's number. "Hi. What's going on?"

"Your mama said you were coming back to town today. Can you come to dinner at our place tonight? Dewey's asking Blue."

"Sure. What's the occasion?"

"Making plans for the holidays. Want to include you two."

Delta held the phone away and stared at it for a second before responding. "Holidays aren't even on my radar, but okay."

She made it to the spa with five minutes to spare. The manager greeted her warmly. "Nice to see you again. You look great."

Her name escaped Delta, but the woman sounded sincere. "Thank you."

She was approached by a blonde girl who looked bare-ly eighteen. "Hi. I'm Robin. I'll escort you back."

The way her mouth worked, Delta guessed the girl seriously missed her chewing gum. Hopefully she wasn't chatty.

"So," Robin said as soon as Delta was comfortable, "I understand I worked on your ex mother-in-law yesterday."

# Chapter Forty

Distaste shimmered up her spine before Delta eased out a breath. *Wow. The military should have intelligence this thorough.* She tipped her head once.

The girl looked up through thickly-coated lashes. "She didn't waste any time cuttin' everybody here into little pieces, so I don't expect your divorce was friendly."

Delta still didn't comment, just shook her head. She wouldn't be drawn into making a gossipy remark.

The blonde continued. "Sure thought she was something special. 'I'm moving to a tropical climate. Be sure you do a nice job. I'll be wearing sandals on the plane,'" the girl mimicked.

Delta froze. Her ex mother-in-law was moving to a tropical climate? Was Slayton's father sending his wife out of the country to protect her from prosecution?

She choked out a laugh. Everyone in that family was out for themselves and themselves only.

"Do they own an island or something?" the girl asked.

"Not that I'm aware of," Delta said. *But you're close.*
The remainder of the appointment was quiet.

The hour drive to Peck's Bluff gave Delta time to pon-
der the information she'd come across. It looked like her
ex's family planned to skip the country. And she thought
she knew where they were heading. Something must have
happened to tip the balance way out of their favor. What
to do about it spun round and round in her mind, building frustration.

Saying nothing would guarantee their unimpeded escape, and she would have them and probably their lawsuit
out of her life forever. Her elation turned to ...

The only word she came up with was apathy. The
crushing depression she'd felt only a couple of weeks ago
had, because of the sale of Brisco's Folly, and Blue's in-
volvement in her life, virtually disappeared. The appreciation of which made her smile when she pulled to the side
of the road, found a number in the papers Blue had given
her, and dialed.

The INS agent who answered was very interested in
her information. When Delta commented on what Slayton and his parents would be abandoning in this country,
compared to a probable fine and slap on the wrist, he
laughed.

"Aside from having their sole source of income shut
down and owing every creditor in town, a prominent Cuban-American judge has been assigned to the case." He
paused. "It's all public record."

It was Delta's turn to laugh.

She met Blue at the Jameson's front door, stepped through and hugged him tight. "I got some interesting news, today."

"Since this morning?" he teased.

Delta nodded. "Let me grab my coat and I'll tell you in the car."

Blue stepped inside. "Your parents at home?"

She slipped her arm into her coat sleeve. "Nope, out playing Bridge."

He backed her against the closet door and nuzzled her neck. "Missed you, today."

Warmth slid into her middle and Delta momentarily forgot her train of thought. She sighed and held his face between her hands. "Keep that in mind for the next sixty years, Richmond."

The look he gave her canceled every doubt she ever had about permanence with him. She wanted to take him upstairs to her bed and stay for about a week. Instead, she slipped her hand in his and led them outside.

Blue started the car engine, adjusted the heater, then turned to her. "Okay. What's your interesting news?"

"I went to the day spa for a mani-pedi," she said, wiggling her fingers under the dashboard light. "The girl who did my nails worked on my ex-mother-in-law yesterday."

Blue cocked an eyebrow. "*Amazing.*"

She reached up and pressed his lips together. "Listen and you might learn something."

"Hmn hmn."

"The evil one demanded an extra-special pedicure because she was moving to a tropical climate and would be wearing sandals on the trip."

Blue gently took her hand away from his mouth. "Moving?"

"Yep. That's what she said. I think it's true. I also think they're planning to leave the country."

"Why?" Blue said. "Look at what they'd be leaving behind. Besides, she might have meant south Florida. It's tropical."

Delta shook her head. "Trust me. It's not Florida or any place else in this country. The key word is *look*. They look rich and successful and connected. The truth is, their house is mortgaged to the hilt, their cars are leased, her jewelry is paste and their credit is maxed, and their so-called friends are standing back. It's all like you said. A house of cards."

Blue waved his hand to cut into her stream of words. "Whoa. We'll get to how the manicurist knows about your ex's family and their financial affairs in a minute. I want to know how their moving would affect the lawsuit."

Just like Blue to worry about her, first, Delta thought. She was one lucky woman. "I guess if they left the country permanently, it might be dismissed."

"That's good news," Blue said slowly. "Too bad it would also mean they'd skip out on being punished for breaking those immigration laws."

"Bummer of a decision," Delta said. "What would you do?"

The interior of the car was dark, but Delta knew his face would reflect the honesty in his voice.

Blue hesitated a moment. "If I came across that information, and I was in your circumstances, I'd do the same thing you did."

An aborted gasp escaped Delta. "How'd you know?"

He unsnapped his seatbelt and leaned to hug her. "Because you would understand you signed a legal document – unfair as it was – and you would also want to stand up for those workers who couldn't stand up for themselves. That about it?"

Delta made a dismissive sound. "That's all you know. I came very close to letting them fly into the sunset and calling it good."

A chuckle near her ear bathed the side of her face in his warm breath. "You ratted them out, anyway. That sense of fairness is one of the things I love about you." He kissed her temple. "Now that I know the end of the story, tell me the beginning."

That he knew her so well delighted Delta. She gave him a quick kiss on the jaw and pushed him back to his side. "We're running late. Drive. I'll fill you in on the way."

It was a couple days before Halloween, but Patience's house was in full spook mode. Tattered webbing drifted from the porch overhang and something crumpled and black watched with glowing red eyes from the corner of the swing. Delta laughed in appreciation. No way would any kids be out this far in the country trick or treating. Patience did it for herself. Correction. Herself and Dewey.

It looked like the deputy had been busy, too. There was a large pile of freshly chopped firewood stacked against the side of the house.

Dewey met them at the door in stocking feet. He looked happy and entirely at home. "Hey, guys. Thanks for coming on short notice." He nodded to Delta. "Patience is in the kitchen."

"We're glad to be here," Blue said, and the guys walked toward the chairs bracketing the fireplace. One of them was a larger overstuffed chair across from the one Patience usually occupied. Delta noticed that was the only change to the room.

She went into the kitchen to find Patience stacking dishes. "Things seem to be going well," Delta said, tipping her head toward the living room.

The redhead grinned. "We're kindred spirits, lovers, altogether made for each other."

Delta laughed out loud. Patience had always been too busy to date much, so when she'd fallen in love, she reached out and took hold of her future with both hands and reeled it in. "Wow. I'll say it again. I'm happy for you."

Patience set down the stack of plates she was holding. "You and Blue working things out?"

Delta felt her face flush. "*Things* are amazing."

"I'm happy for you, chickapea." Patience looked at Delta closely. "Something else going on. You have that tiny crease at the top of your nose."

"Oh, that," Delta said. "Some sneakiness, courtesy of Slayton and his parents. I'll tell you the story over dinner. It's pretty entertaining."

"Goodie. I hope the lawn jockey's in trouble."

Delta smiled. "You could say that. You could also say Slayton's ex-fiancée, Melissa owes me, big.""

Patience leaned forward, setting down her fork. "You think they were planning to go to some islands halfway around the world called the Maldives? Why would they go there?"

"My guess is because Slayton has an uncle who moved there twenty years ago due to a discrepancy in the books at the investment firm where he worked. A lot of retirees lost their life savings but the Maldives don't have an extradition treaty or diplomatic representation with the United States and it's a tropical paradise. So he's been there ever since. Which is convenient for them."

"And a Cuban-American judge has been assigned to preside over the case." Patience chuckled. "That's what I call Karma."

Delta sighed in contentment at the end of the meal. At a break in the conversation, Dewey nodded at Patience and they met, standing by her chair. He put his arm around her, blushing. "We're getting married middle of

December and were hoping the two of you will stand up with us."

Squealing and clapping her hands was all Delta could manage. Her heart was truly happy for her friend.

Blue shook Dewey's hand. "We accept." He shot a grin at Delta. "You okay with that?"

Still not trusting her voice, Delta went to Patience and hugged her. Before she let go, she asked, "Who proposed?"

# Chapter Forty-One

Patience laughed. "Who proposed? Guess you could call it a draw. He started and I finished."

Blue couldn't get over the changes happening in their lives. Dewey and Patience had known each other casually for years, but it took her honest declaration of attraction for Dewey to realize he'd been fishing in the wrong waters. His friend had never looked more genuinely happy.

Envy sliced into his thoughts and Blue turned to Dewey. "First Van, now you. Pretty soon I'll be the last single guy in town."

"There's a cure for that," Dewey grinned, bobbing his eyebrows toward Delta.

She turned to catch the look and tilted her head in question.

"Later," Blue said as Delta kissed Dewey on the cheek and gave him a congratulatory hug.

Blue grinned, hugging Patience. "I'm not missing out on this."

The four sat and chatted details for a while, then Delta yawned. "Sorry. It's been a long day."

Patience nodded and stood. "I still have to get up at four to make pies, so I'm officially kicking you out."

The warmth of the house gave way to a deep chill hanging in a thick mist. Blue pulled Delta close as they walked to the car. Inside, he turned on the heater. "That's really something. The two of them under each other's noses all these years."

Delta hunched into her coat, arms crossed. "Yes. Right under each other's noses all these years."

He couldn't tell from her voice if she thought that also applied to them, but he took it as a good sign. A sharp stab of lust made him lean and kiss her. "I'm crazy about you, you know."

Delta winked. "Thinking the same about you." She tipped her head. "What was that look Dewey sent my way?"

"He suggested that I, too, could end my sad bachelorhood."

"Oh," she said, shrinking further into her coat.


Blue grinned into the darkness as he warmed up for his run. He liked it like this. Cold enough to smell the weather, but not too cold. It had been a couple of days since he and Delta returned from Atlanta and the more time they were able to spend together, the more he believed they'd make it to permanence.

His paranoia had cooled since his accident, but he chose to run in the nearly deserted streets rather than the dark trail. At least he had an occasional pool of light to see by.

As he passed the Canfield house, Blue was surprised to see Charlotte's car in the driveway. Delta was right. His cousin's dramatic meltdowns must burn hot, then fizzle out.

He shook his head. Charlotte couldn't get a break. Marriage didn't work out, no pile of ready cash from her inheritance, and now a desperate alliance with a character like Braxton.

Charlotte and her problems faded as Blue concentrated on his surprise for Delta. Since he'd paid cash, he had immediate access to the house and had met with the contractor the day after they returned from Atlanta

The flooring factory investment looked like a done deal, too. The managing director had received the okay from the owner on the terms for the financial infusion. Blue had a meeting with them this morning.

Reaching the turning point in his run had him kicking into high gear and totally happy with his decision to stay in Peck's Bluff.

His run helped burn off some of the energy Blue would rather be burning off with Delta. They'd both admitted they loved each other, and thinking about the sex made him nuts. Okay, now he was completely warm.

The managing director walked into the owner's big office and shook Blue's hand but would not hold his gaze before taking a chair. What had happened to change the man's attitude toward him since their last meeting? Maybe the proposed financing had a term they decided they didn't like.

"Guess I'll find out," Blue muttered to himself, as a private door opened and the factory owner walked in. He was a tall, thin, man with a florid, stern face. He held up a hand for Blue to stay seated and took his chair behind the desk.

"I'll get right to it," the owner said. "When I received your proposal, and had you checked out, I thought it was a Godsend."

Blue had done background checks on the owner and company officers, too. They were clean. The owner was a strict Southern Baptist whose policies ran to promoting those as like-minded as himself. Where the law allowed.

A look of disapproval set in around the man's mouth. "Until I received this." He held up a sheet of yellow lined stationery.

"It cautions me about doing business with a man of low quality."

*Low quality?* Blue almost smiled at the antiquated phrasing, but took a deep breath, hoping he looked sincere. "What does it say?"

His serious question seemed to work. The owner continued. "I usually don't acknowledge anonymous letters, but this business has been in my family for over a hundred years, and I can't afford rumors about my choice of associates. My family and employees depend on me."

The man slipped on a pair of glasses and peered at the letter. "It refers to *overnight dates* with a local divorcee and your purchase of a house for the two of you. Your meetings at a roadhouse with another divorcee, and your intention of ruining the name of a fine old Atlanta family are also mentioned. Can you shed some light on these charges?"

Damn. Someone was out to torpedo Blue's project, and they'd picked a good way to do it. But he wasn't stupid. The owner was forty or fifty years his senior, staunchly religious, and worried more about his reputation than getting a badly needed financial injection for his company. He needed to play to the man's concerns.

"I understand your reluctance," Blue said. "But I put this proposal together to help the town where I grew up. I'm moving back permanently. I also think my private business should stay private." He held up his hand as a frown creased the owner's brow. "But I'll address the *anonymous* accusations and leave the decision to you."

The owner gave a slow nod.

Blue took a breath. "It's true. I am dating a divorcee whom I hope to marry, soon. She was in an abusive marriage and is lucky to be out. True again; I purchased a house, but I bought it for renovation and resale, not to co-habit with my girlfriend. I live with my mother." He could see he'd scored with that last bit of information, so he went on. "The other divorcee is my cousin. She's going through a tough time right now and I'm helping with her finances." Blue lifted a shoulder. "Not my style, but she likes roadhouses."

The managing director leaned a little closer.

"That fine old family the letter mentions, is under scrutiny by the INS for breaking several federal laws and endangering the lives of their illegal workers," Blue continued. "The investigation that's ruining their name is the byproduct of an entirely different issue."

He sat back. "As you undoubtedly noticed, my name is on the list of prospective investors. I don't put my money anywhere without knowing everything there is to know about the recipient. You and your company passed with flying colors. I hope you'll make the same decision about me."

Bands of red appeared on the old man's cheekbones and the tops of his ears. He gave a whisper of a smirk and tore the sheet in half. "Well said, Mr. Richmond. I believe in giving the benefit of the doubt to the man who's willing to stand face-to-face."

Things went very smoothly after that and the papers were signed in short order. When he left the office, Blue was restless. And pissed. He'd never had to explain his personal life in order to invest money. He also didn't like that an anonymous somebody tried to trash his reputation. His candidate was Braxton. Charlotte's explanation that he was scouting tracts of land in Florida sounded weak. Braxton might have decided to hang around for the fun of screwing with him and Delta because they blew off his proposal, and by extension, his commission. Charlotte would be able to provide him with the gossip he needed to write the letter. Blue hadn't seen the guy since he'd run into Charlotte at Tinker's over a week ago. Maybe it was time for a conversation.

He drove home to change and found the transportation company he'd hired to drive his car from Chicago had arrived right on schedule. No more borrowing his mother's. It would also be easier to approach Braxton in a car he'd never seen.

Less than an hour later, Blue gave up. No red truck at either of the motels, Tinker's, or any other bar. He'd checked out the Canfield house before driving into town. Charlotte's car was still there, but no truck. Of course Braxton might have sent the letter, then left for greener pastures.

His foray into private detection was stalled. Blue looked at his watch. Too early for lunch. Mackie's would be packed for at least another hour. Might as well go out to the house and see what progress had been made, then call Delta. He'd only seen her for a few minutes off and on the last couple of days as she'd been busy finalizing plans for a renovation in Roswell.

The scene in front of his house made Blue smile. He'd been able to get Stanger, the general contractor he wanted and was not sorry. The guy was enthusiastic about working with green products and quickly brought in reliable subs. There were trucks and vans everywhere, but Blue was most excited about the furniture delivery van.

An hour later he called Delta. "Wanna go to lunch?"

"Hi. Sure. Then I need to make some modifications on the preliminary drawings for the Center. I didn't get very far in the rain the other day. Oh, and I got some news about Slayton this morning. I don't know whether to celebrate or be depressed."

"If you decide in favor celebrating," Blue offered. "I can help."

"I'll bet," Delta said wryly. "But I am hungry. So, meet at Mackie's for a quick lunch, then I can get some sketching done."

"Sounds good. See you in ten."

The lunch crowd had thinned and Patience nodded toward the back booth where Delta sat, when he walked in.

"Dewey been in?" Blue asked her as he joined Delta.

Patience shook her head. "Called to say he had to go in for an emergency briefing."

They ordered and Blue took Delta's hand across the table. "What's this about Slayton?"

Delta pushed out a huff. "I heard from the agent I spoke to the other day at the INS."

Blue had expected another stall tactic regarding her settlement. "What's happened?"

"He thought I should know that Slayton and his parents were caught at a small private airfield in south

Florida. They'd paid a pilot to fly them to Cuba. No flight plan involved. The pilot said he had no idea they were trying to skip the country or where they were headed after Cuba. They're being detained for transport back to Atlanta where they'll be arraigned."

She lifted a shoulder. "The agent said they were caught due to the information I gave him."

"Wow," Blue said. "They didn't even wait until the suit was settled. Maybe you really can get the courts to dismiss."

Delta shook her head. "That's the depressing part. Nothing's resolved. Slayton and his parents took the easy way out. Just dropped everything and ran. Cowards."

"So, what's the celebratory part?"

"Same thing."

It took Blue a second to get what she meant, then he burst out laughing. "I pick celebrating."

"Me, too," Patience said as she walked up and set a white bag of food and two disposable drink containers on their table.

Delta looked at her friend. "What's this?"

"Your order," she said, tipping her head toward Blue. "Per his phone call."

Delta squinted at Blue. "Richmond?"

"Got a surprise. Let's go."

How could she turn down a man who looked like a nine-year-old about to attack a stack of Christmas presents? She tried to look stern, but felt all warm and squishy as he pulled her out of the booth.

"This had better be good. I'm a busy woman."

Patience snorted. "Good looking man who's about to feed you *and* got a surprise for you? Just go with it."

Delta let herself relax and be led outside to a car she didn't recognize. "This isn't your mother's Toyota."

"Nope. Had my car driven down by a service. Got here this morning."

She stood goggle-eyed. The sleek, navy blue coupe was top-of-the-line decadence. It made her Honda look like a Lego car.

"I thought you said you didn't do much driving in Chicago."

Blue opened the passenger door. "Didn't. Have a client who owns a dealership and I got a screaming deal."

Delta settled into a luxurious interior and looked around. *An attorney who charges a thousand dollars an hour, now a high-end car dealer.* She was beginning to understand the level of clients Blue dealt with.

He handed her the food and got in. "Ready?"

"Is this the surprise?"

He turned to look at her. "No. Hey, are you okay? You just turned pale."

*Wow. Just wow.* "Uh, I'm good. One of Slayton's friends has a car like this. They played golf together and Slayton always talked about owning one. I never thought...."

Blue took one of her hands and rubbed it between his slowly. "I bought it as an investment. There's a five year waiting list for this model. Besides," he grinned. "It'll rack up a lot of tickets going to your place in Atlanta."

Delta stared. Blue was the most unassuming person she knew.

Her earlier assessment of his financial standing needed an adjustment, that's all.

When she didn't answer, he continued. "I know you don't care how much money I have, and if it'll make you happy, I'll sell the car."

Delta started at the sincerity in his eyes. She pulled him to her, almost toppling one of the drinks in the console. "You will not." She kissed him and grinned. "This will make Charlotte turn green."

"If you say so. Wanna drive?"

"Um, I don't know where we're going."

Blue frowned. "Then sit back and prepare to be amazed."

Delta reveled in the comfort as they drove out of town. Her interest piqued when Blue turned down River Road.

# Chapter Forty-Two

Delta sat straighter, looking out the windshield. What had Blue been up to? Then she saw it. The 70's ranch house they'd stopped at a couple of weeks ago. The real estate sign was gone and the house was almost unrecognizable. Fake brick had been stripped from the front, and the exterior was being primed for painting. The crumbling walk to the house was also gone. Replaced by pretty, ornate stones set in crushed gravel. The once overgrown lawn was under assault by tree trimmers and a gardening crew.

She turned to Blue as he pulled in behind a painting contractor van. "What's this about?"

He grinned. "I haven't applied for my contractor's license yet, but the local I'm working with is really good. Come on in. Have a look around."

Delta's heartbeat accelerated. "Blue Richmond. You didn't *buy* this house?"

His grin was still in place. "Another great deal. And you're killing my buzz. Let's go in."

She sighed. He'd said prepare to be amazed and every step proved him right. Even at this time of year the landscape looked alive. A sign taped to the front door warned. "Locked! Living room floor being refinished. Use kitchen entrance only." They walked around the outside, where she noticed a continuation of the pretty stone and gravel path from the front. This one led to the river.

Inside, the kitchen renovation was only half done, but she recognized upscale green materials in the farmhouse sink and counters made of molded ceramic cement. Incredible light shone through large double-paned windows. Delta laughed. "I love it and I definitely want to see the rest, but ..." She held up the food. "No table and chairs."

Blue made a small bow. "One more room. We can eat there."

Delta's stomach replied with a growl as they went down a hallway. She slowed to peek into the living room. No smell wafted from the shiny, wet floor. The original hardwoods had been reclaimed and given a new life, without a nasty-smelling chemical sealant.

Blue waited at the end of the hall. "Master suite," he said and opened the door to step quickly inside.

She crossed the threshold expecting sawhorses and folding chairs. Words froze in her throat as Blue closed the door behind them.

It was perfect. He had done this for her and it was perfect. The room was large and filled with light. At one end, tall French doors reflected gleaming wood floors and led to a terrace. Just inside, two small club chairs flanked a little table topped with a vase of flowers. On the opposite wall sat the black regency bed, covered in a silk cream duvet with pale teal silk shams. The rest of the room swam in a blur as tears brimmed. "You did good, Richmond."

"Hey, hey," he said, taking her in his arms. "Waterworks? This was meant as a happy surprise. That privacy issue I told you I'd work on."

She choked out a laugh. "Liar. This is the exact room that designer and I talked about. And if the rest of the house is going to be staged like this, it'll sell as soon as it hits the market."

"Not selling," he said. "At least not right away. This is for us, for now. If you want it."

The lightness hovering in her chest bloomed into a sharp knowledge. There was no question this man holding her had one hundred percent of her heart. "I want it."

Blue held her away from him, studying her face. "I have other plans, too."

Delta eased from his embrace and walked to the table where she set down the food with trembling hands. Her personal floodgates were open; Gran's passing, inheriting Brisco's Folly, the lawsuit, the Molly Brisco Center, the fire, making love to Blue, falling in love with him. Dewey and Patience taking the leap. All within a half dozen weeks.

Now this.

Blue had been there for her at every turn and was slowly sliding them into permanence whether he realized it or not. Delta searched her heart and found she no longer had any resistance to the idea.

She shook her head, turning. "Other plans?"

Blue nodded, his look sending ripples of heat straight to her toes. "Not saying, yet. One more step to complete."

Delta lifted a shoulder, feigning disinterest. "Whatever."

He made it across the room to grab her before she finished squealing. "Then again, I might not share," he said.

She kissed him soundly, hugging him to her. "Don't believe you."

Blue held on tight. "I know you need the afternoon light for sketching, but how about a date later? And for future reference, this room is strictly off limits to all contractors, the terrace doors lock from the inside, and that's one-way glass in the windows."

"No, sir," she giggled. "Really?"

"Really."

Delta moved her head to kiss his jaw. "Thank you for this," she said. "It's wonderful and I'm looking forward to this evening."

"Me, too," he said, and broke into laughter as her stomach growled.

* * *

Blue pulled up to Mackie's and parked behind Delta's car.

"Thanks," she said. I'll call you in a couple of hours."

He still didn't have a clue where Braxton was and until he knew, Blue was sticking with his gut. "Mind if I went with you?"

"Not at all." Delta smiled. "As a matter of fact, that's a great idea. You can give me some input from a contractor's point of view."

They drove to an area that served as an unofficial parking area for people who came to walk the unofficial trails. Theirs was the only car in sight, but two bicycles lay at the edge of the thicker growth. Blue hadn't been out here for years and walked behind Delta down a narrow path, careful to avoid the Spanish moss. Some species were home to tiny biting bugs.

In a few minutes they emerged onto a level, dry clearing that had several trails leading out of it.

"Here we are," Delta said, flipping open her sketch book. "I envision most of what we just walked through as parking spaces and bicycle racks."

Blue looked over her shoulder at a rough draft of a circular building with glass windows all around. It had solar panels on top and a small greenhouse structure to the side.

"Thought I'd throw in a small hydroponic display," she said.

He grinned. "Lots of natural light, solar energy, fits nicely into the landscape. Looks good, Jameson. I need to apply for my contractor's license. I think you have a winner."

"Thanks," she said. "I don't think we'd have to take down too many trees to get good exposure on an east west slant for the solar panels."

Before he could respond, they heard urgent shouts and two boys pounded down one of the trails into the clearing. They looked about ten or eleven.

When they saw Blue and Delta, the boys stopped short.

Blue started toward them, but Delta held onto his arm. "They're frightened," she said quietly.

Hands in his pockets, Blue stood still. "What's all the shouting about? You guys okay?"

"Back there," the boy in the lead said. A lady's tied to a tree. She's not moving and we think she's dead."

# Chapter Forty-Three

Delta had her phone out, punching in numbers.

Blue stayed where he was, tipping his head toward the area behind boys. "Can you see this lady from the trail?"

They nodded. "About thirty yards back," the taller one volunteered.

"Good to know," Blue said. "This is Miss Jameson. She's calling the Sheriff. I'm going to check on the lady, and I need you to stay here until help arrives. Okay?"

The boys visibly relaxed, nodding in unison.

"They're on their way," Delta said, slipping her phone in her pocket. "I'll bring them back when they arrive."

Acid poured into Blue's stomach at exposing Delta to a possibly grisly scene. "You sure?"

She had paled, but shoved him gently. "Yes. Go."

Blue's instincts told him this wasn't a game and his heart hammered as he loped down the trail from which the boys had emerged.

It ran fairly straight until forced to the right around a large pine. Even though he was looking for her, the shock of what Blue saw him had him gasping, "Charlotte, no!"

She was very still and almost unrecognizable. Her head hung forward, lank hair bunched under a rag tied to hold a wad of dark material in her mouth. Duct tape held her fast at shoulder, waist, and above the knee.

Blue slipped his pocket knife out and cut the rag, gently pulling the material from Charlotte's mouth, revealing a split lip and swollen cheek. Her head lolled and she moaned. His hands shook and anger sent his pulse pounding. "Charlotte, it's Blue. Help is coming. I'm cutting through the duct tape to release you from the tree. I'll hold you up."

"Kill him," she whisper-croaked.

"I'm so sorry," Blue said, pulling the tape from her legs and waist. Sirens wailed in the distance as he split the last piece of tape and Charlotte's full, dead weight slumped toward him, shoulder first.

The knife slid from his fingers as Blue caught her and laid her gently on the ground. "Charlotte, I don't know if you have any broken bones or internal injuries. Hold on and the EMTs will be here soon. I'll wait with you."

She grasped at this arm, her eyes glassy and caked with a mixture of dried tears and mascara. "Son of a bitch beat me and took my money."

In his gut Blue already knew who'd done this. "Braxton?"

Charlotte nodded, then her face twisted in fury, a gasp escaping as the expression reached her split lip. Her fingers tightened then, and she started shaking hard, her feet scrabbling against the ground. Blue pried her ice cold fingers from his arm. "We'll worry about that later, Charlotte. You need to relax and get warm. I'm taking my jacket off to cover you."

He tucked his jacket as gently as he could around her torso while trying to gauge the distance of the sirens. They were close.

Charlotte stared over his shoulder, rasping, "My hands and feet hurt really bad." Tears slid from the corners of her eyes. "Sometime in the middle of the night, I fell asleep. When I woke up, I tried to move them, and couldn't."

*Jesus. She'd been here since yesterday?* Blue swallowed, his throat dry. She was damned lucky she hadn't been discovered by some predatory animal and attacked. The thought made his stomach roil. There was no blood other than that on her mouth, and she was conscious and talking. That was a good sign. "Hey," he said, hoping to keep her spirits up. "When you're all better, we'll go dancing at Tinker's."

Charlotte's gaze found his. "Blue?"

"Yes?"

"You can't dance worth shit."

It must have looked strange to the EMTs as they rounded the curve in the trail, he on his knees and she on the ground, both laughing.

They were beside her in an instant, asking questions and taking his jacket off to examine her.

"Oh, God. Charlotte!"

Blue's concentration on his cousin broke at Delta's voice. He took two long strides to wrap his arms around her. "She's been here since yesterday. Braxton hit her, took her money, and left her here."

Delta's face was pale, her voice hoarse. "He meant for her to die."

They watched as the two medical technicians carefully lifted Charlotte and laid her on a portable gurney, covering her with a blanket. When they started to pass, Charlotte stopped them. She looked at Blue. "Thanks, darlin'."

He nodded. "We'll come see you when you're doing better."

He and Delta followed the trio back down the trail.

"Dewey got the dispatch," Delta said. "He's talking to the boys."

Light in the clearing had shifted to dusk. Blue saw Dewey close his notebook and turn, his and the boys' attention drawn to the figure on the gurney.

His friend took a step, when he recognized who they were carrying. To his credit, Dewey faltered for only an instant. "You gonna need to use the siren?"

An indicator of the criticality of their patient, Blue guessed.

"Just lights," the man in the lead responded, continuing to hurry. "We're barely six minutes out."

The boys stared at the procession, the oldest one turning to Blue as they passed. "She's not dead?"

"No," Blue said. "She was very lucky you guys found her when you did. You should get on home, though. It's almost dark."

The taller boy elbowed his friend. "We're gonna be in the deputy's report. Wait'll we tell'em at school we found a almost dead lady."

After the kids left, Dewey turned to Blue. "Joe's been phoning the department every hour since midnight. Said Charlotte got a call and went for a walk yesterday afternoon. Charlotte never walks anywhere when she can drive, so they thought something might have happened to her when she didn't come back in an hour. We've had a BOLO alert since this morning." He glanced down the trail. "Did she say who did it?"

"Braxton," Blue replied. "She said he beat her and took her money."

Rigid lines bracketed the corners of Dewey's mouth as he scribbled in his notebook. "I'll interview her at the hospital after I look at the scene and take some pictures. She should be stabilized by then." He took a deep breath and rubbed his forehead. "The boys were here looking for specimens for their Boy Scout Forestry badges. They'd taken another route in and were circling back when they came across Charlotte. What were you guys doing here?"

Delta picked up the sketchbook she'd dropped. "Preliminary drawings for the Molly Brisco Memorial Center."

Dewey made another note and looked around the dusky clearing. "Okay. Anything else?"

Delta frowned, trying to remember something. "Braxton's probably long gone by now," she said. "But he took me to coffee one night a while back trying to convince me to go with his client." She shuddered. "He told me he was from Ponchatoula, Louisiana. Still had lots of relatives there."

Dewey pulled his lips in. "Good information. His rap sheet shows him from New Orleans."

Blue's mouth opened. *Delta had coffee? With Braxton? At night?* An icy trickle slid into his stomach. Braxton was a loose cannon. Anything could have happened. What had Delta been thinking?

The trees blurred with the skyline and he could hardly see the tunnel of foliage he and Delta had walked through to get to the clearing.

A large black tactical flashlight appeared in Dewey's hand. "I'll walk you to your car." He turned grinning. "If that navy blue job's the one you had driven down from Chicago, it is one fine ticket magnet."

Blue heard Delta snicker softly.

At the car, they thanked Dewey, got in, and latched their seatbelts. Delta sighed.

"You okay?" he asked.

"Mad at myself," she said. "I was so desperate to get out of my financial fix, I wanted Braxton to be legitimate, so I didn't listen to my instincts. Or you. Charlotte wanted out, too. Look what not listening cost her."

"Luckily, Charlotte always bounces back," Blue said. "And I think his offer was genuine. Given his methods of acquiring the property, though, I don't think its intended use would benefit anyone but the owner."

Her shoulders dropped. "No camp for disabled kids?"

"I doubt it," Blue said, starting the car. "Where to?"

"Want to have dinner at my folks' house, then call to see if Charlotte can have visitors?"

"Okay. I have some legal stuff to talk to your dad about anyway."

"Like what?"

"Things."

She made a huffing sound. "Very mature. Mention it, then not tell me. Is keeping things from me going to become a habit of yours?"

"Ha!" Blue said.

"Ha?" she replied. What's that supposed to mean?"

Blue sighed. "It means I'm going to pay for bringing this up, but when and why did you have coffee with Braxton to discuss his offer?"

"Oh, that," she said, cutting her gaze to the windshield. "Remember the night after your accident when you pressured me to stay in Atlanta because you thought Braxton was dangerous, but you had no proof? Then you intimated my decision was based on lashing back because of my treatment at the hands of Slayton?"

*His fear for her had almost cost him their relationship.* "Yes."

"Your demand made me so angry; I paced the side-walk to cool off. Braxton drove down our road and we talked about his offer. I asked him to take me to coffee and finish his pitch."

Blue didn't say anything for a minute, his heart thumping at the thought of Delta alone at night with scum like Braxton.

"I told you the details a couple of days later after breakfast when you had me trapped in the alley behind Mackie's. You didn't ask where I got the information."

That was true. He hadn't. He'd been so happy that she hadn't written him off, he never asked for the source of her information. Blue looked at her profile. He opened his mouth, then closed it. Here was a stubborn, determined woman who would continue to surprise and sometimes piss him off. She would chafe at his misguided attempts to protect her because she was an adult and had earned her independence the hard way. He smiled and put his ticket magnet into reverse. "Just checking."

# Chapter Forty-Four

Dinner table conversation at the Jameson's centered around Charlotte's abduction and Joe's assertion that all law enforcement agencies were rife with incompetence.

"Braxton was in love with that bright red special edition truck," Delta said. "Find that and he'll be close by, regardless of the charges against him. There are no doubt lots of places to hide a truck in a small town where you have relatives."

Suzanne Jameson had been very quiet during the meal. She spoke up. "Winnie called me, worried out of her head. Since they haven't caught this person, yet, they're posting an officer at Charlotte's door."

"It's very unlikely he'll be back," Blue said, trying to reassure Delta's mother. "Braxton probably blamed his unsuccessful attempts at buying Brisco's Folly on Charlotte, so he roughed her up, took what money she had, and left. No reason for him to return."

Suzanne Jameson brought her hand to her throat. "I don't know what's happening in this town these days. Thank goodness bad things happen in threes and it's over."

Delta raised an eyebrow, but gave her mother a hug. "We're going to check on Charlotte tonight if she can have visitors. I'll let you know how she is."

"Thank you, honey."


"Yes, it is," Charlotte shouted, her voice filling the otherwise quiet hallway of the small hospital. "This whole ugly mess is your fault. If you hadn't stuck your nose in and *stole* my inheritance, none of this would've happened. Get out!"

Delta and Blue stepped aside as a nurse hurried toward the room. They peered in to see Aunt Winnie standing by the bed, tight-lipped, and the nurse dragging at Joe's arm. "You'll have to leave. You're upsetting my patient."

Joe twisted away. "This is a family talk and none of your concern."

Charlotte cried as Winnie patted her shoulder. "Make him go away, Mother. I hate the sight of him."

Blue took Delta's hand and stepped back, not wanting to intrude. Too late, as Joe had spotted them.

His small, pointed chin hitched upward at Blue. "Convenient that you found her," he smirked. "You had to dangle your damn swampland in her face. When that thug beat her up for the money *you* gave her, you suddenly become the innocent visitor. I wouldn't put it past you to have arranged the whole thing. If she had died, you could raid her accounts and make off with a bundle before anybody was the wiser."

"Shut up, Joe."

Astonished, Blue followed the stares as they all turned toward Aunt Winnie.

"I mean it," she said to her husband. "That's enough out of you."

Charlotte wiped her eyes, her chin mirroring the same angle as her father's. "See? Everybody's tired of your lies and whining."

"Same goes for you, Charlotte," her mother said. Winnie turned to Blue and Delta. "I'm sorry about the rude displays of temper. We've been under a lot of stress." She stood on tiptoe, kissed Blue's cheek, and hugged Delta. "Thank you for your help today."

Blue was stunned at this turn of events. Delta seemed to be flustered, too. "You're welcome," they said in unison.

Winnie turned to her daughter. "Get some sleep. I'll be back in the morning." Then to her husband, "Let's go."

"I'm not ready to leave," he said stubbornly.

"Suit yourself," Winnie replied, as she took her coat off the foot of Charlotte's bed. "I'm driving."

Blue pressed his lips together, stifling a smile.

Joe followed his wife out of the room. As he brushed by Blue, he regained his swagger. "I'm not done with you."

"Right back at you," Blue said, holding the older man's gaze.

The nurse straightened and bristled, back in charge. "Five more minutes. She needs rest."

Delta moved to Charlotte's bedside. "You're looking much better. My folks didn't want to crowd in, but they send their love. Is there anything I can bring you?"

Charlotte rolled her eyes. "I don't suppose either of you snuck me in some cigarettes? I'm dying for a drag."

"Sorry," Delta said, lifting a shoulder. "Anything else?"

"Yes," the blonde replied. "I'd like Harlan Braxton's man parts on a platter. Failing that, I'll settle for his head."

Blue sucked in air and felt his own man parts retreat slightly. "Uh, they're working on it. You'll probably have to settle for him going to prison."

"Only if he gets beat up on a regular basis," Charlotte said, easing her weight to one side. She tipped her head slightly at Blue. "Thanks again for being there, cuz."

"Feel like talking about it?" Blue asked.

His cousin sighed. "Dewey already asked about a million questions, but I guess you deserve to know for not saying I told you so."

Charlotte glanced at the doorway to her room. "There's not much to tell, and I'm leaving out about how stupid I've been." She took a shallow breath. "He called yesterday afternoon and said to drop everything, he'd pick me up down the block from my folks' house in five minutes. 'We're going to Atlanta to celebrate. I got the property in Florida and we're getting a fat check in a few days. Bring whatever cash you have and I'll add it into your share.'"

Her mouth twisted in disgust and she gasped, bringing her hand up to carefully touch her lip. "Bastard knew I'd just withdrawn the first monthly installment you'd set up for me. He was all dressed up and even had an open beer waiting. Told me I could smoke in his truck and said we'd shop for a hot new outfit to show me off in the fanciest club we could find."

Tears started in her eyes. "Next thing I know, I'm tied to this tree and he's slapping and punching me and screaming that it's not enough money for what he's had to put up with. Doctor said my ribs are badly bruised and they found GHB in my system. It was probably in the beer." She grabbed a tissue and wiped her eyes and nose, her voice becoming a hoarse whisper. "When he gagged me, I thought he was going to beat me to death."

"That's enough," Blue said, shuddering at the thought of what went through his cousin's mind. He was seeing a vulnerability he'd never seen in her. "I'll find the meanest D.A. in Atlanta to prosecute him. Braxton'll be an old man before he sees another pretty girl like you."

Charlotte's tears flowed freely, now. "Thanks."

The nurse reappeared in the doorway. "Time's up."

"Wait," Charlotte said. "Blue, could you come back in the morning? There's something I want to talk to you about."

Blue cut his gaze to Delta.

"I get it," Charlotte sighed. "You're a couple. But this is personal, darlin'. If you want to share with Delta later, that's your choice."

He couldn't imagine what that something personal was, but he'd learned Charlotte found out things, and, he suspected, kept them to herself until they became useful. "Sure. Nine, okay?"

Charlotte nodded and lay back, closing her eyes.

"That was disturbing," Delta said, as they walked down the hall. "Uncle Joe didn't blame Harlan Braxton or Charlotte for her situation. Which is a new twist, even for drama central. And speaking of twists, props for Aunt Winnie. She showed some real Parker spine."

"I think that's been building for a while," Blue said, noticing Delta didn't even mention crazy Joe's version of the events. He would tell her about Joe, someday soon.

Delta shivered in her jacket. The heater in Blue's beautiful car worked fine, she just couldn't get warm.

"Hey," Blue said, glancing at her. "Still cold?"

She hugged herself. "Maybe I should've worn something heavier."

"We'll be at your folks' in a few minutes."

Delta had been turning over Charlotte's close call in her mind. She made a decision. "Let's go to the house on River Road."

Blue did a double take. "It's not very warm there."

"I want to lay a fire in the bedroom, make love, then take a naughty shower."

She watched his profile as happiness animated his expression.

"Really?" he asked.

His boyish enthusiasm made her laugh. "Yes."

"Here's a stupid question. How come?"

"Charlotte's ordeal," Delta said softly, her shivers diminishing. "She was a hundred feet from us and it's November. If those Scouts hadn't decided to work on their badges.... It made me realize life really is too short. And I want you in more of mine."

Blue pulled to the curb, stopped the car and turned to her. "Why are we stopping?" she asked.

"This is because you're freaked about what happened to Charlotte?"

He didn't seem angry and Delta certainly didn't want to hurt his feelings. Blue deserved the truth. She faced him in the half-light. "It started out that way, but that's not the way it ended."

He leaned forward and kissed her. "You just made my entire week."

Delta felt a wonderful peace and warmth, and admittedly, desire. "I love you, too. Now, do I have to beg for car sex or are we going to your house?"

He laughed and hugged her, then pulled into traffic. "*Our* house, but I kind of like that begging thing."

"Pushing it, Richmond."

"Okay," he said, and sped up.

Blue had installed automatic lights outside the house and the difference was dramatic. The house looked well-cared-for instead of new, and perfect in the mature landscaping. When they entered, the living room floors shone with a rich light and the taupe-colored walls drew the eye to white crown molding.

In the master suite, Delta's joy changed to a sinking feeling. No logs on the grate. "If the electric heat is working, guess we'll have to use that." She turned and found she was talking to an empty room.

A half minute later, Blue came in carrying small chunks of lumber. "This stuff is untreated," he said, beaming. "I cut it up and left it in the garage on the off chance you'd agree to spend some time here with me."

A lump formed in Delta's throat. He wanted nothing more than to spend time with her, and lately she always had something else to do. "Blue?"

He brushed at the sawdust and splinters on his coat sleeves. "Yes?"

"I'll do better."

He looked up. "At what?"

Delta's heart pounded. "At not making decisions where you come in second. I've used work and my marriage to Slayton as excuses to avoid any personal interactions for so long," she made a gesture to include the room. "I want you to know how much you're appreciated."

Blue took her in his arms and kissed her deeply, then just stood, holding her. After a minute, he said, "Matches."

Delta burst out laughing. "Turn on the electric heat. I'm not waiting for you to borrow a cup of matches from the nearest neighbor."

He took two long strides to the small table at the bedside, opened a drawer, pulled out a string of condoms, and tossed them on the table top. "Again, just in case." He pulled back the comforter, then walked to the thermostat and turned the heat on. "I personally guarantee you'll get warm, but we'll use this as backup."

His look undid her. Delta took off her jacket and giggled as Blue swooped in and lifted her onto the bed. Cool temperatures or not, Blue's caresses brought Delta to an immediate sensual rush. She vaguely remembered incoherent begging and urging him on as he brought her to completely over-the-top satisfied. Delta sighed, her pulse tripping fast. "I could get used to this as a way of getting warm."

Blue slid his hand across her waist, and spoke close to her ear. "Say the word."

# Chapter Forty-Five

Blue felt like a million dollars the next morning. He kicked his run into high gear, not able to wipe the smile off his face. Delta had made it known in words and passion how much she wanted him. It may have been premature yesterday, but he was glad he followed his instincts on one more killer surprise.

An hour and a shower later, he slipped in their favorite booth at Mackie's, next to Delta. Dewey occupied the seat across from them.

"I already ordered for you," she said to Blue, kissing his cheek.

"You sound like an old married couple," Dewey remarked.

"Not so bad," Blue parried, smiling. "Not so bad at all."

Patience came to the table. "I heard about Charlotte this morning. I'm so sorry. Tell her I said take care, the next time you see her."

"I will," Blue said. "She's feeling pretty low." He looked at Dewey. "Any word on locating Braxton?"

The deputy shook his head. "Like looking for a black cat in the dark, last night. Hopefully those Louisiana boys'll have some luck today."

"Speaking of cats," Patience said, pinning Blue and Delta with a stare. "The two of you got happy and relaxed all over your faces, like the cat got busy into the cream."

"What? You two are the only ones that can get busy?" Delta asked, turning pink.

Blue put his arm around her, loving her sense of humor. "Good comeback."

After they ate, he checked the time and kissed Delta. "Got a few things to do at the house, then find out what Charlotte has in mind. You want to come?"

"Thanks, but no," Delta said. "I'd just be a third wheel. Besides, Mr. Buchanan left a message at my folks' last night. He wants to discuss a new development regarding the Averill House. Said he'd call back at 9:00 this morning."

"Knock him dead," said Blue, sneaking in another kiss. "Can I pick you up this afternoon? I want your input on the materials for the second bathroom."

"Okay. Around one?"

Blue nodded. It was just as well. While she was distracted, he could put the final touches on his surprise.

He pulled into the hospital parking lot a few minutes before nine and noticed Aunt Winnie's car. Blue wondered if he was going to have to deal with Joe's insults and threats. Again.

Inside, the hallway was much quieter than last night and Blue heard soft voices as he approached Charlotte's room. He peered around the doorjamb and saw Aunt Winnie and Charlotte. His cousin actually looked worse. Although the swelling had gone down, the bruises had flourished into a yellow, purple, and green landscape. He sucked in a short breath. For the first time since he'd taken up kickboxing, Blue thought how satisfying it would be to punish Braxton punch for punch.

"Hey, Charlotte, Aunt Winnie."

His aunt stood gripping her purse, pale and shaky. Her greeting subdued. "Oh, Blue."

He stepped quickly into the room, his pulse accelerating as he feared bad news. "Charlotte's condition? Did they find something else?"

The older woman straightened her shoulders. "No, honey. She'll be fine. Please excuse me. I have some business to take care of." She brushed Blue's cheek with a dry kiss and left.

Charlotte pushed at the tray suspended over her lap. "Had to get food down before they'd give me something for the pain."

Blue swiveled the wheeled tray away and headed for the chair beside her bed.

"Close the door, cuz."

"Sounds serious."

Charlotte let her gaze drop away. "I was going to talk to you before I left, but that looks to be sooner than I thought. Mother and I are leaving for Atlanta when I'm released. She's setting me up in a small, one bedroom condo. I can't stay here anymore."

"Are you worried about Braxton?"

She shook her head. "He's gone, and good riddance to the coward. I'm leaving because of my father and my shame."

Blue thought he was about to hear a sordid account of some childhood abuse and realized he wouldn't be surprised. "You don't have to tell me, Charlotte."

"Please. I have to get it off my chest."

Charlotte sighed. "My father's a sick man." She held up a hand, forestalling any response. "He's obsessed with you and Aunt Caroline. Has been since before you were born. It makes him crazier every day."

Blue couldn't help himself. "What do you mean before I was born? My mother was happily married to my father."

"From what Mother has told me, yes, it was a short, but extremely happy marriage. The point is, my father never accepted that Aunt Caroline chose someone else over him."

"I don't understand," Blue said, the air in the small room growing close.

Charlotte lay with eyes half closed. "I found out when I was fifteen. I wanted a new prom dress and Father said absolutely not, I'm not made of money, yada yada. Well, this geek at school had a crush on me, and I asked if he had a bug I could borrow. I was all spy woman, going to tape it under my father's desk to eavesdrop on his conversations in hopes I'd hear something to make him let me buy the dress."

Blue just stared, still poleaxed by the bomb she'd dropped about Joe and his feelings toward his mother and him.

Charlotte rolled a little to one side. "Instead, I found a manila envelope taped to the bottom of the drawer. "Inside were dozens of pictures, picnics, birthday parties, all kinds of events. Except, everyone else had been cut out, leaving just your mother. Others of her at times I'm sure she didn't know her picture was being taken. There were also creepy pictures of you at all ages. They'd been cut through your neck, but not all the way through the picture." She rubbed her fingers together. "Can I have some ice water?"

Blue had been concentrating, and jumped at the request. He turned to the wheeled tray, getting Charlotte a drink.

She took a sip and continued. "You'd already left for Chicago a few months before that, but everything began to make sense to me. All the times I'd stayed hidden and overheard him say mean things to you, I thought it was because you were being punished for misbehaving, but that wasn't the case. Now I know it was jealousy."

Charlotte had heard her father intimidate and belittle him and never said anything? A cold, but useless anger stirred through Blue.

Tears rolled down Charlotte's cheeks. "I was so stupid and selfish. The only thing that mattered to me was that dress, so I confronted him. It was the weirdest conversation I've ever had." She pointed at the box of tissues, and Blue obliged.

"He looked at the pictures spread on the desk and did this shaky little shrug thing. 'I was here, first,' he said. 'Caroline would have noticed how much I cared, sooner or later, but I never had the chance. Once he showed up, he was low quality you know; they were inseparable and married within six months. He died before his son was born. A son that should have been mine. So, you see, Blue's father ruined everything.'"

Charlotte tucked her chin. "I'm so sorry, darlin'. I told him he was sick in the head and I was going to tell Mother. He got all quiet and started sliding the pictures back into the envelope. When I reached out, he grabbed my wrist and twisted it. 'You're only fifteen and high strung. I turned down your askin' for a new dress, so you made up a nasty story.' His voice and eyes were so scary I ran out of the house. After that, I stayed out or in my room as much as I could, until I got married."

Blue felt a lump pushing at his chest bone and constricting his breathing. "He said my father was low quality?"

Charlotte gave him a funny look. "Yes. He uses that phrase all the time about people he thinks are beneath him, why?

"Something that came up recently," Blue said, scrubbing his face with his hands. "Why are you telling me this, now?"

"Because he's at it again. When we found out you were related to Grandmother Parker and back in Peck's Bluff to stay, something in him must have snapped."

It was surreal. Like driving past a car wreck and not looking. Blue didn't want to know about the carnage, but asked anyway. "How?"

"I guess all the nonsense he'd built up in his head finally became too much. Darlin', I really do think he's a sick man, but let me finish." She took another sip. "After I found out he'd gone behind my back and cheated me out of two years of the life I wanted, I went wild. Even considered running him down with my car. Then Harlan showed up. Started sweet talkin' to me about the high life we could have in Atlanta. How we'd split the commission check right down the middle. Bastard."

Blue cleared his throat. "What does that have to do with Joe and me?"

Charlotte shook her head. "Sorry. It all just comes bubbling out." She sighed again, and held out her hand. "Hold on tight darlin' because you're gonna hate what I have to tell you next."

Blue reached for her hand and found it trembling. She looked directly at him this time, and he could see being Joe's daughter had taken a big toll on her.

"I had some really bad nights after I found out I wasn't coming into my inheritance right away. Came home drunk every morning, then slept all day. That's when I saw him. The morning you had your accident. He was wearing that ugly white polyester shirt and creeping down the slope to the river. So I followed him, keeping out of sight." She squeezed his hand. "He rolled that wagon into your path."

Icy disbelief washed through Blue and his throat went dry. "You saw him?"

Charlotte started babbling. "I saw my father kick at something, but I swear I didn't know what or why. I was still half drunk and didn't figure it out until later. I went to the hospital to see for myself that you were okay."

"He hates me enough to want me dead?"

Charlotte shook her head, then moaned, putting her free hand up to her forehead. "It's all about control and getting attention. Of people, situations, money. Don't you see? You're making Aunt Caroline happy. You're a financial genius. You're helping the town's employment problems. In a little over a month, and all by yourself, you're doing everything he's never been able to accomplish. He hates you because you're not his son, but he's a coward. He probably wanted to see or hear you fall for his own pleasure."

It surfaced into Blue's memory, then. The rude re-mark Joe had made in his office when they had the confrontation regarding Charlotte's portfolio. Joe had said "You hit your head on that jagged rock …" The doctor had said a tree root or rock was her guess as to what had caused his head wound. How had Joe known it was a jagged rock unless he'd seen it happen? And he had done nothing to help.

Horror choked Blue's throat. "What about Delta? What do you know about her *accident?*"

Charlotte seemed to shrink before his eyes, her fingers reaching for the pale, hospital blanket. "That was Brax." She twisted the blanket edge. "He got so angry when I couldn't convince you to accept his offer, he bought one of those fireplace lighters. I'd told him how much Delta loved this big old, ugly house and how it hadn't been lived in, in years. He went out to set the place on fire, but the thingy he bought didn't work. He was going to drive into town and get a new one, when he heard about the fire. He laughed and laughed, then slept it off. The next day he left for Florida." She cried harder. "I was afraid of him by then and since he wasn't the one who actually set the fire, I let it go. I didn't find out about Delta until later."

"I have to get some air," murmured Blue, standing.

Charlotte pushed her hair back, looking even worse because of her crying. "I know you and Delta don't have any reason to forgive me, but maybe in a few years?"

Blue didn't feel generous enough to give her any assurances, so he didn't speak.

"Had that comin' darlin'," she said, sighing. "I'm leaving, with a small adjustment to the plans I told you about a while ago. Mother's going to take care of me until I'm well, then come back here. Told her I'd keep in touch with her as long as she didn't tell father where I was. I'm truly done with him. Wish she was, too."

Blue leaned to kiss Charlotte's forehead. He didn't want to leave her like this. "Thanks for filling in the holes."

He walked to the door and paused, turning. "Good luck, cuz. You won't be around, but I want you to know I plan to marry Delta, as soon as she'll have me."

# Chapter Forty-Six

"Congratulations!" Charlotte winced and put her hand to her lip. "You guys deserve to be happy. I mean it."

Blue winked. "Haven't asked yet, so don't spread the word."

Stuffing his hands in his pockets, Blue headed for the parking lot, his brain on overload. He made it to his car, when Joe pulled in one car over. Without processing his actions, Blue walked around his car and the one between them. When Joe got out, Blue held the older man's car door open, trapping him.

His uncle produced an instant sour look. "What do you think you're doing?"

"Having a long overdue chat. We have time because Charlotte just told me she doesn't want anything more to do with you."

A red flush crawled up Joe's collar. "That's a lie."

"Nope," Blue said. "We had a long talk about you and some pictures and my mother. And last but not least, my *accident.*"

Joe's flush turned gray at the edges and he tugged for control of the door. "Charlotte's a liar. Always has been."

"How do you know they were lies if you don't know what she told me?"

The older man ceased struggling, but hadn't lost his look of belligerence. "I'll go in and make her tell the truth. You can't stop me."

Blue felt a complete lack of sympathy. "You're not going anywhere until we come to an understanding."

Joe resumed pushing at the door. "I'm not going to agree to anything. You're no good."

"I used to believe that, too," Blue said, gaining momentum. "When I was a little boy, and an older man, a friend of the family, kept telling me how I didn't fit in or was worthless because I didn't have a father." Blue leaned closer as Joe shrank toward the driver's seat. "Come to find out the older man was sick and jealous. You still are."

"You have no right ..." Joe blustered.

"Neither did you," Blue said. "Even less so, because people trusted you around their children."

Joe wouldn't meet his gaze, but the Canfield chin jutted straight out. "I don't have to do anything you say, and I'm going to have you brought up on charges for keeping me here against my will."

"No, you won't. You're a pathetic coward who torments children when you think no one is looking, and writes poison pen letters to try and make people you're afraid of look bad." Blue saw Joe's age-spotted hands tremble.

"Here's what's going to happen. You will burn those pictures. You will stop stalking my mother. You will not be allowed to speak to my wife or any children we have without my presence. *And*, if you're smart, you will get counseling."

This time Joe did look at him. He snorted. "You can't make me do any of that."

Blue smiled. "I'm moving back permanently. And I have the resources to check into every financial deal you ever made."

Joe cut a sideways glance, but his posture belied his bluff. "Nobody'd care about any of that."

"You were a loan officer at the bank. They might be interested. Especially since they offered you an early, *unsolicited* retirement."

Blue could see he'd struck a deep chord.

"That's private information. None of your business," Joe stammered.

"I made it my business when I found out you were stealing from your daughter."

Joe looked toward the hospital. "If Charlotte's put out with me, it's you who's talked her into it. But she'll come around." He gave a curt nod. "You're coming after me for personal spite, pure and simple."

"Imagine that," Blue said. "Being spiteful because someone tried to kill you."

The older man sank onto the driver's seat. "I want to talk to Winnie."

Blue let go of the car door. "It won't be pleasant. Charlotte had a conversation with her, too." He stepped back. "I'll keep in touch."

Joe drew an audible breath and slammed his door as Blue walked away.

Blue pushed out his own pent-up breath as he got in his car. He sat for a minute, trying to decide how he felt after confronting Joe. Not really vindicated or virtuous, just hollow. He suspected Charlotte's father had some very ugly demons in his past. That was too bad, and for Joe to deal with. As long as he stayed away from Blue and the people he loved.

Blue decided a brisk jog through Brisco's Folly would clear his head.

His hair was still damp from a shower when he showed at the Jameson house to pick Delta up. She answered the door and went into his arms.

"What's this about?" he asked.

"Where've you been? Aunt Winnie's here with your mother. Winnie's very upset, nearly incoherent. Something to do with Joe leaving."

"Whoa," Blue said. "Slow down. Run that last by me again."

Delta took his hand. "In the kitchen."

Blue let Delta pull him into the Jameson kitchen, his pulse pounding, dreading what he would find.

They walked in to see his mother and Aunt Suzanne hovering near Winnie Canfield, who sat with her hands around a cup of tea, determination stamped on her features, dry eyed.

Until she saw Blue.

The tea sloshed in her cup and she stood, eyes starting to brim. She walked the few steps to hug him. "I am so sorry, honey. Charlotte told me this morning, but I didn't know for sure until Joe came home. I forced him to tell me the truth."

She had taken on her husband's burden and Blue saw the last support of the Canfield family fail. He hugged her back. "Old history, Aunt Winnie. Nothing for you to worry about. Promise?"

She nodded and stepped away, tugging at her sweater. "I want y'all to know I'll be gone for a while. I'm taking Charlotte to Atlanta and staying with her until she's well. I've also offered to make a down payment on a condominium. In exchange, she's agreed to get a job and make the monthly payments." The older woman lifted her hands then let them drop. "I think she's learned something about taking responsibility for her actions in this whole ugly mess." She took a deep breath. "In the meantime, I've told Joe to be gone when I return. I want him out of the Parker house."

Winnie held up her hand to forestall questions or explanations. "He did some things in the past I only just learned about and he won't be returning unless my conditions are met. Namely, full apologies to the Richmond family, and professional counseling. If both of these terms are not completed, he's gone for good."

Apparently, Blue wasn't the only one who thought Joe needed help.

Delta squeezed Blue's hand in the total silence that met Winnie's declaration.

Until she'd mentioned the Richmond family, Blue hadn't considered who Aunt Winnie had told about Joe's obsession. He looked at his mother, but she was concentrating on her half-sister.

"If you or Charlotte need a place to stay while all this is being worked out, please come to me," Caroline Richmond said.

Winnie put her hand to her mouth and nodded.

Blue turned to Delta. "I need to talk to my mother for a minute. I'll fill you in later."

Delta kissed his cheek and let go of his hand.

His mother was still wearing her coat, so she buttoned it and turned toward the back door. "Let's take a walk."

"This seems to be the time for revelations," she said, skirting shallow spots on the river path that were deep with sodden leaves. "I know it's too late, honey but I have to take some of the blame for what happened to you."

"No, Mother."

She went on, holding his hand as if he'd cast her away. "Please listen." A cloud of her breath huffed out. "I loved your father so much, and after I lost him, I was barely functional. After you were born, I let go. I let us get absorbed into the everyday lives of the Briscos, and Jamesons, and

Canfields, thinking you'd be safe." She shook her head. "I was stupid and wrong. Even when you started to withdraw, I thought it was because you didn't have a father and that you would outgrow it." Her face stiffened. "It was very selfish of me."

Blue had never seen his mother like this. It scared him. "Stop." He took her shoulders. "I can't imagine losing someone you love without losing part of yourself. I feel the same way about Delta."

His mother's eyes sparked at this and he went on. "Joe fooled me, too. He's a very sick man. Has been since before he came here. I've dealt with it, and him. Promise me this is the end of blaming yourself."

Indecision warred across her features. "You were so young. I was supposed to protect you."

"It's over," he said, holding her gaze. "How about I give you some grandchildren to spoil? Deal?"

Life flashed into her face and she nodded, going into his arms. They stood on the river path in the shelter of the trees, listening to the rush of water.

When they re-entered the kitchen, his mother's self-possession was back in place. She hugged Delta fiercely, then turned. "Suzanne, if you can spare some more tea, I think the three of us need to talk."

Delta looked at Blue curiously.

He tipped his head toward the hall to the front of the house.

She complied, stopping to get a jacket out of the closet.

Once in the car and on their way, she turned to Blue. "That was dramatic. "What's going on?"

"Let's get to the house," he said and Delta nodded.

This time when they pulled up, there weren't nearly as many trucks. Delta started to open her door.

"Wait," Blue said, turning in his seat, determined to be honest, "I want to get this out."

He told her everything. About Joe's obsession with his mother and his hatred of Blue. At the end, Delta lifted Blue's hand to her cheek. "I'm so sorry you had to deal with that. I always thought Uncle Joe had a mean streak, so I just avoided him. None of us knew how deep the cruelty went."

"We're lucky to have ended up with each other," Blue said, pulling Delta to him for a deep kiss, then putting his forehead to hers. "This isn't how today was supposed to go."

She grinned. "Did you have naked in mind?"

"I always have naked in mind." He grinned back. "This is something else. Want to take a short walk?"

Her glance was questioning. "Sure."

Blue headed them in the direction of the Averill House, his heart pounding, his whole future on the line.

The closer they got, the slower Delta walked. Finally, she stopped just before the curve where the house came into view. "I don't want to go in this direction," she said. "Buchanan told me this morning that he was pulling out. Somebody contacted him about the property and made him and his wife an offer they couldn't turn down."

"I know," Blue said and took her hand, tugging her along. He watched her face, hoping the giant pink bow, ludicrously hanging on one of the charred posts, was still upright.

Delta saw the bow and stopped to process its meaning. "You bought the Averill House? Why?"

Blue took a deep breath. "Because I suck when it comes to picking out wedding presents."

"But who ...?"

"Geez, Jameson. Help me out here."

She got it then and jumped to wrap herself around him, nearly taking them to the ground. He kept his balance as "Yes," kiss. "Yes," kiss. "Yes," kiss, rained down on his face.

He got a word in edgewise. "I knew the house would seal the deal."

Delta stopped kissing him and slipped to the ground. She grabbed the lapels of his jacket. "Not the house, not the other house, no houses involved. You could come to me in sackcloth, Richmond. It's you."

A lump blocked his windpipe for a second. "Okay."

She kissed him hard, then turned, sprinting toward the ruin. When he caught up, she twirled around. "What did you promise the Buchanans, our firstborn?"

Talking about having children with him thrilled Blue to the core. "Told him I'd give them their choice of the lots we plan to build on, plus a certain architect's design services at a reduced price. That clinched the deal."

"Oh, giving away my services," Delta said, then stopped. "I can't possibly top this as a wedding present."

"Already thought about that," Blue grinned. "Soccer mom van and car sex."

Delta's laughter echoed from the woods at the river's edge. "Done."

## The End

# About the Author

People who hear voices are not always in need of counseling. Sometimes we are writers listening to our muses. Dee-Anna started listening when she was ten and got a small, powder blue, working typewriter for Christmas.

Born of stubborn Welsh-English stock with a little Cherokee thrown in, DeeAnna grew up the oldest and bossiest of four siblings. Life spun out with wins and losses: she wanted the snow queen crown in the winter pageant at nine, and ended up in the snowflake chorus, but won the title of mathalete the next year. Light her fire baton in junior high? No problem.

She has lived beyond breast cancer and believes in strength, passion, dancing with fate, and keeping your powder dry.

DeeAnna lives in the fresh air and sunshine in Southeastern Washington State with her first husband and HRH Pandora, the miniature pinscher.

Please visit DeeAnna's website at:
www.deeannagalbraith.com

22780357R00223

Made in the USA
Charleston, SC
01 October 2013